MW01141102

This is a work of historic fiction. Certain names, characters, and incidents, except for some incidental references and people, are products of the Author's imagination. There are historical accuracies and many historical facts. Some of the characters in this work actually existed and were a part of America's history. However, there are many fictional scenes and references that do not refer to or portray any actual people or the events that they represented.

This Book contains adult themes and criminal acts. There are scenes of extreme violence, drug use, profanity, sex, and coercion. This Book is not meant for everyone, it's entertainment is designed solely for adult readers.

CHAPTER 1

He walked up to the automobile while the confused victim rolled down the window. As soon as he reached the car, he pulled his sawed-off shotgun out from beneath his coat and pointed the snub-nosed end of the barrel into the man's face. He quietly told the man to step out while he opened the door with his free hand. "Now walk towards the back of my truck," said the Telephone Man.

It was another hot and wet Spring morning, somewhere in Florida. After tossing his victim into the back of his truck, he pulled back onto the road and drove straight to a fish camp on the back of a bayou near the Gulf of Mexico. He loved to fish. It was the only way he knew how to commune with his notion of God. He would always find a nice, secluded area, away from all the other campers near some oak shaded place and back his converted bread truck into the camp facing towards the road.

As soon as he parked the truck and surveyed his surroundings he put his gloves on and walked to the back of his truck. The victim was still sleeping from the knock out gas and bound to a round post running down the length of his back and shoulders. Behind the truck, under an old oak branch, the

Telephone Man drilled a large metal auger stake with a curved hook at the end into the ground, strung a rope over a large branch then tied it to the victim. He got back into his truck and drove forward until the man was hoisted three feet above the ground. After quietly gagging and blind-folding his victim, he grabbed his cast net from a bucket in the bread truck, took off his socks and shoes, rolled up his trouser legs and took off towards the beach with a rather proud smile on his face. It was just another job for him but he seemed to always find pleasure in combining work with leisure. It was a hubris he never mentioned to his bosses but his old lady knew it and she never really liked it but tolerated it anyway.

It wasn't easy supporting his family but he would do whatever it took. Perhaps that is why he loved to drink, fish, hunt, and rut. Which was usually the order of things in his world besides work and that just seemed like another four-letter word to him. His real name was Ed Goodwin, he worked for Ma Belle. He was a lineman and he did it all but mainly worked as a telephone man. That was how he obtained his code name.

He originally began working for the Sullivan boys in Pensacola and they happened to work for the Dupont family that had just recently created the St. Joe Company in Florida. Alfred Dupont was a new player in Florida but knew how to run an empire as proficient as any other robber baron. When the industrialist moved to Florida in the 1920s, Mr. Dupont had just recently married again and discovered that his new wife's brother was not only a financial wizard but also had a knack for finding the right sorts of people to do certain jobs that needed to be done.

Edward Ball was his name and eventually became one of the most influential men in Florida. Mr. Ball became Alfred Dupont's right-hand man. He knew how to get things done and immediately hired the Sullivan's, in Pensacola, to help with the uglier side of management. The deep South of the 1930s was just like any other times in the South after the Great War, it was mainly a hot, sleepy poverty stricken back water region, that mostly stayed forgotten.

The Law was purchased, prejudiced, and proud. It was right to be white and Yankees were not welcome. It was important to know who was who and how to stay cool. That was one of the lessens that young Ed Goodwin learned when he was growing up off the bayous in lower Alabama.

A few hours later he came walking back into his camp with the biggest shit eating grin a man of the South could muster. His fish bag was chalked full of mullet and sheep-head fish. He had also snagged a branch of milkweed that he knew God must had placed there just for him among the refuse that had washed up to shore. He had everything he needed. Just as he arrived he noticed the fellow began to wiggle and muffle a moan or two. From somewhere in his outfitted bread truck, he took out a wooden square box with a large black handle, a tank of gas, and several corn sacks full of thrown together supplies. After setting out a small camp fire next to the hanging man, he began to set up his fishing camp.

First, he extended his roll out table from the truck that could double as a perfect fish cleaning station for him and the boys. Then he pulled out a metal cook stove, attached the tank of gas, pumped pressure into another cylinder and lit up a larger than usual flame in the stove's box.

During the entire time he gutted and prepared all the fish he caught, he never said a word. Instead, he wound up wooden radio box, found his favorite radio station on the AM and listened while he cut just the flayed meat of the fish, saved part of the innards and kept all the heads in a metal bucket.

An uneventful fried fish dinner later, he cleaned himself off and just walked off into the night looking for some hooch and hopefully some girls that he could tickle. It wasn't long before someone pulled over, stopped and asked him if he needed a ride. He took off his hat and introduced himself with the name he used when working for the Sullivan's.

"Mr. I would love a ride my name is Paul and I've been fishing at this here camp. I've caught all the fish I need, I'm full and I would love to look at some pretty ladies and have a drink some where's if that's not too much to ask." The driver in the Buick slapped his right thigh and let out a holler. "Well hop in Mr. Paul, my name is Floyd and I'm heading to a card game where I'm sure there's pretty girls and something to drink."

There it was, Ed's gift. The Sullivan boys always said he had the knack of knowing when and where he needed to be even if he didn't know it himself. Which was exactly how he was noticed by the Sullivan brothers in Pensacola.

Chapter 2

Every city in the South had their under-bosses, especially the port-cities. His family had moved to Pensacola from lower Alabama when he was fourteen years old in 1920 and it was a good place for young Ed to learn his trade. The port of Pensacola was rife with sailors, shipping merchants, whores, and stevedores.

It was a cut throat's paradise, where those who own fleets of ships controlled the brothels, speak-easys, and the local law could make anyone disappear. A virtual proving ground for anyone tough enough to want to prove themselves. The Spanish Influenza had nearly wiped out the sea port's residents the previous year. The Sullivan's lost nearly all their hired ruffians and was forced to do all their dirty work themselves and it was about this time that some local banker in town had gotten drunk, raped a sea captain's daughter and thought because he owned a bank that there would be no retaliation. He was dead wrong.

Ed was glad to be away from all the sick and dying folks from the last year. Seeing all those dead bodies lying around the downtown still gave him nightmares on occasion. He hated to see anything dying, he would rather help put a life out then watch any sort of animal needlessly suffer. Perhaps that's why he loved to fish. Yet, last year's horror had taught him how to kill and young Ed had learned some very important rules: Never talk about it, never get caught, and learn to enjoy life to its fullest. That was why he was glad to be cast-net fishing along Pensacola's bay. The mullet were running and he was having a good time filling up his fish bag.

As he was putting another fish into his bag, he looked up and could just barely make out the shapes of three men on the beach. He had waded out as far as he could at dusk and the tide was low so he went out far enough where it was difficult to see him from shore. The men were making loud noises and young Ed thought they were calling to him. Perhaps they needed his help. With a sigh and a grunt, he made his way back towards the shore. However, it wasn't long before two of the men turned around and pointed their pistols toward young Ed. "Come here boy," said one of the men with a gun pointed straight towards Ed's face. He walked right up to them with both slumped shoulders and a large netted bag with dozens of flopping fish inside. Looking down between the strangers was one beaten to hell, well-dressed man, with bruises, cuts, and two black eyes.

Both Tom and Byron Sullivan knew what had to be done but it had been a while since they had gotten their hands dirty and killing the scumbag banker was not something they really relished doing. As soon as young Ed dropped his cast-net and asked what they wanted, Byron knew just how to handle this dopey looking kid. "Hey, boy, you know who this man is?" No Sir". This here fellow decided to rape a little girl from Captain Rocheblave's house and he thinks no one is going to do anything about it but you see, my brother and I've been hired to take care of him and then you come along to witness this catastrophe. What do you think about that, Boy? Ed pulled his shoulders back and looked straight into Byron's eyes and simply asked, "What do you want from me, Sir?" Tom smiled at his brother and then took his gun and emptied the chamber except for just one bullet. Then he adjusted the gun and handed it to his brother Byron. "Seeing is how you're a witness, then we only see it as proper that you do the deed. There is only one bullet in this here gun and it's locked, loaded and ready for the kill. How's about you put just this one little old bullet in Mr. Banker's head and none of us will be any wiser, hmmm?"

Ed blinked. He had just learned from the previous year, that killing was a paid service and not to be taken lightly. Killing the lame and dying flu victims was something he wished to forget. "How much?" Immediately, Byron pulled out a ten-dollar bill and held it out in front of him as an enticement. Ed couldn't believe his eyes. He had never seen so much money in just one single note. His mind began to race with the anticipation of spending it. He dropped his fish and cast-net walked over behind the banker, pulled out his filleting knife and simply sliced open the banker's throat from behind. "There is no need to waste a bullet Folks", said young Ed. "You'd actually hand over your gun to a stranger even with only one bullet, now that's one for the books. Lord Misters, what were y'all thinking?"

Byron stuffed the ten-dollar note into Ed's front pocket in his coveralls. "What's your name kid?" Asked Byron, with a look of complete astonishment and a bit of amusement. For some strange, mysterious reason Ed's instincts told him that he shouldn't use his real name when doing something criminal so instead he gave them a different name. "Whatever you want to call me Sir, but most folks call me Paul. For another ten dollars, I'll be glad to deliver this person to where ever you want?"

Tom couldn't believe this kid. He didn't know whether to shoot him or buy the boy a drink. There was something about the kid's lop-sided grin that spoke of greater mischief. Byron spoke first, "Yeah, you see that ship out yonder in the bay. If you can take him to that boat moored at the foot of that ship, drop the body in and yell up to the sailors, the job is done. I'll pay you another ten-dollar note." Both brothers smiled at each other knowing full well that the boy would have to find a small skiff to manage that.

"Consider it done." Young Ed stripped off his overalls and shirt, wearing only his underwear, walked over to the dead banker, picked up both the banker's wrists, and dragged him out to the water where he floated and swam the body out to the ship. The Sullivan brothers had never witnessed such an adept swimmer before.

The Casino on the beach happened to need a life guard but it wasn't easy finding anyone that could swim this well. Nor was it easy finding someone that could do the type of work that the Sullivan's needed with that much proficiency and willingness, while keeping quiet and loyal.

Ed finally made it back to shore, he was heaving, yacking, and fell down on the sand next to both of the brothers, sitting on the shore smoking cigarettes. With two rather large smiles both Tom and Byron stuffed a five dollar note in both of Ed's hands and patted him on the back.

"Hey Paul, how's about you come work for us? The pay is good, the benefits are great and we could use a fellow like you as well." Young Ed looked up and smiled, "There is only one problem, gentlemen.

You see, I have a special need and I kind of require a sort of help to get things done. I need money and lots of pussy. They happen to be the two things that helps me sleep better at night." Both of the brothers began to laugh hilariously and Ed joined in with a twinkle in his eye. The Sullivan brothers just shook their heads. This would be the beginning of a very long employment.

Ed when he first began his apprenticeship
with the Chief & Gunny.

Chapter 3

By the time he made it back to his camp on the bayou, the sunrise was just beginning to commence, and the birds could be heard singing in the early morning's day. Everything was still a little dark and the hanging man was not moving about. After rolling out his bed-roll in the truck, Ed grabbed the stalk of milkweed and walked over to his newest victim. He pulled the cover off the man's head and broke the milkweed stalk and waited for the milky latex like sap begin to puddle at the end of the stalk. Quickly, Ed dabbed each of the man's eyes as he held the victim's eyelids opened. Making sure the gag in the mouth was secure, he slumbered back into his truck and passed out with happier thoughts of the early night's women.

A few hours later he awoke to the sounds of moaning. It didn't take very long to revive the camp fire. He made a cold fried mullet sandwich, some coffee, and sat at the camp fire watching the man hang there while listening to his favorite station on his wind-up radio box. A quick smoke and a long piss gave him the relief he was looking for before Ed made his next move. The hanging victim was still moaning, his eyes had begun to swell, tear up, and turn red. Ed knew the man could no longer see anything but shades of light and darkness. It had almost been twenty-four hours since he had hung the man up.

He walked over to his victim and removed the man's gag. Then he walked back to his truck and retrieved a soft dark leather-bound note book. He sat down at his carving table and opened the book, sharpened a pencil and hesitated a few seconds. "If you yell or scream, I will gag you and begin the torture. Do you understand?" The hanging man was still breathing heavy but now Ed could hear the man's breaths become deeper. The victim nodded his head up and down.

"What did you do with the money that was loaned to you?" The hanging victim looked over at his direction and whispered, "They stole it." "Who?" "My partners at the law firm, they want to buy another business," the man stammered. Ed began writing down the statements. However, he didn't like where this story was heading. "What other business," asked Ed? "Can I at least get something to drink first?" Ed put his pencil down, walked over to the man and stuffed the gag back into his mouth. He then reached down and grabbed one of the burning logs and held it under the hanging man's crotch just long enough for him to feel the burn.

This was a waiting game and Ed knew how to play it well. After his victim began to calm down, he removed the gag and walked back to his note-book and picked up his pencil. "What other business?" "Concrete and asphalt," was all the man said. "Why do they want to go into that type of business?" "They are building another highway soon and my partners want to seize the contracts through our relationship with the governor." "What kind of relationship does your firm have with the governor?" "We handle his finances and keep his personal business private," explained the exasperated man.

Ed continued interrogating his victim until he felt he received enough information. It eventually became dark again, and from underneath the truck he pulled out a metal lunch box and opened it. Inside was a thermos half full of liquid-knock-out- juice, a pair of leather gloves, and one rather thick handkerchief. An hour later, Ed's camp was packed up, and he was driving down the road with the victim sleeping in the back of the bread truck.

Chapter 4

Sometime later he found a deserted bus stop where he dropped off his victim knowing it would still take another day or so before the man's eye sight returned. After leaving the fellow asleep and clothed on the bench, he drove off down the road with one job done and two more to complete.

It wasn't long before he found what he was looking for. Just outside of the Tallahassee city limits, he pulled up to a junction of telephone poles and power lines. He parked his truck next to one of the telephone poles and disappeared inside his truck. Minutes later he reappeared with his pole climbing kit and uniform on. It didn't take him long to shimmy up the pole. With his work tools, and one soft leather-bound note book tied to his belt, he made it up to the top of the pole in just a few minutes.

The view was good and the sun had just begun to rise giving him the needed light to see what he was doing. Sitting there strapped to the telephone pole, he pulled out his special phone, connected it to the right line and dialed up Mary Louise, his favorite and the cutest operator in that county. "Hey Mary Lou, this is Paul calling from down the road. How're you been doing, Sweet-heart?"

Mary Louise's giggles where not only loud but rather strange sounding to Ed. She remarked, "It's been forever and a coon's age, Paul. What in heaven sake have you been up to?" She was imagining his square jaw, chiseled chin, and lop-sided grin. Ed was someone that always gave her a good time but never promised her anything else. "The company has been sending me all over God's country, testing lines, fixing lines, running lines, securing lines, and everything else in between." "Well I suppose you need something or else you wouldn't be calling me," she said in her most kitten like voice. "Yes please, I want a bath, a dinner, and you Mary Lou," he said back. Coughing back into the phone line, Mary Louise was having a time, trying to clear her throat. "Do you need a place to stay tonight?"

Her heart was beating faster and she was already thinking of ways she could get her brother to sleep somewhere else beside the tiny house they shared. "That would be wonderful Mary Lou, I still have work to do but how about after seven o'clock this evening?" Before Mary Lou could control herself, she rambled on that her brother was her roommate and might disturb them but that she would love to cook him dinner that night. "No problem Mary Lou, I don't mind a bit, it's you I want to see any way." "Hey Mary Lou, could you tell me where the conjunction to Governor Carlton's office is please? I really need to secure the lines for him or I'll be in a heap of trouble with the phone company?" Mary Louise immediately gave him everything he needed to know. "I'll see ya' then Sweet-Pea," he said in a hurried tone of voice.

Ed knew he didn't have much time. Most folks that used the phone for business almost always called their partners in the morning to confirm the day's business and Ed knew that he needed to be at the right place at the right time. Hurriedly climbing down from the telephone line, Ed raced off in his converted bread truck and made his way to the area that Mary Lou mentioned.

Ed strapped his tool belt back on after parking his truck and scurried up another telephone pole, where he attached his work phone to onto another telephone line. This time, however, was a little different. It was a dead line that was unused at that time. However, Ed knew to wait. And it wasn't too long before the operator patched someone through. It was another lawyer. Lately, it seemed like attorneys where sprouting up like wild turnips. He could smell a Yankee a mile away and this one sounded just like a New Yorker. The man kept talking, giving him just what he needed to know.

Wow, thought Ed. He was always amazed at how freely people spoke over the phone. After writing down everything worth noting, he climbed back down the pole and drove off in a different direction. It wasn't long before he pulled up right next to the president of the state university's office. Dr. Conradi was one of Ed's favorite conversationalist. Ed had been listening to Dr. Conradi and the Purity League go at it for some time now. The Baptist preachers were not very subtle in the way they protested and destroyed any material that was contradictory to their church doctrines. It was a rather fickle business with the University boys. Lately though, Ed's bosses were itching to find out who the next union leader was going to be. They knew that the ministers in the Purity League would be choosing the new labor union boss, not the union.

Ed scurried out of his truck and up the next telephone pole as fast as he could and hooked his unique phone onto the right line. Within minutes, he could hear Dr. Conradi complaining about the Purity League sending certain female student's threats about another one of their thesis being published at the University. "It's got to be that preacher, Templeton. I know it's got to be him, he's always poking around, trying to upset the women professors. That man is obsessed with bringing a halt to educating young girls," replied the voice talking to Dr. Conradi. "Where does he come from, I mean where does he live?" "He's staying with some family member from the church I'm sure. He is probably staying with the Prechet's over at the old Wiggin's farm. There have been a few tent revivals lately at that location." "Perhaps you should talk to the Colonel concerning these threats. He's got two daughters that will be graduating soon." "Well that's a good idea. Thanks, Mr. Ball," said Dr. Conradi as he ended their conversation.

Ed began his descent down the telephone pole when he noticed a man across the street get out of a delivery truck and start walking towards Dr. Conradi's office. The man looked like he had a box of long stem roses in a box, but Ed knew better. As quickly as he could, he climbed down the pole, released his tool belt, grabbed some gear, and crept over behind some azalea bushes near the entrance to Dr. Conradi's office. As the man got within hearing distance, Ed began to roll out telephone wire from a spool and crossed directly in front of the man, blocking his way. "Excuse me sir," was all Ed said as he looked up from rolling out the line directly in front of the stranger. The man annoyingly walked over the line as he shot him a dirty look and muttered something under his breath.

Ed waited a few seconds and then sprang into action wrapping his arms around the man's head from behind into a vice grip, while dragging the fellow behind the bushes. Ed was not a very tall man but he was thick and quite strong. After a couple of minutes of squeezing out the air from his victim's lungs, he let go and quietly got up and opened the box the man was carrying. Sure enough, it was a sawed off shot gun. Twilight was on them and the light was dimming quickly. He removed the spool of wire, walked back to his truck with the box and came back to gag and restrain the man after knocking him out again. Then he waited till it was dark, lifted the fellow over his shoulders and walked back making sure his new victim was secure and sleeping soundly in the back of his converted bread truck. Then he made off towards his favorite Tallahassee girl, Ms. Mary Lou. Upon arriving after sundown, he pulled up to her little Bungalow, grabbed his overnight duffel bag, secured the bread truck, his victim, and walked over to Mary Lou's front door. She was already waiting by the door in a pink and saffron dress with a look that told him everything he needed to know.

"Wow, you are indeed a sight Ms. Mary Lou. There ain't a more beautiful gal in this whole city." She blushed immensely and opened the door for him to walk in, hoping that none of the older ladies in the neighborhood were watching. But Ed knew the trick and nearly bounced inside the house with the ease and mischievousness of a Cheshire cat. However, right as he entered her house, he quickly grabbed her by the waist and snatched her into his arms while looking directly at her without blinking an eye.

"I want you Mary Lou, but I need a bath. Could you help get me get cleaned up," he replied, before he took a deep sniff of her presence and gave her a kiss on her lips. Mary Lou giggled, smiled and kissed him back. "Yes Sir," was all she said as he released her and she led him to her bathroom holding his hand with a smile and a passionate anticipation of the night's alluring pleasures. This was their ritual and she was as devout as any devotee. She turned on the hot water before she began to undress the only man she had ever worshiped besides her Savior. The room would become steamy in more ways than one. He always encouraged her with each step, coaxing her on, with statements that spoke to her inner ego. She could not help but do every nasty and sinful thing he asked for, it was as if he could control her deepest thoughts and she relished everything he said.

Her dress would be ruined after they were finished but that didn't matter to Mary Lou. She would help Ed release himself and in returned she would be there to clean him and worship his body. Afterwards, she would feed him and he would take her to her bedroom for more. He enjoyed Mary Lou thoroughly, she was pliable, gullible, and devoted. He worshiped her body too but it was with a savage animal lust that she desperately wanted. Mary Lou never knew that he had listened to her and her girlfriend's discussions over the phone. It was these insider notes that allowed him to seduce her as easily as eating pie. She finally drifted off to sleep sometime during the night but he eventually waked her up in the early morning hours with a kiss and told her that he had to get back to Panama City before too late in the morning so he could get to a new work site. Mary Lou sat up in bed and immediately asked when she would see him again. "Soon, I'll call you at the end of the week, Sweetheart," was all he said as he kissed her again and left the house.

As soon as he got back to his truck he could hear the man scuffling around in the back. He started his truck and drove off towards a lone country road. Before too long he pulled over and waited a second to look at a map and administer his knock out cloth over the man's mouth. Then he drove off again where he soon found the entrance to an old farm and parked beside a cow pasture.

Quietly, he walked to the back of the bread truck, pushed the man over onto his side and pulled his pants down exposing the man's behind. He reached into a cleverly hidden compartment inside the back of his bread truck and pulled out a glass vile of concentrated acid. He opened the container, spread the man's ass cheeks and poured a few drops onto the man's anus. Then he pulled the man's pants up, refastened them and then dragged the man out of the bread truck.

As quickly as he could, Ed lifted his victim over his left shoulder and began to walk down a very dark lane towards the old farm house. As soon as he could see the house an old hound dog began to bark. He dropped his victim on the ground, untied him, removed the gag, and pulled out a note scribbled on a scrap of paper and shoved it into the man's shirt pocket. Then he jogged back to his truck where he backed out of the lane while keeping his headlights off. A few miles down the road, he spotted a telephone pole and pulled over next to it and began assembling his gear and note book.

Sometime before sunrise he received his first phone conversation. It was no surprise to him that the voices where stressed and terrified. Apparently, the old Reverend Templeton discovered

Ed's newest victim that morning and was seriously disturbed. Somehow, he and his companions in the farm house believed that Dr. Conradi had hired a perverted homosexual goon that molested one of the preacher's devoted followers. When did church followers become knock-off-men, thought Ed. These people were a little too zealous, he thought, but he knew that his bosses would want to hear his report as soon as possible. The note that he left on his victim simply read, "You're Fucked." The rest of their speculation was purely their imagination. This would buy him and his bosses enough time to make their next move. Once again, he finished taking his notes and quietly climbed down the pole and drove off back down the country road as quickly as he could.

Chapter 5

When he finally made it back to Pensacola, he drove directly downtown to the San Carlos Hotel, parked his truck in the back and immediately headed towards the private service entrance. When he reached the seventh floor. He sat down on the last step and breathed in deeply. He hated using the stairs but he knew the elevator boy would ask too many questions. After a minute of regaining his breath, he made it to his boss's suite and knocked on the door.

When the door opened, Mr. Goldring met Ed and invited him inside. Both the Sullivan brothers were sitting in chairs looking out towards Pensacola Bay. "Pour Pauli a drink, Saul," said Byron Sullivan. He took the glass of whiskey from Mr. Goldring and began to drink it slowly down in one sip. "Now I've got my story telling voice on fellows. Are y'all ready for the low down, gentlemen?"

Tom immediately motioned for Mr. Goldring to refill Ed's glass and Byron stood up and asked him to sit down and tell them everything. He pulled out his note book, sat down, took another sip of whiskey, and began to recall everything he heard and did that week. After his debriefing, the Sullivan brothers wasted no time in giving new orders for him upon which Byron reached into his coat pocket and handed an envelope to him.

Tom reached into his wallet and handed him more money as a bonus for doing extra work. "We appreciate you thinking on your feet, Paul, but we are going to need these folks to disappear soon." "We'll let Mr. Johnson know that your back and we'll call you sometime this week for your next assignment," remarked Tom Sullivan. He showed them his gratitude and headed back down the steps after his debriefing.

Within a few minutes he was already back on the road heading toward the west side of Pensacola. He was always exhausted when his assignments were over so he quickly headed towards U street where he lived a modest domestic life.

By the time he pulled up to his house and parked the truck, his wife Mabel had ready a plate full of buttered corn bread, a bowl of cooked collard greens, and a mug of black coffee waiting for him on the dinner table. As soon as he walked in the door little Arthur ran up to his daddy and jumped into his father's arms. Ed hugged his son, sat him back down and walked over to his wife, reached around her waist, kissed her on her cheek, and pinched her right breast.

She quickly kissed him back while holding her husband's hands down. "Sit down Sweetheart and eat," chided his wife. He didn't argue. He was famished and tired. After he ate and told them how much fish he caught and telephone wire he had strung, Ed winked at Mabel and she immediately picked up little Arthur and told him to go play in his room. It wasn't long before Arthur heard those funny noises his mother made when his daddy returned from out of town.

Early the next morning, Ed awoke and reached over to his wife and pulled her underneath himself. Already exhausted from the previous night, Mabel just laid there and held her husband until he was done. She was always afraid to turn him down before he left for the day and she knew this was his way of marking his territory. She dared not interfere. After turning her over and finishing his deed, he got dressed and headed off to relieve himself in the bathroom. Mabel began her daily routine and started fixing her boy's lunches for the day. As soon as they all ate breakfast together, Ed ruffled Arthur's hair and gave his wife a kiss goodbye.

His job at the telephone company was a hot and grueling affair but somehow, he always made time to do his telephone work and make his rounds collecting money for his real bosses too.

Sometime around noon he pulled up to his favorite downtown brothel in Pensacola's Haymarket. The local Madam always paid on time and completely understood his addiction to her working girls. In fact, Madam Mirabella fully enjoyed the attention he gave her and the girls and she always welcomed his protection. Nobody ever stiffed her or mistreated her girls and she was able to walk proudly down Palafox and Garden street, without anyone giving her a sinful stare. Business was good for Madam Mirabella and lately her new-found whiskey deliveries made her business grow substantially.

A few hours later after he dropped off his collections to Mr. Goldring. He was able to make it back to his home to begin his afternoon ritual. After cleaning up, he put on a clean cotton shirt and walked over to the outside garage, turned on his barber pole light and opened the garage door exposing a make shift barber shop-salon with a barber's chair, a refrigerated ice box and a large radio inside tuned to his favorite station. On one side of the garage he had a church pew bench where customers were able to wait in line while they were able to sit comfortably.

Within a few minutes an old man walked in and greeted him. "Well hello there Mr. Edward. How's it going?" Replied one of his loyal customers. "It's been hotter than hell Mr. Weisman." "Come on in and have a seat here," said Ed as he lowered his barber chair and waited to wrap a sheet around the fellow. "A trim and a shave Mr. Weisman?" He asked as the older man nodded his head. By the time he was done shaving Mr. Weisman, there were two more men waiting for a haircut and shave.

Sometime later Mabel rang the dinner bell that he had been placed just outside the back-kitchen door announcing dinner time for her husband in his make shift barber shop. After closing up, he quickly cleaned himself and made his way to the kitchen. When dinner was done and Mabel began to clean up the kitchen, young Arthur and his daddy walked into the living room and Arthur turned on the family radio and tuned to his favorite show. Ed sat down in his recliner and closed his eyes listening to the Rin Tin Tin Radio show. An hour later the phone rang.

He could hear Mabel talking and got up. "Mr. Goldring says you need to meet him tomorrow morning over at the Casino before seven o'clock, says the telephone lines are down and they need fixing." He just shook his head and walked back to his room and crawled into bed.

It took him sometime to ferry across Pensacola Bay and over to the beach the next morning. However, while sitting in his truck during each ferry crossing, he could see how much progress they were making building the first bridges across the bay and the sound. Everything was changing so fast. It wouldn't be too long before people would be driving to the beach whenever they wanted. As he watched the ferry chug along, he began to reminisce.

His first job was on Pensacola beach in 1921. Back then Prohibition was still young and his new bosses had made him a life guard and night keeper for their new nightclub called the Casino. They had it all back then, money, power, and all the booze and pussy a fellow ever needed. Things were simple for him back in those days. All he had to do was keep an eye on Pensacola's wealthy during the day and help the Jews run the Casino and brothels at night. The Sullivan brothers even had workers build him a modest concrete bungalow on the sound side with running water and an outhouse. During the summer he simply lived on the island, fishing, working, and learning how to live.

That was when he first met Gunny Fletcher and Chief Mimms. They were his real teachers. The Sullivan's needed professionals and they were the perfect candidates. Both the Gunny and Chief were retired veterans from the Navy and the Marine Corps and they were very good at their jobs. He was quickly placed in their hands by the Sullivan's and they were told to make him learn, listen, and obey.

Young Ed, at the time never knew just how deep he had placed himself in the service of his new bosses. Gunny Fletcher and Chief Mimms were strict and thorough with him. The first time he saved a swimmer from the rip tide and brought the boy back to the beach, he knew to not make a fuss about it. He was simply doing his job and had remembered the second rule his new teachers taught him. Never, ever brag about your success. That only brought unnecessary trouble. That was the beginning of his learning days and a long apprenticeship with the Gunny and Chief Mimms.

Horses were not animals that he was fond of much. The first duty he had was to always feed, clean, groom, and water Gunny and Chief's horses. Without them it was quite hard to cover the island due to almost no roads. There was nothing but white sand dunes with scrub oaks and sea oats covering the entire island. One morning he forgot to clean the stalls of horse shit and Gunny nearly went mad. Ed never thought an older man could beat him so bad that he couldn't cough without wincing for an entire week. These new teachers terrified him but in time they would teach him much of what he needed to know.

When the last ferry landed on Pensacola beach, he already had his truck turned on and was waiting for the all clear to drive off the landing. It didn't take him long to reach the Casino and he could already see Chief Mimms sitting on his horse watching men unload another boat of liquor being delivered by one of Pensacola's sea captains. Prohibition was impossible to control in an old port city, with so many fleets of ships coming and going from the port of Pensacola, it was simply too easy for smugglers. There was no law on the beach except Chief and Gunny and no one ever wanted to get in their way.

He walked into the Casino and immediately met Mr. Goldring and his associates, Mr. Bert and Mr. Myron. "What do you gentlemen need?" asked Ed. "We have a little problem in the back room, Pauli." Said Mr. Goldring, "We need it to disappear." Mr. Myron motioned for Ed to follow him. When they got to the back-room Mr. Bert opened the door. He immediately saw a young negro girl's body gutted in her midsection with her innards hanging halfway out laying on top of an old wool blanket.

"Jesus Fucking Christ!" Ed whistled and took his hat off. Mr. Goldring quickly closed the door behind every one and began to tell them about the message from the local clan. "Apparently, the

Star Lake Country Club boys, AKA, Pensacola's KKK chapter, didn't like negro girls being prostituted on the beach and this was their message."

"Well Hot-to-mighty dam boys, I guess they didn't get the memo," declared Ed. "What memo would that be?" asked Mr. Bert. Mr. Goldring beat him to the punch, "The memo that said, we are the ones that are in charge," stated Mr. Goldring. He looked at Mr. Goldring and waited. "Get rid of the body and come back for your new assignment Paul, I'll be waiting at the Ferry. There is a boat moored down the beach with a new kid in training. Be gentle," said Mr. Goldring. After collecting the body and putting it in the back of his truck, he made his way to where Gunny was waiting.

He drove down the beach a little ways on the Gulf side, and eventually saw the old Gunny and a slim boy pulling ashore in an on old sailing skiff. He backed his truck towards the shore and opened the back of his converted bread truck. The kid's eyes were as wide as saucers and already he knew the boy must have started his training from Gunny. "What's your pleasure, Gunny?" asked Ed. "Go ahead and take Jimmy with you and show him the ropes," said the old Gunny "and don't waste any time." Gunny got out of the boat and simply walked off back towards the Casino down the beach.

Ed told the boy to help lift the body into the boat. With everything else he needed, together they rowed the boat far enough out to sea to set the sails down and off they went. An hour later, he dropped the sails and turned the boat around. "Is this the first time you've helped the Gunny and Chief with work like this?" asked Ed. Jimmy looked at him and said "This is the second time."

"Grab that concrete block son, and tie this here rope through it good with a tight knot. You do know how to tie a knot don't you?" "Yes Sir," said the boy. "The Chief has already taught me over seven different knots." Ed remembered each one of the Chief's knot tying exercises he too had to learn back in the day. "Good, then tie it good and watch how I tie her to the block." He pulled out a long thick iron needle with a welded eye ring at the end, tied the end of the rope though the end of the needle and immediately threaded the needle through the skull of the young negro girl. Jimmy vomited over the side of the boat. "Why did you do that," asked Jimmy.

"Her body will be eaten by the fish and eventually fall apart but her skull will stay here on the bottom of the Gulf. You don't want her ghost to haunt the island, do you?" Asked Ed with a twinkle in his eye. "Now help me push her over." Together they threw the girl's body over the side of the boat with the concrete block and rope.

During the trip back towards the island he could tell this boy was not cut out for this sort of job. He would have to learn it soon or become the Chiefs fodder and the Gunny's problem. Young Jimmy just kept looking at the horizon with a thousand-mile stare, not saying a word the whole time back. Not anyone could do this sort of work and thrive Ed thought. "Only the strong could survive this world and be successful," he could remember Gunny saying to him when he was learning his trade.

By the time he made it back to the shore where his bread truck was parked, it was high noon and the heat was becoming too much to handle. "Take the boat back and report to your station as soon as possible," relayed Ed. The boy remarked "Yes Sir" and did exactly what he was told. Ed grinned to himself and took off in his truck down the beach. Gunny was already forging this lad into something tougher than when he first met his teacher thought Ed. The bosses didn't tolerate slackers and he had the scars to prove it.

When he pulled his truck up onto the ferry to wait until it set off for Pensacola, Mr. Goldring got out of his car, walked over to the back of his truck. Ed got out and went to the back of his truck and opened up the back doors. "How about it, Mr. Goldring?" asked

Ed. "Excellent Paul. However, this incident needs addressing tonight if you know what I mean," said Mr. Goldring.

He pulled out an envelope from his coat and handed it to him saying, "Everything you need to know is written down. The person in question is a local judge and it's best for the Families to show their disapproval of this sort of blatant disrespect. Perhaps a little overt demonstration of our point. Nothing too vulgar, mind you, just a strong message and reminder of who's in charge," said Mr. Goldring with a smile and quiet demeanor. Ed tipped his hat and said "Yes Sir Mr. Goldring, I will see you tomorrow afternoon." "Good day," declared Mr. Goldring. Thirty minutes later Saul Goldring watched him drive off towards Brownsville with another important job to do.

Sometime late that night, a boat pulled up to the dock of a beautiful craftsman bungalow overlooking Bayou Texar. Ed jumped out and tied his boat to the end of the dock, removed his tool bag and quietly got out and headed towards the house. Half way across the yard an old yellow retriever barked at him from a dog house and he quickly reached into his pocket and pulled out a pig bone and foot. He threw a large chunk of it towards the dog and jogged up to the house. The old dog got silent quickly and began slobbering over the pig's foot. Minutes later, he opened the back door with a special tool he had made and went looking for the maid's room searching for the servants. Sure enough, there was a young negro girl sleeping in the bed and no one else in the room. This judge had his own perversions, thought Ed, as he crept up to the bed and held the cloth over the girl's mouth.

Upstairs he found the judge and his wife sleeping in different bedrooms. This job was going to be easier than he thought. A few minutes later, he was headed to the boat, with the judge, hog tied and thrown over his shoulder. He dropped the judge into the boat as softly as he could so he wouldn't make any loud noises. Then he walked back towards the house again to make a clear and obvious statement.

He immediately went to the judge's private office, found the liquor and poured himself a drink. Then he walked back upstairs and closed the doors to the master bedroom. For a few seconds Ed contemplated having his way with the wife but there were some things even he wouldn't do and rape never interested him. The judge's wife was still knocked out when he cut her throat with one of his shaving blades. He walked back downstairs and repeated his performance on the maid, wiped off his blade and returned to his boat throwing the last bit of meat to the old retriever. The women would never know who their killer was and neither would the police. But the judge would know of it right before he cut off his head and fed his body to the fish in the bay. Sometime in the early dawn hours of the morning, a paper boy rode by and saw a man's severed head with a note in its mouth sitting on the top step of the courthouse in downtown Pensacola. The clan would get their message without any further delays.

The newspaper had their sensational story the next day and the San Carlos Hotel was busier than ever that afternoon when he pulled into the service entrance. Apparently, a senator, with a rather large entourage was staying in one of the suites upstairs. By the time he made it up the flight of stairs he was out of breath again and in the company of a few fellows hanging out smoking cigarettes in the stair way. "Who do you guys work for," asked Ed as he sat down and caught his breath.

"Senator Roosevelt," replied one of the guys. "Hey, did you hear about that judge that lost his head down at the courthouse?" Asked one of the men. "Apparently, there was a note in his mouth that said he was a nigger lover. What do you think that means?" Asked the other guy. Ed stood up, brushed his clothes off and said

"I guess he likes dark meat," as he started to walk to the door leading to the corridor. Both of the fellows began to laugh and one of the guys remarked, "Yeah, probably so."

After knocking twice, Mr. Goldring answered and showed him inside. "Fix old Pauli a drink Saul, he deserves it." Byron Sullivan offered him his seat and walked over to the desk to retrieve Ed's payment. "We sure like your punctuality Paul," said Tom Sullivan after toasting him with his glass of whiskey. "Indeed, I say, you're getting better and better. But don't let all this success go to your head. Remember what Gunny and Chief taught you, Paul." "How could I ever forget," he stammered. Even the mentioning of his mentor's names by his bosses still made him a little nervous.

"Looks like you're going to have go on a little vacation this time for about two weeks," said Tom Sullivan. "Mabel's been itching for me to take her somewhere, does the assignment include company?" "Yes, I believe that would be fine. This time you will take the train to St. Augustine and await further instructions. Saul will make the arrangements." Ed looked up and motioned with his right hand towards Mr. Goldring. "I will need two tickets please?" Mr. Goldring just nodded his head.

When he told Mabel that night she was so excited that she nearly wet herself. "We will have to let momma watch Arthur while we're gone," Mabel said, after they had made love again. "Are you sure you don't want my folks to watch him?" Mabel shot him an intense look and declared, "No thank you sir. Your daddy is too mean and your momma is too busy raising young'uns of her own to look after another one." He didn't bother to argue the point. Raising children was her department and he would leave it up to her anyway.

The next day he hopped onto one of Pensacola's trolleys heading downtown on Lakeview Avenue. His truck was being outfitted with another set of tires at his brother, Alto's garage, and he loved riding the trolley up to East Hill where there were a few housewives that he liked to look in on every now and then. However, this trip was more for business. He had just come from a house in East Hill where he bought a pair of green diamond earrings and a white diamond wedding ring from a Jewish diamond merchant working out of his home.

He knew that the green diamonds would look stunning against his wife's flaming red hair. Diamonds always fascinated him and he especially enjoyed watching how women behaved around them. But that wasn't the only reason he was visiting. It just so happened that his former boss's son had been blinded at the end of the Great War and he looked in on him, from time to time.

They had become close friends after the Chief asked him if he would go by his son's house and give him a haircut every so often. It didn't take the trolley long before it pulled up right in front of his friend's home. He jumped off the trolley and made his way up to where the blind veteran lived.

After he knocked on the door, Simon Mimms hollered "Coming," and immediately he saw his friend shuffle towards the front door. "Hey partner, how's it going?" Asked Ed. "Fair enough, Pauli. What brings you by?" "I've brought my barber bag with me, you're over a month due. Besides your daddy don't like it when you start looking like a rag-a-muffin. And you know that," argued Ed.

"Give me some gossip, Pauli. I want to hear it all," replied Simon, as he sat in a kitchen chair on the back porch of his home. Ed draped a sheet around him and began to cut his hair, telling him about current events in the Family business. He had a natural way of telling stories where he used certain types of meaningful details that captivated his audience.

That was one of the things that made Simon like him so much. Simon's need to stay aware of current events made him still feel important, so when Ed told him any news, that was exactly what he wanted. Friends were something of a commodity with Ed and he endearingly fostered as many of them as he possibly could. He eventually worked late through the evening trying to catch up on all his telephone work at the company. By the time he came home it was too late to open his barber shop. All he wanted to do was eat, rut, and fall asleep. Which was exactly what he did.

Chapter 6

The next evening, after working a hard day's work for the telephone company, he arrived back home and began to assemble his work kit that he made just for those specialty jobs that he did for the Sullivan brothers. There was one leather satchel inside another larger old sea trunk that carried his weapons, clothes, and other tools of his trade and profession. He gave his wife a smaller sea trunk and brought it inside for her to pack.

Mabel couldn't believe it when she opened the trunk and found the set of riding clothes he had bought and stored inside the trunk. She immediately asked if there were going to be stables where they were going and could they go riding. She knew that Ed never really liked horses and just had to ask because of the clothes in the trunk. "Yes, yes, yes, and yes" he said. "There are stables, horses and we're going to go for a ride along the beach, just like you always wanted to do, Mabel," replied Ed. His wife grinned, squealed, and hugged her husband as tight as she could.

The following morning, Ed and Mabel sat comfortably on the train heading for Tallahassee. It was during this time that he pulled out the letter Mr. Goldring gave him the day before. All the letter said was to check in at the Ponce De Leon Hotel and wait for further instructions.

Easy enough thought Ed, but the instructions were a bit vague, so he began to wonder. Usually, Mr. Goldring's letters were a little too wordy with more emphasis on the specifics. He eventually put the letter away and watched his wife sleep across from him on the train with a smile on her face. Later that day while they were eating in the dining car, he noticed that there was a bus boy cleaning off one of the tables and was sneaking a bite from the discarded plates. He paid it no attention but sometime later, he walked down to the restaurant cars and found the same bus boy smoking a cigarette standing outside of the kitchen car.

He opened the door and walked outside of the car on the moving train and lit a cigarette as well and leaned up against the train watching the scenery change in front of him. "How's it going, kid?" "My shift is over and I'm still hungry," said the dimple faced boy drawing a puff on his cigarette. "How long do you work on this here train?" Ed questioned. "I only work on the Pensacola to Jacksonville line," the boy answered. Ed leaned back, took a drag off his smoke, blew it out and asked the boy if he'd be interested in another job.

The boy introduced himself as Johnny and then asked him what kind of job it was. Ed introduced himself as Paul and began to spin a tale about being a detective looking for certain folks riding the train from Pensacola to Jacksonville. "How much would it pay?" asked Johnny. "Well, every time you give me something worth knowing I'll give you a dollar starting with this one right here" he said as he pulled out a silver dollar from his coat pocket and handed it over to the slack jawed kid.

"If you can keep your mouth shut, your eyes and ears open and deliver to me the right information, then you might just get a better pay off," related Ed. Johnny kept looking at the silver dollar in his hands and licking his lips. "Sure, boss, no problem," said the boy.

Ed pulled out a few photos he brought with him and handed them to the kid and began telling Johnny what he wanted him to do. A few hours later, he and Mabel switched trains and headed towards St. Augustine. By the time the trained pulled into their destination it was already late in the evening and it was too dark for Mabel to see anything.

When they walked into the hotel, the scene nearly took his wife's breath away. She had only read about places like this and never dreamed of actually staying in a place like it. The Ponce De Leon Hotel was a Flagler hotel and it showed. The ceilings, arches, floors, with plants and palms decorating the well-lit lobby brought about with awe struck wonder.

He thoroughly enjoyed watching his wife take it all in knowing that she was going to have the time of her life. After checking in, a bellhop was assigned to them, Ed received his room key, along with a letter from the hotel's clerk.

They reached their rooms and the bellhop showed them inside and opened the veranda windows that allowed the sea breeze to blow into the room. Ed tipped the boy and sat down to read his letter while Mabel went around and inspected the room. The next morning a well satisfied Ed awoke with another erection and pulled his wife back underneath him. "Jesus honey," moaned his Mabel as her husband entered her again.

"How many times are you going to get off Sweetie," asked his wife as he began to pick up his rhythm. He held her closer to him and began to speak to her about what they were going to do that day as he pumped faster and faster until finally he exploded inside his wife and collapsed on top of her. Mabel kissed him gently on the forehead and began to tell him how much she loved him.

Sometime after breakfast, they dressed for riding and made their way towards the stables. He had already made arrangements with the stable master earlier and knew that there would be horses waiting for them. When they arrived, the stable master introduced himself and showed them to their horses. Both of the horses had saddles and tack already fitted on them. There was a gray mare named Paige and her chestnut gelded son Samson. Mabel was shown to Samson and Ed awkwardly mounted Paige. The horses were actually rather tame and docile and before long he and Mabel made their way down to the beach to begin their journey along the shore.

By the time they raced their horses back to the stables the sun had already climbed high in the sky. They had spotted two pods of dolphins and various schools of fish that the dolphins were hunting. Watching the predatorial performances of the dolphin pods excited and amused him. The day was shaping up to be wonderful for them and he knew that sometime during their trip he would give his wife the diamond earrings and ring she never had yet had always wanted. He continued to wrestle with when he should give them to her.

While they enjoyed their lunch, he reached inside his coat and pulled out a wad of bills. He pulled enough money out for his wife to see and handed some to her saying, "I want you to go buy some clothes for this week and get a few evening gowns too. It looks like we will be attending a Ball while we are here, I'll have to get fitted for a tux as well." Mabel's eyes had opened even wider in complete astonishment. "Aw, come on now, you're just fooling me, right?" Asked Mabel while counting the money. He just stared at his wife and let an awkward moment creep by. She couldn't believe her husband. He was treating her like a queen and she was a little afraid that she would suddenly wake up from a dream.

Knowing that she was out of her league, he led his wife to the hotel's concierge for help. Besides, he didn't know the first thing about picking out evening gowns and it seemed way to effeminate anyhow. So as soon as he felt comfortable that she was being properly looked after he departed and went back to the room to retrieve some of his trade tools. When he was done he left the room and walked up the stair way to the top floor, entered the hall leading to the upper most suites and found the room.

He quietly turned the key that was slipped to him by his contact man and walked inside the room. He walked to the window, looked out, and sat his satchel down and opened it up. Inside were various parts of a bolt action long range rifle. Gunny personally made this particular gun and had trained him in its specific uses. Without making much sound, he assembled the gun and began looking out the window using the scope on his rifle. As soon as he was satisfied, he placed the gun and bag underneath the bed and left the room undisturbed.

Later that day he laid down on his bed and was reading the local newspaper when Mabel unlocked the door and walked inside the room with the bellhop in tow. "Thank goodness the concierge helped me out, I would have never known how or what to have gotten. Oh, Edward, you should see what I look like in my gowns," swooned Mabel. He got up and tipped the bellhop. When the boy closed the door, he reached over and grabbed his wife and kissed her warmly. "How about a little whoopie before dinner?" Asked Ed with a lop-sided grin and a look of sheer mischief on his face. She didn't argue with him. Soon after they had finished making love both Ed and Mabel dressed for dinner and returned to the restaurant. She was thoroughly fascinated and he was completely enjoying himself.

The week crept by slowly for him as he waited for his phone call, although he was sure that Mabel's week probably flew by with all the excitement she was having. The evening before, they had taken dance lessons that the concierge arranged for them and they enjoyed all the attention and their new-found skills.

His wife was having the time of her life but he was simply too anxious to get his job done. The following morning, he received the much-awaited phone call. After shooting skeet down the beach some ways, they headed back to the hotel for lunch. Ed looked at his watch and told his wife to go ahead and find a table at the restaurant.

Then he made his way up to the suite where his gun was hidden. There was an undisturbed view from the window and his victim was the only person standing in the way of Mr. Charles Mott. Ed didn't really know who it was that he was about to kill but he did have an inkling that it had something to do with the destruction of the Southern Sugar Company.

He had been putting together a rather large portfolio over the last year for his bosses concerning the sugar company and he began noticing the larger pattern of what was happening. The Southern Sugar Company lately was so poorly managed that it didn't take long for the northern industrialist to begin their hostile takeover of the industry. Sugar had become a staple everywhere in the world. The war industry had to have it and the Families wanted it all for leverage against their enemies.

He kept watching his victim in the park across from the hotel until just the right moment, took a slow deliberate deep breath then pulled the trigger and watched his victim fall. Several minutes later and he had broken the gun down, stashed it back at his room and was walking back into the restaurant where his lunch was just being delivered to his table. "Thanks, Mabel, for ordering, I had to go to the bathroom. Would you like to know when we will be going to the Ball?" Inquired Ed as he sat down and draped his napkin across his lap.

A few days later he got another telephone call. This time however, he was going to have to be a little more daring but far more surreptitious with his deed. The next victim would be attending the annual Flagler Ball. Although it would be a little different this time, the results would still be the same thought Ed. He was just going to have to be a little subtler. The following afternoon after waiting for his wife to finish dressing herself and putting on what little makeup the concierge advised, Ed decided to present her with the green diamond earrings. She nearly screamed with utter delight as he helped fasten them to her ears.

They were clip-ons as she never had her ears pierced, because he wouldn't permit it. However, she felt like she was floating on a cloud in absolute heaven. Never in her life had she ever dreamed of living such a glamorous experience, much less be married to a man that treated her this way.

A few minutes later they stepped out of the room. She couldn't help herself from smiling so much. She was with the man of her dreams clutching a little silk purse and wearing a coral evening gown with silver slippers. He wore his tux and together, they looked fantastic. She was a little nervous but he soon calmed her with his soothing affirmations of her beautiful clothes, hairdo, and jewelry.

Flagler's Ball was a smorgasbord of who's who for Florida's State Legislature. It was where many politicians in Florida came to obtain the patronage and support from the industrial class for their candidacy and it was exactly where Ed needed to be that night. He and Mabel danced that evening until she could take it no more and she excused herself to attend the ladies powder room.

As soon as she was out of sight, he reached inside his coat and slowly pulled out a small glass vile from his inside pocket and gently poured its contents into his champagne glass. A few moments later he was walking in front of one of the politicians and suddenly, tripped and fell, spilling his drink unto the politician's coat.

Immediately, he began to profusely apologize and acted like he was trying to clean it off the politician's coat. Representative Darcy was not pleased but excused the fellow for being a little too drunk and ignored him as he left to play a game of cards with a potential client. An hour later, the cyanide began to creep into the representative's skin. Within moments the politician fell over dead holding the cards in his hand close to his chest.

The next morning the hotel employees were gossiping amongst themselves in the hotel lobby. Apparently, one of Florida's legislatures died of a heart-attack playing cards. None of the guest seemed to care though. Their indifference was obvious.

Everything had worked out perfectly for Ed. The only problem he had would be helping Mabel adjust to her old life style when they returned home. While riding back on the train to Pensacola that next day, he stood up in front of her and knelt down on one knee. He pulled out the diamond ring and gave it to her, thanking her for waiting so long to get a proper wedding ring.

She was over the moon and beside herself as she looked at it on her finger. He explained to her that the trip was something that they would not be able to do for quite a while because he had spent way too much money but he didn't care as long as she would cherish her memories forever. Mabel cooed into his ear that she would be pleased for years to come, knowing that her favorite man in the world loved her so. Together they fell asleep on the train still holding hands until the next stop.

Sometime after lunch, he noticed Johnny, the busboy, and he looked at him but continued his meal. An hour later they met each other for a smoke on the back-kitchen car. "Hey Johnny, got any news for me?" Johnny took a drag off his cigarette and began to tell him about who and what he saw over the last two weeks.

After Johnny finished his news, Ed reached into his coat pocket and pulled out a dollar for him. Johnny took the money and thanked him profusely. Ed told him to keep up what he was doing and that he would see him in a few weeks, tipped his hat and walked back to where his wife was sitting.

Ed & Mabel's trip to St. Augustine

Chapter 7

Sometime early that night they reached Pensacola's train station and headed home after picking up Arthur from Mabel's mothers. However, when they arrived back home on U St. There was a sheriff's car parked in front of the house with two police officers standing outside smoking cigarettes. Ed knew the officers. He got out of the car and invited them to come in for a cup of coffee. Sheriff's deputy Willis looked at him and nodded his head saying sure but they would sit on the front porch instead.

By the time Mabel brought a tray with cups of black coffee on it, he had heard enough of what he needed to know. There was an election soon and he was needed by the department to do some detective work. He never turned down any job the police asked of him and he never asked for a payment either. The law enforcement in the county and city had always been on the Families payroll and he knew better than to pry where he didn't need to go.

It was just a simple form of extraction and extortion that they were looking for and that was easy as eating pie for the Telephone Man.

The next day he began his routine work on Pensacola's downtown telephon lines. Within a few hours he had discovered where the right line was located and was already setting his special work phone to it when he looked down and saw Mr. Wentworth walking by smoking a cigar, heading down on Garden street. Few people ever saw the man during the day. He was usually held up at the newspaper building, managing and editing. Whenever Ed did get to see the old man he was usually gambling at the Casino on Pensacola Beach.

Eventually, he found the conversation that he wanted to hear and began writing down what he needed to get. There was another mayoral race and the Sullivan's obviously wanted their man to win. Mr. Henry Armstrong Jr. would be the next mayor of Pensacola and Ed was going to make sure his bosses would get their man. It wasn't too long before he received all that he needed and began to climb back down the pole. By the time he delivered his report to the police chief downtown it was already too late to open his barber shop so instead he headed off to Madam Mirabella's place for some whiskey and a little fun.

The next morning, before sunrise, the phone rang and Ed got up, and answered it still half asleep. "We need you at the courthouse basement this morning," said Mr. Goldring. "What time you need me there?" "An hour from now, please." "Yes Sir," was all he said before he hung up the phone. Winter was approaching and the nights started to become colder. He dressed himself appropriately and headed off towards the courthouse. There were two police officers at the entrance to the basement of the courthouse when Ed parked his truck. They let him inside and he immediately could hear the screams of someone in agony in another room.

Mr. Wentworth was apparently the one screaming. Mr. Myron was in a room down the hall sitting next to the old newsman, who was tied to a chair. Mr. Myron was holding the man's hand out as he pulled the terrified man's thumb nail out with a pair of pliers. Within minutes the newsman passed out and went limp. Tom Sullivan and Mr. Goldring ushered Ed out and into the next room where they began to tell him about Mr. Wentworth's gambling debts and how he was going to repay them.

They began to discuss what they wanted him to do. The Sullivan's choice of candidate, that also controls the clan, would be Tom Wentworth Jr.. Mr. Goldring assured Ed that Mr. Wentworth's son Tom, would be the perfect candidate for the position but needed some persuasion. They were already collecting from the tax collector's office and besides he had already done a few jobs for the bosses to their approval.

What they needed was to find something to black mail him with so they could keep him on the books. "What about Mr. Wentworth senior in the other room," asked Ed. Mr. Goldring looked at Ed and said, "Don't worry about him, he'll write what we want him to write after today. He'll be on the hook for quite a while, I suspect. In the meantime, go back to Mr. Johnson at the telephone company and tell him that you're good till tomorrow."

By the time he drove his truck from the downtown out to Ferry Pass, the morning cold had already begun to burn off. Florida winters were never too cold and that was the way Ed liked it. He drove by various dairy farms sometime after lunch and began to think he wasn't going to find where he was looking for when suddenly, he heard a car horn and watched as Mr. Wentworth Jr. drove around him as fast as he could. Ed picked up his speed and began to follow him without being too conspicuous. The tax collector eventually pulled onto a lone driveway and parked his car.

The old farm house was dilapidated and nearly falling down. As quietly as he could manage. Ed stalked up to the house and looked inside the back window and noticed a gray haired old lady with nothing on but a black rubber corset with a whip in her hand and a mask on her face. What in the world was going on wondered Ed. Wentworth Jr. was on his hands and knees pleading for forgiveness and trying to unbutton his shirt while staying in the prone position.

It was a demeaning act that she apparently enjoyed forcing on her compliant victim with apparent pleasure. Ed went back to his truck and found his Kodak camera, took off the flash and crept back to the old farm house where he began clicking away at the most humiliating scenes that he had ever seen. An hour later and he had all the evidence he needed for the extortion that his bosses wanted.

It always amazed him how people were never good at covering their incriminating behaviors while they were holding a public office. When he finally got back to his house that afternoon, he went to his garage, locked the door, and went to the back where he had a makeshift laboratory designed for chemistry, ballistics, and also doubled as a darkroom when needed. After finishing all the sets of photos gathered from the mission he attached them to a close line strung up for drying them out and left the room to let them finish processing.

While waiting in his shop he sat in his barber chair with a clip board, blank sheet of paper, pencil, and a rubber eraser. Ed could draw nearly anything he could recollect from memory. It was a skill he'd picked up from an artist on Pensacola Beach when he was life guarding. The artist was an eccentric female college art instructor with a taste for young men. He learned not only how to draw but much of what and how to please a woman. Within a half an hour, he had all the set of pictures processed, dried, and stored in a folder with all their negative, too.

After cleaning up his laboratory and closing the door behind him, he had just enough time to open the curtains and turn on the barbershop pole announcing that he was open for business. Within a few minutes a loyal customer walked up and asked for a haircut. "Sure thing Mr. Fleisher," said Ed as he stood up, put his clip board away and made ready to give the man a fresh haircut and shave.

The next morning found him climbing up another pine pole, fixing telephone lines when he suddenly remembered to call Ms. Mary Lou. After finishing his current work, he climbed back down the pole and drove off looking for another line to place a call to his favorite Tallahassee girl. Moments later he was up another pole, placing the call through to the company's dispatcher. Nearly all the telephone operators in Pensacola loved him. He knew them all and something about each of their families. It wasn't long before Betty Fay put him through to a special line that he and only a few executives could use.

Mary Lou soon answered. "Hello Mary Lou, how's your brother been treating you?" "Is that you, Paul?" "Sure is, Mary Lou." That's when she began to tell him things about herself that he found quite uninteresting but he listened. After she rambled for a while, he excused himself and began to tell her how much he missed her voice and that he wouldn't be down that way for a while but he would be calling her sometime soon.

Mary Lou didn't mind so much as long as he listened to her rant, which was exactly what she did for the next twenty minutes while he sat there and casually rolled several cigarettes for later use. She told him that she would wait patiently for his next call. A few minutes after the phone call he drove off down the road towards his next job. Later that afternoon when he finished his collections and made it back to his boss's office at the San Carlos Hotel, he nearly tripped over an old hobo sitting in the service entrance to the hotel. "What the hell," said Ed as he stumbled over the sleeping hobo.

Within a few seconds, the hobo jumped up and sprang at him with astonishing speed and pinned him against the wall, holding the back of Ed's head in a vice grip. A few seconds later, the hobo released him and removed the hat and fake beard he was wearing. Gunny Fletcher had caught him off guard and he immediately knew it.

"Jesus H. Fucking Christ, Gunny. Now what do I have to do to pay you back for this embarrassment?" huffed Ed as he and Gunny began to walk up the stairs together. "Well, start observing your fucking surroundings, Paul, the way the Chief and I taught you, Boy. How many times do I have to show you, kid. Not everything is as it appears to be. Always stay on the alert especially when something is not as it is supposed to be" replied the old Gunny.

Ed shook his head and kneaded his sore jaw as they climbed the stairs. "Oh yeah, I'll take either a ten dollar note or you can let me punch you in the gut for your mistake." Ed stared at him for half a second and then pulled his wallet out and handed Gunny a ten-dollar bill. He knew how strong Gunny was and didn't care to feel the excruciating pain. The Chief and Gunny always collected on their punishments and lessons that they taught him and some things seem to never change.

A few minutes later they were both sitting in the Sullivan's office, being briefed on their next job. Mr. Goldring explained to them that there was a problem in the Blocks. The Belmont DeVilliers community, otherwise known as the Blocks, was Pensacola's largest negro community during the 1930s and lately there had been a large amount of heroin being sold there.

Apparently, the smack had eventually made its way to the employees of the lumber and paper industries and that had the big bosses seriously upset. Their work force was already being depleted by the newly found addictions and they wanted it stopped. Within a few days they quickly found out that the one to talk to was a negro man named Hercules Green, a rather ostentatious hustler with a knack for disappearing like a ghost only to reappear somewhere across town. Gunny didn't believe in ghost but decided to watch Hercules incognito.

Ed continued to work on Pensacola's phone lines while eavesdropping on various phone conversations as he went along. Over the next few days they were able to piece together how Hercules got around so fast. Somehow Hercules Green had two negro doppelgangers, one from Titusville Florida, and the other from Century. All three together allowed Hercules to be in several places at once and made it possible for Hercules to run his dope from somewhere in South Florida to Pensacola and then to Detroit. It was a confusing relay system. Gunny was none too impressed and decided to hatch a plan to round up Hercules for further interrogation.

Gunny went undercover as a traveling sales man that was hopelessly peddling hair tonic for negro barbershop owners that he claimed worked best on black folks. Hercules Green was receiving a new hair cut in the barbershop in the Blocks when Gunny entered and began to demonstrate his wares by giving free samples out to the owner for his approval as well as future sales.

As soon as Hercules was finished and was paying for his hair cut, Gunny closed up his suit case and they headed for the front entrance door about the same time. As soon as they were outside, away from the customers, Gunny pulled out a small wooden baton from inside his coat and knocked Hercules over the head and dragged him to his car. There were several colored fellows watching from in front of the store and saw Gunny perform his daring maneuver.

They all began to run over to help their fellow friend but were quickly astonished at how fast Gunny slipped his baton away and pulled out a black revolver and pointed it at them saying for them to stand down or he would kill every one of them without so much as giving a damn. Gunny even cocked the hammer on his gun to prove the point and they all began to back away. After slipping his gun back up and lifting Hercules into the passenger side of his car he got in and drove off with many of the men starring at the tail end of his vehicle in complete confusion.

On the first Sunday of the next month, Ed sat in his truck outside the back of the Police Department and waited for Gunny to return from inside the police station. Hercules Green was being interrogated inside the police station and Gunny was leading the questions. When Gunny eventually returned, Ed was ready to get going. As he drove Gunny back to the bay front, Gunny told him that he would be going on another train ride but this time it was going to be Miami. Gunny would be the point man on this next assignment and Ed would be the scout. There would also be a meeting in Jacksonville with the big bosses. Ed considered, the less he knew who was in charge, the better. However, the Telephone Man was their creation and he knew that he would have to do whatever they asked of him no matter what.

Chapter 8

The following afternoon, Ed sharpened his razor blades as he sat in his barber chair and listened to the radio. Cleaning, sharpening, and mending his tools of his trade became a monthly ritual for him. Every knife blade would be sharpened and oiled, each gun would be methodically broken down, cleaned and reassembled and everything carefully inventoried just like he was taught by Gunny and Chief.

He even had a make shift chemistry lab that fit inside a heavily worn suitcase that usually remained locked and stored underneath his work bench in the back of his barber shop. Each and everything he would need would be seen to and made ready for use. Remembering what the Chief and Gunny had taught him sometimes brought back feelings of pain and sweat began to form on his brow. Those lessons were hard won and excruciatingly learned. He wouldn't let them down. For he knew what would follow if he did.

Gunny sat on the train the next morning looking like Mark Twain in a brown and tan suit reading a newspaper and smoking a pipe. Ed sat further back and kept an eye on him until he noticed young Johnny passing by walking towards the rear of the train. After a few minutes, he headed back the same way. Johnny was standing in the rear of the train smoking a cigarette when he found him. "Got any news for me, Kid?" "Yeah, there's been a whole bunch of Yankees riding lately. The men in those pictures you showed me, well I saw a few of them leaving the train station in Jacksonville yesterday evening." Ed put a silver dollar in Johnny's coat pocket and told him to keep his eyes peeled for any more suspicious behavior. The boy smiled and thanked him again but asked him if he was interested in something special to help ease his pain. "What would that be," asked Ed. Johnny pulled a piece of paper from his coat, unfolded it and began to explain to him that it was a wonderful drug called heroin and it helped make a person forget all his pain and woes.

Ed immediately seized the package and asked him where he got it from. Johnny could tell that he was none too pleased and quickly told him that he was given a little sample by one of the negro cooks in the kitchen car. Ed looked at the boy rather seriously and said, "Johnny, if you ever want to know what it feels like to have one of your ears cut off and your right eye plucked out by a rusty knife then go ahead and keep doing this here drug, Boy.

If I were you, I would tell which cook wanted you to sell this shit on the train or I'm going to do just that." Ed shot the boy a look so cold that poor Johnny began to stammer and quickly told him which cook it and apologized for offering it to him. Ed just shook his head, looked at the heroin, tossed it overboard, and told Johnny not to worry but if anything like it ever occurred again that he wouldn't be so nice. However, he told him to report to him as soon as possible when and if anyone else tried to offer him that very same drug and to make sure that he got their name. Young Johnny immediately asked him where would he find him so he could tell him if it ever happened again.

Ed looked at him sternly told him he would find Johnny where ever he was and he would hear of it sooner than he realized because he had eyes and ears everywhere in Florida. The boy swallowed his next thought and nodded his head and replied "Yes Sir."

Several minutes later he was in the kitchen car with Gunny holding the negro cook's hand over a gas flame on the stove. Gunny was not a very talkative man. He would ask a simple question and expect a specific answer. The other kitchen staff were standing outside the kitchen car trying their best not to fall off the small area they were shoved into. It didn't take very long for Gunny to get exactly what he wanted to hear and had Ed release the cooks arm and hand.

"I want you to act like this never happened. In fact, I want you to tell your boss that he has a new boss and his name is Mr. Sullivan. Do you understand me, Boy?" Asked Gunny. The cook nodded his head and immediately began to say Yes Sir several times before Gunny motioned for Ed to let the other staff back into the kitchen. A day later and he and Gunny stepped off the train in Miami. Gunny checked into his hotel room and Ed found his contact man just across the tracks at an old boarding house run by a fat Cuban matron named Mrs. Perez. Within a few minutes of casual conversation, he discovered where he needed to be.

The Ambassador nightclub ran a few slot machines in the back and a numbers racket as well but the main attraction was show girls. However, that wasn't why he was there. He needed to find who was in charge of the negro heroin trade in the South that had lately become an issue in Pensacola and he was determined to find out who was in charge. After a few questions placed here and there, he was back outside the building, walked around to the back, found a telephone pole and began climbing it. A few minutes later he had connected his special work phone to the right line and was listening to the club's manager discuss his very own presence to another fellow on the line.

The club's manager happened to be calling an officer in the local police to check on a stranger staying at the boarding house down the street. Ed called Gunny and told him about the conversation. Together they made their plan. By the time he made it back to his room at the boarding house he had just enough time to shave and change his clothes. As soon as he sat down and lit a cigarette there was a knock on the door. He answered it with a "Yeah, who is it," remark. "It's the police, now open the fucking door," said the voice on the other side. Ed got up and opened the door to find a pock-marked face of a police officer with a club in his left hand. Suddenly and without much time to react he was pushed back into his room with the officer's Billy-club and told to have a seat.

Ed did what he was told and sat down while he relit his cigarette that had gone out during the abrupt encounter. "What's your name, Boy?" Asked the police officer as he surveyed the room. "Stanley, Sir" was all he said. The police officer opened his old sea trunk and began to look inside the draws. Ed interrupted him by standing up and suddenly the police officer swung his Billy-club around but missed him as he ducked and sprang on top of the police officer while trying to shove his lit cigarette down the officer's mouth. They began to wrestle each other on the floor as Gunny stepped inside and simply hit the surprised police officer over the head with a pair of brass knuckles.

As the bewildered officer regained consciousness and opened his eye's he looked down between his legs and saw Gunny with a bloody sheet draped across his shoulders and a look of sincere concentration after just finishing up sewing the incision he made in the officer's genitals. It was only a minor operation but it looked and felt like much more. The officer let out a muffled scream to realize that he had no voice.

Ed looked down at their victim and told him not to strain himself too much, it wouldn't do him any good and would just make the hurt even more worse. That was when Gunny began to tell Officer Jankowski that God gave every man just two testicles. One was for fear, the other loyalty. And now Gunny owned his loyalty. Officer Jankowski would be left with only fear.

Gunny lifted the officer's hand from his bound arm and began to tell the police officer why God gave man only ten fingers.

Suddenly, Officer Jankowski was more receptive to questioning. Ed sat down and opened his leather note book and wrote down everything that was said to them by the terrified police officer.

During their questioning, Gunny introduced them as men of honor and would return him to his beat without further molestation. Although, they were not interested in money they were interested in information. With his gloved hand, Gunny removed a bloody handkerchief with the single testicle in it in his gloved hand and showed it to the police officer while Ed helped pull up the pants of their astonished and terrified victim.

"This is your loyalty to the Family. If you have lied or I find that you have squealed then I will be back for the other testicle Sir." Ed helped the police officer out the door as Gunny carefully walked him outside the boarding house. An hour later he and Gunny headed back to another hotel with Ed's sea chest in tow.

The next couple of days found Ed and Gunny driving to Tampa in a company car. Ed always knew that he worked for the Sullivan's and that they, in turn, worked for someone else but he never really gave it too much thought. After all he was just a cog in the wheel and he knew not to pry where he didn't need to be.

Lately he was beginning to realize that Gunny took orders from another boss as well the Sullivan's and this mysterious boss seemed to be a lot more connected than anyone he had ever heard of before. Where ever Gunny went, there would always be a contact man that was there with everything Gunny asked for. He could really get used to working for an operation like this thought the Telephone man.

Apparently, there was a group of Jewish traders in Tampa shipping the heroin from Cuba to Miami for further distribution. It wasn't long before they discovered the ring leaders. Ed had never flown on an airplane and he was a bit nervous but trying not to show it as he and Gunny boarded the plane. "Don't worry," said Gunny as he reached inside his coat pocket and handed him his flask of whiskey.

The stewardess gave Gunny a wink and walked on by them. "This is going to be a quick flight, Havana is just a quick puddle jump away," replied Gunny as he retrieved his flask. Gunny was right. By the time he began to get use to the sensation of flying they were already taxing into Havana's airport. When they checked into their hotel, Gunny Fletcher made it a point to tell him that he would be traveling with another fellow that needed to use his room.

As Ed unlocked his hotel room he immediately began to smell a musky odor in the room and noticed a man stirring something in a pot on a makeshift cook stove, sitting on the room's wet bar. "What in the world are you cooking?" asked Ed as he looked down at what the fellow was stirring. "Just a little something for Gunny," said the fellow as he introduced himself as Señor Santiago.

"Gunny and I go back quite a way. We met back during the war when the Americans had their way here in Cuba and nothing seemed to ever change," mumbled Señor Santiago as he turned off the stove and removed the pot. Ed sat down and asked what it was he was making for Gunny. "Cow shrooms," mumbled Señor Santiago. "This is a reduction of bovine fecal loving mushrooms. Apparently, Gunny wants to confuse or terrify someone very important."

"How did you learn this?" Replied Ed. "I used to be a professor and medical doctor for the crown," replied Señor Santiago. "Before the war began there was a plague that killed many people on the other side of the island. My immediate family did not survive the pestilence. I nearly lost my mind but then the war saved me and suddenly we lost and I was left to look after my enemy's wounded.

That's when I first met Señor Fletcher. He was just a private back then but he saved my life and now I am forever in his debt." As the former physician poured the solution into a metal flask, he tightened it with a rubber cork and fastened it to a make shift sling. Then he walked out to the balcony and began to swing the flask inside the sling around and around his head making a swirling sound.

After several minutes, he stopped and opened the container inside the sling and began to suck out a purple fluid inside a glass straw and then he blew it back into another clear glass vile. After the vile was full, it was corked and placed inside a cloth bag.

Señor Santiago pocketed the vile, excused himself, and headed off to deliver it to Gunny. Ed sat by the telephone and waited for his orders. Sometime during the night, the phone rang and he answered it. There was a meeting that night in the penthouse suite with Mr. Meyer Lanski and Ed was to serve as Gunny's body guard.

He knew that Gunny never needed a body guard so he was a little interested when he showed up at the rendezvous and found Gunny looking like one of the Rockefellers. As soon as they stepped out of the hotel elevator there were two goons opening the doors and ushering them inside for the meeting.

Mr. Lanski was standing beside the window and was looking out toward the sea as they came inside the room. "Mr. Fletcher or is it Gunnery Sergeant Fletcher and your associate, I don't quite know. How may I help you?" asked Mr. Lanski as they were surrounded by Lanski's goons. Gunny motioned for Ed to stand beside the door while he sat down and retrieved his smoking pipe from his coat and began to light it with a match. "Heroin, Mr. Lanski. You may help me by not selling it in Florida Mr. Lanski." said

Gunny as he drew a puff from his pipe and blew out several smoke rings. Lanski raised his eye brow and told him that he knew nothing about heroin being sold in Florida or anywhere else. Besides he still wasn't sure exactly who Gunny worked for and wasn't exactly sure he liked the accusation.

Gunny kept smoking his pipe as he began to explain to Mr. Lanski that he worked for the American Industrial Families of known repute. "You see, Mr. Lanski, there are big fish in the ocean and then there are even bigger fish in the ocean. All these fish think they know what's what in the big ocean but they are simply too small to see the big whales that can swallow them whole without ever a thought," replied Gunny.

"Now, you're a big fish, and you work with and for another big fish, Mr. Lanski. But you see I work for a rather large and quite impressive sized whale. And he says he doesn't want heroin being sold to his workers in Florida. Excuse me, do you mind if I pour myself a drink," said Gunny as he stood up and made his way over to Mr. Lanski's wet bar. Mr. Lanski watched Gunny and looked over at Ed.

"I can't control all the heroin sales in Florida but what if I could make such an arrangement. What would you give me if I can say, make this happen?" Asked the Jewish gangster. "You want your license to gamble in Florida, don't you?" Replied Gunny. "I didn't know there was such a thing," said Mr. Lanski.

"There isn't but we can create special permission for the right person to own and operate certain establishments and race tracks." Mr. Lanski smiled and shook his head, "How did you read my mind? How can you make something like this happen?" Gunny poured the vile Mr. Santiago gave him into the whiskey flask after he poured himself a drink and hid the vile back into his sleeve without anyone noticing.

As he turned around he told Mr. Lanski that information was a precious commodity to the Families and they never shared such important information. "However, I will send you what you'll need at the beginning of next week. In the mean time I prefer that you make all the right calls and the appropriate decisions. I will be leaving this morning and I need to let my bosses know as soon as possible."

Sometime late that night the most influential man in the syndicate would mistakenly dose himself with Mr. Santiago's solution. Meyer Lanski would come to remember that night and never take a drink of whiskey again. From that day forward, he would only drink kosher vodka that he obtained himself.

He would get his special license sooner than he thought but would never find out who Gunny worked for until it was too late and only after he had to make his executive decision. The more men he sent to find out the more he would lose and that didn't go over to well with his partners in the syndicate.

Their heroin would be rerouted to New Orleans instead of Tampa and he would begin opening his casinos in Florida. There were indeed rather large and impressive whales in the ocean and he had no intention of being swallowed. Mr. Lanski would eventually figure out that Mr. Dupont was the whale that happened to control everything important in Florida but by that time it would be a little too late to change his mind. The syndicate would learn to make way for the American Families of Industry and especially Mr. Dupont in Florida.

Gunny and Ed jumped on a flight that next morning at a Marine Corps base in Guantanamo Bay and they flew directly to the Navy base in Pensacola. He didn't know how Gunny knew this many people but it seemed that every officer in Cuba knew Gunny Fletcher, respected him and gave him whatever he asked for with respect and without any delays. Eventually he would come to learn that Gunny never talked about his career in the Marines but had loyal men that still worshiped him in the Corps.

Apparently, Gunny was supposed to become field commissioned to second lieutenant but something happened and he mysteriously resigned his enlistment before his intended promotion. Ed dared not inquire any further than he already did and left it at that. He too would learn to respect his teacher's methods and history the more he discovered about them. He had called ahead to let Mabel know that he was on his way when he left Pensacola's Naval Air Station. He had just arrived at his house when he saw his wife's extended belly. Yep, thought Ed, I've done it again. "Looks like there is another one in the oven Mabel," said Ed as he walked over to his wife, kissed her on the lips and grabbed one of her breast. "Please, Edward, not outside," begged his pregnant wife."

Chapter 9

"There are men that are beyond reproach, that cannot be purchased, persuaded, or scared. They live solely for themselves and their nation. They have fostered certain notions and ideas of the way they think their country and people should behave. They will stop at nothing to fulfill what they perceive as their righteous duty to uphold and defend this belief in the unity and sacredness of what they call the United States of America."

Chief Mimms kept reading out loud another excerpt in the newspaper. Gunny continued to watch their new stable boy brush down his favorite mare. "Sounds like General Butler is in the race for Commandant," said Gunny. "I bet they pick old LeJeune again," replied Chief Mimms as he scanned the newspaper for more information.

"Well, we've been asked to make a trip on behalf of the top boss, to try and persuade Old Duckboard to come work for the Families when he gets passed over. Either way, you know he's not going to go for it so I'd rather have you be the point man on this next assignment," replied Chief Mimms as he folded the newspaper and handed it to Gunny.

Major General Smedley Butler was, in 1930, one of America's top Marine Corps Generals that became a contender for the Commandant's position. It was an appointment that the American Industrial Families paid attention to like hawks watching their prey. They never deviated from making sure that the appropriate Marine was chosen.

In July of 1930 the right Marine, General Wendell Neville suddenly disagreed with their philosophy, and poof, the general mysteriously died while serving as Commandant of the Marine Corps. Their empire relied on U.S. Forces and the Marine Corps was one of their most effective branches. Whether it was bankers, Wall Street industrialists, or multinational corporations, America's Marine Corp held together the American empire with diligence, terror, and iron hard discipline. General Butler was considered one of the most effective Marines in the history of the Corps besides General LeJeune and LeJeune was past due for retirement, which made General Butler the obvious choice. Mr. Rockefeller wanted him on the Family's payroll and he didn't care what it took or how much money it cost.

General Butler was simply too powerful and too much like a hero for the Families to ignore.

A few months later, late in the evening on Friday the thirteenth, the phone rang in Ed's make shift barber shop while he was cleaning his supplies. He answered in his usual way. "Howdy." It was Chief Mimms on the line and he began to tell him about his new assignment. A week from that day he, Gunny, and the Chief were going to travel to Quantico Virginia, to see a man about a dog was all that was told to him. Every time the Chief said something that vague and ambiguous, it usually meant that there was danger involved. Ed was hoping that they were going to take the train. Flying still scared him a little and he hated to display nervousness in front of his mentors.

However, during that week while he was making his drop off to the Sullivan's he was asked by Byron Sullivan to make sure that he reported back to him exactly everything that he witnessed while working with the Chief and Gunny on his new assignment. This was something he was not used to. There was always a clear-cut chain of command that everyone followed. Somehow his inclination concerning Gunny was starting to become evident and the Sullivan's wanted to know more. "Sure thing, boss.

Is there anything else I might need to know?" asked Ed, as he swigged down the last bit of whiskey in his glass. "Just pay attention, keep your eyes open, your mouth shut, and your ears peeled. You got it?" "Yes Sir," replied Ed as he got up, put his hat on and headed off towards the door. Things were starting to become a little strange, he thought, but a job was a job and once again he would find himself in the very thick of it.

They all took the train and a very thankful Ed sat as a scout during the entire trip. When they reached Jacksonville Florida, they left the train station and were brought to a large estate by the fanciest Rolls Royce limousine that he had ever seen before. In fact, it was the first one he had ever seen and he had a hell of time trying not to keep from smiling and grinning while he was ushered off to the Epping Forest Mansion. He knew that the Sullivan's were rich folks but he began to see that there was a whole class of folks that were richer than Midas himself. This must be one of these whales in that big ocean Gunny had mentioned.

Understandably, Ed was shown to the servant's quarters behind the kitchens. During that night's pre-dinner cocktail hour, he was able to get intimately involved with one of the kitchen maids in the mansion's garage when Gunny found him and nearly ripped Ed's ear off while pulling the two rutting couples apart.

"God Dam it, if I have to fucking castrate your ass I promise you that it will fucking get done. Now pull your pants up and come with me," hissed Gunny as he stood waiting for Ed to dress himself. "I fucking mean it, Kid, do this again and you will lose your fucking nuts, Boy," he replied, Ed followed him back to Gunny's room. That was the last time he decided to mess around during that assignment.

The Chief nor the Gunny ever made false promises and he knew it. The Chief was outside Gunny's room waiting for them. There was a butler and a valet waiting inside to fit Ed for a dinner suit that was more appropriate for that night's dinner. He would be dining with them and apparently, he needed to be presentable. A few moments later and he was dressed like them. That night would become an illuminating event that would shake his notions of propriety entirely. From that day forward Ed would always view Pensacola as a very small city in a rather large and dangerous world.

By the time the dinner gong was rung, everyone enjoying their cocktails had already made their introductions and early evening conversations. He walked into the dining room with Gunny and Chief and sat down between them. He had no idea that John

Rockefeller Jr., Frank Vanderlip, J.P. Morgan Jr., Paul Warburg, Alfred Dupont and his right-hand man Mr. Ed Ball were present at the dinner party. Ed simply listened and answered everything that was asked of him.

Later after dinner he would learn over a brandy and smoke that the night's guest were mainly bankers, investors, and all-around players, of the American Empire. How was he ever going to explain this to his bosses back home or should he have thought Ed. When he was asked by Mr. Dupont what he thought was America's place in the world.

Ed was sort of dumbfounded. He took his time thinking about his answer while rolling his cigar between his fingers and starring at his brandy. Both Gunny and Chief Mimms simply stared at him along with everyone else in the smoking parlor as he began to slowly tell them what he thought.

"Gentlemen, I believe that God has bestowed upon this nation, a great responsibility to manage this world's affairs, as best as we, Americans see fit. We are this world's chosen people. Look around us. All this wealth was carved out by hardworking American sweat and blood. I will say this, if anyone else in this world wants to get in our way than they had better watch out because this train we call the United States of America ain't going to stop for no superstitious, spear-chucking, brown eyed natives or any other uncivilized peoples," replied the Telephone Man.

"Here here," chimed in Mr. Rockefeller. Mr. Dupont raised his glass to Ed and said, "Well done my man, well done. I see Gunny Fletcher and Chief Mimms have done well with their new protege." Chief and Gunny exchanged looks of contentment and began to discuss openly how they were going to approach General Butler. Ed relaxed and began to listen and learn what his new role would be during his new assignment. They were all playing a different sort of game that he had not seen before. Power and money made for a rather interesting sort of company, thought Ed.

The following morning at breakfast all three men were introduced to Colonel Edward House. Colonel House was not someone to be crossed. Everything he said could be taken literally and he immediately began to outline where and when they were going to meet other contacts along the way. After the breakfast and their debriefing, the Chief and Gunny began to relay their plans to the Colonel on how they planned to proceed. Everything was planned but Gunny held his reservations to himself. Reality rarely if ever followed men's plans and tactical strategies left little room for change. Over the next few days Gunny and Chief Mimms created a contingency plan for several what-if situations. Ed was not included with any one of them but remained a scout during the entire trip.

When they, three, eventually arrived at the Marine Corp Barracks at Quantico the contact person was Major Monroe. The local train station was located at a civilian town located on the Potomac River and was completely surrounded by the Marine Corps base. Ed found it strange that a military base could have a civilian town inside its borders.

The town of Quantico was where he would be staying and his job would be to trace the phone lines that ran to the commanding general's office on base. He knew this was going to be a dangerous mission but he had no idea that he would be breaking federal law on the most heavily guarded base on the east coast.

Somewhere along their way to Quantico, a contact person near Norfolk boarded the train and had left him a suit case with a map and set of maintenance work clothes that matched the ones that the phone company that worked on the Quantico phone lines were. Ed didn't know what to think about this type of undercover work but it was all very intriguing to him and its excitement made him feel a little nervous with anticipation. He also found a set of keys inside the suit case. Gunny and the Chief gave him his orders and he soon set out following the instructions as thoroughly as a well-trained professional.

He knew, this time, that there wouldn't be any room for error so he set about doing exactly what he was told with precise coordination and a cold calculated sense of pride. He had never traveled that far north before and the weather was fairly cold. He found the work truck behind the boarding house which he was told belonged to the set of keys that he was given. He jumped in started the truck and headed out of the so-called Q town towards the military base that he was soon to discover was the headquarters for the entire Marine Corps.

He was already starting to feel the cold when he began to climb his first telephone pole in the middle of the Marine Corps base. The wind was whipping around him and his knees began to shake as he searched the right line to hook up his special phone. Within a few hours of climbing other poles and tracing all the necessary lines, he was able to map out which lines were the important ones and which ones to ignore. When he was done he drove the work truck back to the civilian town and immediately made it back to the warmth of his room in Q town.

The next morning found him listening to a phone conversation in a ravine called Whiskey Gulch where several field grade officers lived. This General Butler fellow was surrounded by men that Ed knew better than to mess with or else he wouldn't be going home. He just hoped that Gunny and Chief Mimms knew what they were doing. The dangers of this mission began to be felt and he knew that things were going to quickly become dicey. It was about two days later and all hell began to break loose for their team.

The Chief and Gunny would come to find out what a red line brig meant and all the horrors that it ensued. By the time newly appointed Major General Butler arrived, both the Chief and Gunny were already pissing blood from their bruised kidneys. Ed was stuck in the field listening to conversations about what General Butler was up to and he didn't quite know what was about to happen.

"Good evening gentlemen," said the General as he walked past Gunny and Chief Mimms while they stood in front of the wall behind the red line. "You're making a terrible mistake," moaned the Chief as he tried to lean against the wall but was too afraid to buckle his knees in fear of receiving another beating from the Marines that stood guard.

Gunny Fletcher simply kept starring at the red dot placed on the wall in front of him. The air reeked of fear and wet leather as General Butler studied his captives. The Marine that was sitting in the wooden chair in the middle of the room walked over to the Chief and swung a rubber covered wooden club over the Chief's shins and began to yell at him about talking out of order.

General Butler knew exactly why they were sent to him and also knew who it was that the Chief and Gunny represented. However, he felt insulted and didn't like them trying to manipulate him and the Marine Corps. He was, after all, quite ready and capable of handling the Wall Street bankers or the other American industrialist and he was also prepared to let them all know what he thought and was willing to do to them. "How about this, gentlemen?

You may go ahead and tell Mr. Rockefeller that he is more than welcome to go fuck off with those other, cock sucking, yellow bellied, sons of bitches that call themselves American. Our son's blood is worth more than a general's pension, Folks. Go ahead, take that back and tell them all what I just said. Let them know where I stand. Let them know what I'm capable of doing, and let them know that I'm not afraid of them nor what they may think they can do or get away with. You boys hear me?" The Chief and Gunny immediately responded with a simple "Yes Sir." "I'm going to be fair though and give you two fellows one day's ride before I begin this hunt."

The general studied them closely as he surveyed their reactions.

Gunny looked over at the general and said "you're going to kill us anyway?" General Butler looked at Gunny with an intense look of sheer hatred and stoic resolve. "No. I'm not going to kill you fellows but my hunter-killer team probably will. You boys should know all about the hunt, Gunny Fletcher. I believe you and Chief Mimms used to practice this ceremony in the Philippines," replied the general as he began to put his gloves back on. "This continent is too small for the likes of you two fine specimens of human waste. May your horizons be brighter than tomorrow's future," said the cryptic general as he walked out of the room.

Gunny and the Chief were ushered outside and told to leave the base. Within just a few minutes a 1930 Chrysler pulled up and two men got out and helped the wounded Chief and Gunny get into the car. Ed was a few streets over listening to a conversation concerning the Chief and Gunny when the Chrysler sped by him on its way off the base.

He couldn't believe what was going on but knew that he had to get out of there as fast as possible. When he arrived back at the boarding room and grabbed his belongings, there was already a contact man waiting for him outside the boarding house.

Instead of leaving Quantico by land he would be taking a sailing boat with Major Monroe down the Potomac River. Things were going south way too quickly for his taste but he knew there was only one thing to do and that was to rendezvous with the Chief and Gunny, watch their movements like a good scout and help them in any way that he could.

At first, he thought that he was heading up to Washington D.C. but the Major quickly doubled back and pulled his boat toward the shore where Ed was asked to follow another fellow that was waiting for them on a deserted road near the river bank. An hour later and he and the fellow driving him pulled into the entrance of an old farm house that appeared as if it had been present in one of Virginia's Civil War battles.

Inside was Chief Mimms and Gunny sitting in the front room of the farm house being tended to by a physician and his nurse. It didn't take him very long to see that they were distressed and in serious pain. "We need to get out of the country as soon as possible," explained Gunny to Ed as the nurse began to wrap his rib cage with an elastic bandage. "I want you to follow Chief and take a flight tonight back to Jacksonville and tell Mr. Ball that the "Duck" has flown the coup. We are now in the hunt. Repeat that back to me" said Gunny as Ed began to repeat his words verbatim.

"Are they coming after us?" asked Ed, as he sat watching them redress themselves and begin to leave the house. "Yes. We are being hunted right now and it's either us or them. Remember not to miss your target, Son. A weapon is useless unless you can hit your target. Remember what we've taught you and stay sharp. Now let's get going," said Gunny as he stepped outside and began to walk towards the car.

Within seconds, there were gun shots going off and Chief Mimms fell over in the front yard with a bullet through his forehead. Ed looked over and saw the driver was hit and slumped over the wheel of the car. It felt like everything was moving in slow motion for him as he scrambled through the front passenger's side of the car, pushed the dead driver out and began to drive off with Gunny firing his pistol out of the back of the automobile. He couldn't believe it, the Chief never even saw it coming, they never saw it coming. Like a crazy twisted madman, he drove down the road like a bat out of hell wondering why they were being hunted and how he and Gunny were going to get to Jacksonville, Florida, alive.

Sometime in the early hours of the morning, he and Gunny pulled their car into a private airstrip somewhere in North Carolina. For some reason he assumed that he and Gunny would be flying together to Jacksonville but there were two planes ready to leave when they got there. Gunny gave him a handshake and told him to get on the plane, he was going to head off somewhere else to confuse their hunters.

Ed could only express his fear and acceptance of his duties but kept his promise to Gunny. Both the planes left as soon as they were boarded. Thirty minutes later a group of Marines in civilian clothes arrived at the airstrip and began to interrogate the maintenance workers. Ed sat on the plane in total wonder and complete disbelief. How could these Marines get the drop on them so fast and why in hell were they being hunted, he thought, as he kept pondering multiple possibilities. When the plane landed a few hours later outside of Jacksonville, there was a car waiting for him at another private airstrip.

He and his trunk were delivered to Mr. Ed Ball somewhere between Jacksonville and Tallahassee. Mr. Ball listened to Ed's story and recollection of the past events. After he was done answering all of Mr. Ball's questions, it was made very clear to him that he was going to have to set an ambush for the men hunting Gunny.

Outside the front of Dr. Conradi's office, up a telephone pole stood Ed on top of another telephone pole while he made his notes inside his leather-bound notebook. Earlier that morning he had placed a call to General Butler's office at Quantico and asked to speak to General Butler "Duckboard."

When the general finally answered the phone, he began to quack into the lines several times and simply said to the general, "we send our regards from Florida Mr. General Quack Fuck" he replied with as much disrespect in his voice as he could manage right before he hung up the phone. Let's see how long it would take before these hunters showed up thought the Telephone Man.

He drove the car Mr. Ball had loaned him down an old country farmer's drive way which happened to be the very same one that he had dropped off the fellow that was sent to kill Dr. Conradi but had failed. He parked his car and walked up to the front door of the farm house.

After knocking a few times on the door and several seconds later the door opened with a farmer holding a shot gun in front of him. Ed immediately took his hat off and introduced himself as Stanley Farmer of the Patent Westley Insurance Company. "Mr. Prechet, I presume. We have a rather large check for you from the trust of the honorable Joe Scarlett," remarked Ed as he stood back some ways from the farmer standing there with his mouth open.

The farmer immediately asked who Mr. Scarlett was and why he was getting a check from him. Ed asked if he may remove the check from his coat pocket, the farmer nodded his head and that's when he pulled out his sawed off shot gun from its leather sling and knocked the farmer's gun out of his hands while hitting him over the head with the butt of his gun. He began to hit the farmer in the back of his head three more times when he heard a lady's voice in the other room.

He walked right into three women with his shot gun drawn and told them to lay down on the ground or he would kill them all without a moment's hesitation. He ordered one of the girls to tie up the others and when she was done, he tied her up and checked the rest of them the make sure they were safely secured. After tying the ladies back to back in the kitchen chairs good and tight, he walked over to the bound farmer and threw a bowl of water in his face. Within a few seconds the farmer came to looking confused and a bit angry as he saw the women bound to the chairs and crying their eyes out.

He walked over to the youngest of the women and began to cut her clothes off with a shaving razor. The farmer began to scream and yell so he stopped what he was doing and walked over to the farmer laying prone in the middle of the hallway. "I want you to call some fellers for me Fred," he said as he dragged the bound farmer over to the telephone inside the hall way. "I want you to call the preacher's Templeton, Bower, and Sheldon and tell them that a perverted homosexual feller is about to fuck them all. You hear me Mr. Prechet? Call them and tell them or I will begin sodomizing that young'un in there before I do to you what I will do to them," he replied with a wink and nod.

Sometime later that morning he began to climb a very tall pine tree in a field nor too far from the farm house. He was quite accustomed to using his climbing gear on telephone poles but digging his lineman's spurs into the sappy pine bark was another thing entirely. He eventually made it to the very top and sat way up high in a pine tree watching the farm house with his rifle scope.

He could see everything from that spot giving him a clear and undisturbed view of the entire farm. Within a short time of settling and preparing himself for what was about to happen, several men and pious parishioners that served the zealot preachers, began to creep up on the farm house with guns and the determination of settling matters for themselves. Suddenly, Mr. Prechet the farmer walked out of the house wearing the same clothes that Gunny was wearing back at Quantico and began to call out to his fellow church members that the pervert had already left.

Half an hour later and all three preachers showed up in their cars with several men standing around them with guns and stern faces. As they were all assembling in front of the house, a military truck drove down the lane turned around and three Marines opened fire from inside of the canvassed truck with machine guns blaring and laid waste to everyone standing there in front of the old farm house.

In less than a minute there was no one left alive. As the Marines got out of the truck and began to look for what they assumed was Gunny, Ed began to shoot his marks. Two were killed with only one shot. That would have impressed Gunny and the Chief. The third Marine went down climbing the back of the truck while it sped off down the road.

He couldn't believe his eyes. The carnage before him seemed like such a terrible waste of good man power. However, it was a necessity that needed to be done and a message for the general of what would happen if any more Marines were sent on the hunt. Several minutes later he drove off down the road, found another telephone pole, climbed it, and made the appropriate calls.

Later that morning Mr. Ball sent a clean-up crew to remove all the dead victims including the military men and equipment. Getting rid of that many bodies was a particular problem that only certain specialist could do without leaving behind anything incriminating.

The only thing left alive were the women inside the home. They had hidden themselves in the storm shelter behind the house and were still waiting for the all clear when Ed found them cowering inside the root cellar. He really didn't want to have to hurt them so he just told them from outside of the doors to wait until the next morning before they came out or they too would be killed and left to rot. When he had received his instructions, he was also told that he would be meeting a new and future colleague back at the farm house where he should wait until the clean-up crew could help him with the work that needed to be done.

When he walked back to the front of the farm house there was already three fellows that were sent by Mr. Ball loading up bodies in another military truck and that's when he met Captain Riley the company pilot. After all the bodies were stripped naked and thrown in the back of the truck, Captain Riley told him to hop in and together they drove off while he radioed back to his workers what to do with the rest of the equipment and cars. Ed just sat there and watched as the captain relayed the orders.

After just an hour's drive to another private air strip, he would discover that this Captain Riley operated a rather large plane. The captain drove straight over to the back side of the aircraft and together he and Ed managed to load up all the bodies from the truck unto the plane. Another hour later and they were both flying over the Gulf of Mexico inside the largest cargo plane he had ever seen.

It was quite cold and hard to breath when the captain motioned for him to hold onto the control yoke while he got out and walked to the back of the plane. The captain opened the back door and began to throw the naked bodies of the Marines and church folks outside the plane where they fell down to the Gulf below. Ed was nearly scared to death as he held onto the controller and tried not to move a muscle.

"Tonight, the sharks and fishies are going to eat well," said the captain as he removed his bloody gloves and entered the cockpit to resume flying the aircraft. Ed just looked over and gladly gave the yoke back to the captain. When they arrived back at the landing strip he and the captain cleaned the rest of the blood from inside the plane and burned all the clothes taken off of the victims.

He was quite amazed and very impressed at how fast and efficient the captain worked and at how jovial he was toward him. He knew this was the kind of man that he could work with and learn to appreciate. After the clean-up was completed he was sent back to Tallahassee with another set of instructions. He was told to spend the night in Tallahassee and to take the train back to Pensacola the next morning where he was to settle back into his old job and told to lay low for a while until further instructions were given to him.

He decided there was only one place he could enjoy himself while waiting for the train the next morning. He hadn't had any sex for what he thought was way too long so he decided to pay Ms. Mary Lou a visit before he left. After giving her a call and announcing to her that he happened to be in town that night but would be leaving the next morning, Mary Lou quickly told him that he should come over and see her that night. She would cook him something to eat and they could visit for a while before he had to leave.

He arrived late in the afternoon and took a taxi to her neighborhood without telling the cab driver which house he was visiting. He proudly walked up to her door and knocked on it, waiting for her surprise when her brother answered it and introduced himself. "Howdy," said the young man as he opened the door to let him inside. Ed walked inside, took off his hat and turned around as Mary Lou's brother, former Lance Corporal Sutton of the United States Marine Corps knocked Ed over the side of his head with a pair of homemade iron knuckles.

Mary Lou was not present that night when he was taken to the model T garage in the back of the house and interrogated by her brother. Ed would learn that night that it was indeed a very small world that he lived in and some things just never changed.

Sometime before midnight a very bloody and bruised Ed hung from a hook on a ceiling joist inside the garage and he tried not to scream as the former Marine poked his finger inside of Ed's thigh. There was a knock at the door when it opened and in walked Gunny holding a revolver in his left hand with two fellows standing behind him.

Immediately, Mary Lou's brother ran at Gunny and swung his iron fisted gloved hand towards Gunny's head. Gunny was faster than he looked. He ducked and backed out of the way as one of his men garroted the former Marine and began to choke the life out of him. Ed was cut down and Gunny quickly asked him what was that he had told the Marine. He looked up at Gunny and said "Only that I fucked his sister, his mother, and that I was going to eventually fuck him too," rasped Ed.

That night Gunny had him examined by a physician on their payroll. He was able to travel but was a bit shaken up. Once again, he had no idea how they were able to get a drop on him so fast and so knowingly as well. The faster they were able to get back to Pensacola and lay low the better, thought Ed, as he and Gunny boarded the train the next morning. Once again, he would be the scout and Gunny rode incognito.

For obvious reasons no one seemed to notice Gunny, due to his costume. Probably because he looked and dressed like an old man that had just come back from a funeral. By the time they were pulling into Pensacola's downtown train station the sun had just begun to set and the sky was a bright orange with tendrils of purple peaking down in slanted rays of silent discord.

They visited Simon Mimms and told him about his father's death and how they had delivered their justice. Simon was distraught to say the least, but seemed to understand their grief with a respectable silence. As Ed and Gunny drove back to the San Carlos Hotel Gunny looked over at him and began to tell him what to say to the Sullivan brothers. "Paul, I want you to tell the Sullivan's everything that happened. Don't leave out a thing. You hear me, Boy." said Gunny as he turned off of Cervantes onto Palafox street. "Yes Sir," replied Ed. Something had changed inside Gunny, thought Ed as they pulled into the back entrance of the hotel.

When they reached the Sullivan's offices the brothers were waiting with glasses ready for whiskey and looks of severity and anticipation. Gunny sat down in a chair and looked over to Ed to give him a toast when Mr. Goldring reached under a pillow on the couch, pulled a pistol out and fired a bullet into the head of Gunny. Blood and brains scattered the wall behind Gunny as a very confused and surprised Ed stood, up dumbfounded in complete shock. "What the fuck was that for?" Yelled Ed through the ringing in his ears. "God damn it," he roared. Suddenly, a Marine in civilian clothes stepped out from behind the curtains and nodded his head at the Sullivan's.

There were men already coming inside to take Gunny's body away and clean up the mess. "We may all work for the Rockefellers or the DuPont's but we don't fuck with the D.O.D., Paul," said Byron Sullivan as he poured him another shot of whiskey. "I know this is bothering you but it's too far over our heads to let go, of much less try to run away from. Every knock-off-man in the woods has a hit on the Gunny right now and we don't want to lose you too," said Byron Sullivan.

"The hunt is over and they're both gone Paul. There's nothing we can do about it. It's was the only way to stop this mess. Let it go, Pauli," said Tom Sullivan as Gunny's body was wrapped up by the hired men. He looked over at the body as it was taken out of the room. "are the Gunny and Chief going to get military funerals at least?" asked Ed as he starred at the door.

"They will be buried at Fort Barrancas with full military honors," said one of the Sullivan's. He got up, put his hat back on, shook off his nerves and nodded his head with tears in his eyes. "Go home, Paul." Murmured Byron. "It's been a long mission and your wife probably misses you," said the other Sullivan as he was handed an envelope with cash and sent on his way.

He drove back to his house on U street in a complete daze. The Chief and Gunny Fletcher were dead and not coming back. They were the most important teachers Ed had ever known. When he was younger back when he had left his home and had his falling out with his father, he sort of adopted Gunny and the Chief as surrogate fathers and now they were gone for good. Life was simply too short thought Ed as he pulled into his drive way and heard a bird dog wail while he was turning off his truck.

When he walked up to the front porch of his home, his father, George was waiting in a rocking chair with a smile and a cup of coffee in his right hand. "Why the long face, Edward?" asked his father as he walked up and sat down on the front porch swing.

"Well, Daddy, it's been a hell of a day at work and I'm damn glad to be home," he replied as his pregnant wife and child came out and ran over to him and gave him a kiss and hug. George could tell that Ed's family idolized his son and it made him proud to see that his boy was a working man that could support a family. "Who does the dog belong to?" asked Ed as he sat his son on his left knee. "Her name is Bo Peep," said Arthur while chewing on a piece of candy that his grandfather brought him.

George looked over at Ed and began to tell him that one of his grocery store customers was in debt and had to barter with him to pay off what he owed. Ed looked over at him and immediately asked his father about owning a grocery store that he had never heard of before. George winked at his son and began to tell him about how he was going to make it rich in the grocery business. He slowly shook his head and listened to his delusional father's rant. Laying low for the bosses was going to be more difficult than he realized, he thought, as Ed and his wife headed inside for dinner time.

Chapter 10

At the end of May, in 1931, Ed sat in his church and listened to Reverend Schubert preach a sermon about the Day of Pentecost. Ed and his family listened and patiently waited for the next hymn to be delivered. The windows were open and there was a slight breeze blowing in from outside. Already the days were beginning to get hotter and hotter in Florida. Ladies in the church fanned themselves with paper fans the church provided with little bible scenes and prayers printed on them. The men had their hats off and some wiped their foreheads with cloth handkerchiefs. Mabel held her new born son, Charles, while he slept during most of the sermon.

When the church services were over they all shuffled outside and began to head back to their respected homes. That's when Mr. Coy Kelly walked over to Ed helping his wife get into his new Buick. When Mr. Kelly gave Ed a handshake it was the secret Masonic handshake that only fellow fraternal members of the order recognized. Mr. Kelly offered an invitation to come eat a fried chicken dinner that night with his family on T street. Mabel immediately seized the moment and accepted. Ed smiled and told them they would come over around five o'clock.

Everyone in Brownsville, Pensacola, Florida, respected Ed and his family. Nearly half of the men in the neighborhood got their haircuts every month from him and most of them knew that he worked for the telephone company and collected debts for the Sullivan's and feared him but also admired him as well.

He was easily approachable, would help his neighbors and community with everything he had but he was seen to have a very nasty side that cut through to a darker part of reality that most folks in the South strangely understood and tolerated. The South was still a very violent place to live. Lynching's still existed and during the Great Depression crime was perceived with a different set of ethics. Scratching a living amongst the unemployed caused many folks to lose their pride. Survival simply became a necessary virtue.

Later that night over at the Kelly's, after dinner, sitting and on the front porch smoking cigarettes and drinking coffee, he would learn that there was a new candidate that wanted to become a member of Lodge 15. Apparently, the treasurer of Pensacola Creosoting Company was looking to join the Freemasons of Pensacola. It was John R. Jones, he wanted to be initiated, and he had every right.

He was a white male, protestant, and he was also an up standing member of Pensacola's downtown community. He was also an honest accountant that Ed's bosses wanted to put on the pay roll as well. Apparently, the Sullivan's were looking for a good accountant for Mr. Harbeson who was the hotel's owner and they were hoping to recruit Mr. Jones.

On the ground floor of King Solomon's Temple in Lodge 15 sat all the members of Pensacola's Protestant elites. It was the full moon and the Worshipful Master of the Lodge sat listening to the reports of his fellow brothers as they delivered out loud the history of Mr. Jones in the Sanctum Sanctorum. Ed was not surprised to hear about the man's accomplishments and deeds. Apparently, John R. Jones was a World War I veteran, a swell golfer, honest accountant, and all around American patriot. Just the kind of guy that was nearly impossible to hate and simply too irresistible for the Sullivan's to ignore.

The Worshipful Master heard enough to evoke the rite of the summons and called for a vote. Ed raised his arms and began to speak the words of accordance. All the brothers followed suit and began the proceedings that would open the doors to Mr. Jones's apprenticeship. Sometime soon there would be an initiation but that would have to wait until the next lunar cycle. Moon Lodges were mighty particular about timing and they never deviated from their schedules.

During the next few weeks he checked up on Mr. Jones but found nothing queer or out of place. The man was a simple family man that ran the books for the Creosoting Company. He did, however, find out that some of the company's managers were displaying a lot more wealth than was normal, so he decided to follow that lead instead.

North Hill was one of Pensacola's first suburban neighborhoods to the downtown. Most of the houses were lavish Victorian homes and many of Pensacola's wealthier families resided there which happened to be where the men Ed needed to investigate were living. It wasn't long before he found the rats he was looking for without much effort on his part. Amazingly, the honest accountant was being duped at the company he worked for by his fellow managers and the accountant was completely clueless.

Ed climbed back down the telephone pole and began to head down to Madam Mirabella's to collect that month's payment. As he was stepping back into his work truck he noticed Mr. Flowers from Crystal's pharmacy walking across the road heading down Palafox street towards his business. Ed drove around and honked his horn to get the pharmacist's attention.

"Howdy, Joe, "replied Ed as he pulled his truck over and stopped in front of him. "I need to have a word with you partner. I'm heading over to Mirabella's and last time I was there they said you were a little light on the Listerine, cough medicine, and the other meds you are supposed to deliver. Now, you were a little light this month on your payments, Mr. Flowers. How's about you send some more goods for the girls. I'm sure they could use some more supplies. What do you think Mr. Flowers?" Asked Ed.

"Uh, Yes Sir Mr. Goodwin. I'll get them right now for you, Sir. Could you, please, wait just a few minutes while I bring you everything you need?" "Sure, but don't be too long." Ed answered. He sat back in his truck and lit a cigarette and waited for the goods. Ten minutes later, a delivery boy carrying a box of supplies came out and walked over to his truck.

The kid looked down and began to read off the list of goods. "Here's everything the doc wants you to have, Sir." The boy was not aware of who he was and what the supplies were for but he was about to learn. Ed got out, took the box and put it up in the back of his truck while the boy simply stood there and waited with a goofy look on his face.

He walked back to the delivery boy, grabbed his left hand, twisted it and brought him down to the ground. "Next time you deliver what I need to Madam Mirabella's, Boy and I will not have to come back here to take care of you and the doc. Hear me, Son?" Exclaimed Ed as he twisted a finger and heard it snap. The kid screamed for mercy and he let him go with a kick in his rump as the terrified boy ran off back towards the pharmacy. He got back into his truck and shook his head and mumbled something under his breath. He would be back to take care of the pharmacist later. Sending a boy to him was a big mistake and he didn't like it one bit. He would have to teach them a lesson but for now he had pressing business and he didn't want it to wait.

Every whore house needed regular supplies from their local pharmacist and Madame Mirabella's was no different. Lately, Chrystal's pharmacy was a little too light on paying their protection dues and Ed's favorite girls had been complaining about their pharmacy supplies being overpriced. Something like this simply wasn't allowed in his territory and his reputation was too important to overlook. Respect came in many forms, even if a teenage boy was sent to do a man's job. Business was business and the doc and his delivery boy would have to learn the hard way.

Madame Mirabella was pleased as punch when he delivered all the goods from the pharmacist. He received that month's payment at the same time. He told her all about the agreement with Crystal's Pharmacy and to let him know next week if the girls got what they needed. Mirabella snapped her fingers and two of Ed's favorite girls came into the room wearing next to nothing with mischievous grins on both of their faces. He took off his hat, handed it to the madam and began to walk up the stairs with the girls with his typical lopsided smile and mischievous grin. Life was good for the Telephone Man, he kept a tight shift, and everyone learned to respect him and pay their dues.

Sometime that next week he began to piece together what was going on at the creosoting company. Apparently, there were two fellows in upper management that were miscounting the number of treated logs that were being loaded onto the ships. A discovery was confirmed one evening on top of the San Carlos as Ed looked through his binoculars and counted the stacks of logs in the creosoting yard. Hell, all Mr. Jones had to do is count the stacks in the yard, thought Ed, as he shook his head and wrote down what he observed.

Treated telephone poles and rail road ties had become in huge demand in the 20s and 30s. Every industrialized country in the world needed and wanted creosoted poles. The rail roads, power lines, telephone lines, and telegraph lines needed them and it became a mad rush to acquire them. And Pensacola and its hinterlands still had some of the country's tallest pines and the sappiest stressed timber for miles around.

There were already more lumber yards than you could shake a stick at with several extremely successful lumber barons in control of them all including the Sullivan's. Some of these barons became wealthy enough to back the banks and public utilities. Pensacola's port may had seen better days but the port was far from empty. There were plenty of ships ready to deliver them to their newly purchased countries and sea captains and the lumber barons kept turning a profit. Old port cities tended to always find new business, one way or another, and Pensacola was no different than the rest.

The Sullivan's moved their office when the hotel extension was built and Ed was pleased that he didn't have to return to their old office where Gunny was murdered. He still had bad feelings whenever he walked by them on his way to the new ones. He knocked on the door and was invited inside. He took off his hat, walked in and noticed two men sitting on a couch looking out towards Pensacola's bay through the windows. Mr. Goldring took his hat and handed him a drink.

"Come on in, Paul, and have a seat. This is Mr. Jernigan and Mr. Ard," said Byron Sullivan. Ed gave them a hand shake and a nod. "We were just talking about the canals being dug over in Santa Rosa. Looks like we got another union problem to be solved." Both of the gentlemen nervously got up and began to make excuses to be somewhere else. The Sullivan brothers smiled and winked at each other in front of him. A few minutes later and the two Santa Rosa men both nervously left after making up bad excuses about having to be somewhere else. They quickly excused themselves and were out the door as fast as they could. Both the Sullivan brothers began to simultaneously laugh out loud. A very bemused Ed sat down and finished his drink. Mr. Goldring refilled his glass.

"We need you to break up a simple labor dispute over in Milton, Paul," replied Tom Sullivan. Byron chimed in with some more details and together they debriefed him on what he needed to do. By the time they were done and he had delivered his news concerning Pensacola's Creosoting Company, Mr. Goldring wrote down all the information that he would need to complete his assignments and gave him a written report of what they wanted him to do.

An hour later and he set off with a new set of orders and a need to check in on Mirabella. There was an itch somewhere that he needed to scratch and he knew right where to look.

He sat up in bed as one of Mirabella's girls performed fellatio on him. He was studying Mr. Goldring's notes and imagining several different strategies to finish the job. Marjorie took a breath and looked up at Ed. "Am I doing it alright Paul?" He kept starring at his notes. A few seconds later he looked over and winked. "Oh yeah, Sweetheart, you're the best cock sucker in this here house. And don't you forget it. It helps me think better, Darlin. You have really helped me out. Now don't stop, Baby. Use both your hands like you're doing. That's it, Sweetheart." Replied Ed as he went back to studying his notes.

When he walked back down the stairs he asked Mirabella if Crystal's Pharmacy got her orders right that week. "Yes Sir." Sure enough, a very frightened young man had delivered her goods and to her surprise there were more than enough drugs to keep a madam pleased and a happy brothel entertained. Brothels couldn't run successfully without supplies and medication and he was determined that his favorite whore house would function like a well-oiled engine.

The next morning, he walked out to his front porch and found milk spilled all over the porch. It was pretty obvious that Bo Peep the bird dog had knocked over the milk bottles that the milk man had delivered that morning. A very pissed off Ed walked back inside his house and hollered for his son Arthur to come to the front room. A few seconds later, Arthur ran into to room answering his father's summons. He pointed to the front door and told his son to clean up the front porch and not to complain. Sometime during breakfast that morning he asked Arthur to go get himself a switch from the Privet bush in the back yard. Thirty minutes later a sullen faced Arthur walked back into the kitchen with a tiny switch no thicker than his little finger. "When I asked you if you locked up Bo Peep last night in her kennel, what did you say?" asked his father with a look that terrified Arthur and his mother. Arthur began to cry and stammered something about closing the gate but Bo Peep must have gotten out. He walked over to his son, picked him up and sat him back down in his chair. "Next time make sure she's secured or I will not be so nice." Replied Ed as he walked back to his room and continued to dress for work.

The last telephone line on his work schedule was working soundly and he had just finished for that day's company work. But he wasn't done for the day and he knew that he would not be opening his barber shop that evening. He had too much Family business to attend to and he would probably be a bit too worked up when he got home so he decided to stay late at Mirabella's to blow off some steam before he came home that night. He called his wife and told her that he'd be working late over in Milton but to keep him a dinner plate ready for when he got home. Mabel told him she would.

A few hours later he pulled over at a service station in Pace and put his metal grieves on his arms and legs. They were padded on the inside and covered with thinly hammered steel. Gunny had made them and taught Ed how to use them to fight dirty in a brawl. After fitting his fighting armor on under his clothes he got back into his bread truck and waited for his crew to arrive.

The Brownsville Boys were what most folks called them but to him they were simply the Fellows. They were a mixture of American ethnicities. Jews, Irish, Polish, and all around American mutts. The Sullivan's encouraged Ed to assemble a team after Gunny was taken out because they simply didn't trust the Department of Defense and business was doing pretty good. To them you couldn't tell the American Great Depression was ever happening. Money was flowing in, in all directions and management wanted everything to keep running smoothly.

A Buick, a Chrysler, and a Ford pulled into the Pure Oil service station and parked next to his bread truck. He motioned for them to follow him and off they went through Pea Ridge and toward their destination. When he pulled up to the lumber canal works and parked his truck he could see fifty or so men standing around the canal dig site and they were holding their arms together blocking the work getting done on the canal. He got out and walked around to the back of his truck, opened the door and pulled out a medium length steel rod from inside the back door. He turned around and all the Fellows were standing in a circle behind him and were carrying similar weapons and gear.

He looked over at Giger and made a remark about wearing a leather football helmet to settle a score and they all laughed. Giger just shook his head and said that it gave him luck and it would keep his noggin safe. Giger was another Okie hobo that had recently come into town off a train and desperately needed work. Several months of training and refinement turned him into another man entirely. After impressing Ed on the last assignment with all the collections from the bookies at the dog tracks, gambling dens and businesses with seamless ease, he was starting to become a favorite with him and the group. Management always rewarded success and he kept up the tradition.

After making sure that they all knew not to shoot anyone but to bust skulls and bones instead, they nodded their heads and answered, "Sir, Yes Sir" at once. Timing was essential for his plan and he knew that he would have only this one opportunity to fix things with the company while Santa Rosa's finest were busy in downtown Milton concerning a negro protest over worker's rights.

Imagine that, thought Ed, as he and his crew walked towards the strikers. He made Hercules and his followers create a diversion in the down town about the very thing that he was about to stop while making the colored folks in Milton the scapegoats at the same time. Hercules didn't seem to care one way or another. He was simply too afraid of what the Family would do to him and his community to realize the bigger picture.

The men lining the canal with interlocking arms were singing another protest chant when his men walked over to them. He called out to his fellows to spread out and do as much damage as they could and inflict as many casualties as possible down the line. The Fellows grabbed their hats, tightened them to their heads, and began to do what he said. This song is too much noise pollution, thought Ed, as he swung his steel rod down the line swinging up and down as fast as he could. His crew saw what he was doing and quickly followed suit.

Suddenly, interlocking their arms together wasn't such a good tactic after all. It was complete poetic violence and mayhem. Twelve very well-trained men took on fifty determined strikers. It was not a fair fight. The Fellows used steel rods, clubs, baseball bats, tire irons, and rail road hammers. They simply decimated them and broke them down to a few pockets of desperate men trying to fight their way from the melee. They were not successful. Breaking bones and crushing skulls was an old traditional form of dealing with would be unions and uppity folks in the South and most people simply accepted it. Business was business and the lumber company would get the canal built with other Santa Rosa farmers and laborers.

Later that evening, he was upstairs at Mirabella's pounding his way to sexual oblivion. A very stoned and satiated Telephone Man drove back to his house on U street and ate everything his wife cooked for him. After showering and cleaning off, he took his wife to bed and continued to fulfill his sexual urges. Whatever that pharmacist had given the girls at the whore house had made his libido twice as potent and it was already pretty intense as it was. Mabel was shamelessly satisfied and tired that night. She was a little sore and began to beg him to stop after a while. It wasn't too long before he went to sleep and a very relieved wife got up and cleaned herself and went back to bed. Ed dreamed of violence and sex that night as his wife held him with another baby in her womb.

Chapter 11

The next day he drove his work truck through the Blocks and found the barbeque joint he was looking for, parked his truck and waited for Hercules to come out with a box full of pork. Hercules came out of the building and sure enough he had a box and a sinful smile. When he arrived in front of the driver's side of the truck, he handed Hercules an envelope of cash and took the box of pork. "You're not worried about them Milton folks?" asked Ed. "Hell no, Mr. Paul, them boys will be thinking it was them Milton niggers. "Sir, they think we alls look alike, Sir." replied Hercules as he counted his cash from the envelope. "Nice doing business with you, Sir," said Hercules as Ed started up his truck. He tipped his hat and drove off down the road back to work.

He came home in time to open up his barber shop. He had just finished washing his hands when his first customer walked in and sat down in the barber chair. "Mr. Phillips, how's the grocery business doing these days?" replied Ed as he draped a sheet around his customer. "Not good." Apparently, your father is letting every Tom, Dick, and Harry in the neighborhood run a line of credit over a mile long.

How do you suppose he's going to collect that?" Mr. Philips turned his head and looked directly at him. Ed just sagged his shoulders, looked at Mr. Philips and said, "Sorry Floyd, he knows better than this. I will make sure and have a talk with him." He had already warned his father not to involve him in the grocer business or there would eventually be consequences but his old man simply assumed that his son's reputation would be enough to make people pay. He reassured Mr. Philips that things would change and began to cut a much-relieved customer's hair.

The Sullivan's were able to swing things for Ed to distract his father with a more tempting treat near the Navy base in Warrington. The forest was being cleared for new roads close to the Navy base and the work crews needed competent foremen. Only problem was that there were too many men that were better experienced and desperate for the work. However, it wasn't what you knew but rather who you knew and he needed to get his daddy out of the credit collecting business before he too would be shaken down.

The pay from the Navy was good and the job came with respect and even a pension. It wasn't too hard for him to convince his father to take the job for a few days in order to see what he thought. Which was just enough time for the Goodwin Grocery store in Brownsville to mysteriously burn down one morning while the old man was working at his new job. George came back that evening and found his business nothing but a burned out building and ashes. A very sad and stricken owner held his hat in his hand while he looked around at the damage that was done.

Ed pulled up a few minutes later in his truck, stopped and got out. "I just heard about the fire, Daddy. What happened?" Ed looked surprised but was cautious enough to play his part and keep his poker face in check. His stricken father looked over at him and just raised his hands and claimed that he had no idea. They poked around through all the debris. Eventually, he showed his father an outdoor ashtray near the bench George had placed by the front entrance. It was completely melted to what was left of the wooden bench and brick wall. "You think maybe someone's cigarette caught the bench or ash tray on fire, Pop." Remarked Ed as he and father studied the evidence.

"I guess so but how did the rest of the place burn so quickly and where in heaven's sake is the fire department?" George Goodwin looked around and cocked his eye brow up while looking at his son. Ed took it in stride. As if on cue, two fire trucks pulled up with sirens blaring.

A very tired, dirty, and soot covered fire crew stepped off their trucks and walked over to the wreckage. George began to fuss and cuss about what happened. He gave them his opinion and kept ranting on but most of the fire men ignored him. Another truck pulled up and the fire chief got out and walked over to Ed. "This is the third fire today. Were there any fatalities or injuries?" He shook his head no when another fireman came over and reported his findings. George walked over and asked him what he said. That's when he told his father that there were two other fires that day in the city.

Apparently, the fire department didn't get the call until it was too late and they couldn't leave where they were. Ed's father just looked at his son as if he were making it up and immediately began to ask the Fire Chief what was going on. He could tell by looking at his old man that he had finally accepted the lost and surrendered himself with regret and despair. It was not a pretty site.

Later that night, he and his family joined his father's family for dinner. Ed's mother, Wanda, was pregnant again with her tenth child and the years of hard work and hard living were already etched into her face. He brought a large box full of fried pulley bones and gave it to his momma for that night's dinner. Outside George was smoking a cigarette and stewing about his grocery store. Ed came outside to join him and lit a cigarette and sat down on the front porch swing. "Hate to ask, Pop, but did you have any insurance on the store?" His father looked over at him put out his smoke took a deep breath and claimed that he was going to get some whenever he started making more returns.

"Well shit fire and save the matches, Pop, didn't I tell you to take some out when you started this crazy ass adventure of yours? Does Momma know about this?" George shook his head no and put his hands over his face. Ed was relishing the moment. He had won. He finally had his old man over a barrel and he was determined to never let him off the hook. "Well, Pops, if I were you then I wouldn't quit this new job. Looks like you're going to need it more than ever.

"By the way, how is your job going, are they respecting your orders as foreman?" Suddenly there was a glint of optimism in his father and Pop immediately began to tell his son all about his new job. A few minutes later and they went inside and ate dinner. Little did George know that his son had taken out an insurance policy on the grocery store building and he would be paid handsomely. It just so happened that there were two more businesses the Sullivan's needed off the books. They happened to burned down at the same time, which made for a rather serendipitous pay off for the Brownsville Boys.

A month later on the ground floor of King Solomon's Temple in Lodge 15, sat the newest apprentice, Mr. Jones. He was being initiated in the Sanctum Sanctorum. The Worshipful Master asked the sacred questions put to the new initiate and was answered with eloquence and precision. The other Master Masons murmured their approvals. Ed looked down and finished the ceremony and they all began to complete the end of their ritual. At the conclusion of the meeting the Senior Warden spoke up and announced that there would be a dinner dance at the Zelica Grotto Hall at the beginning of the next month and extended the invitation to their newest member. Mr. Jones graciously accepted.

About three days later, Mr. Jones got an anonymous letter from a concerned member of his lodge. It said he should count the pole stacks in the creosote yard and have a look at the size of the houses in North Hill that his colleagues lived in. A week later and the honest accountant discovered the discrepancy. Ed told the Sullivan's and they in turn made it known to the hotel owner that Pensacola's favorite accountant was nearly ready for the purchase. All they had to do was wait and sweeten the pot a little. Both the

Sullivan brothers decided to purchase a 1931 Cadillac car that had mistakenly arrived in the port that year but was purchased by a local banker. That banker just so happened to work for Mr. Ball and within a week he was delivering the auto to the Sullivan's with an attitude to match his wealth. The Sullivan's got the car.

Mr. Jones even took it upon himself to drive all the way to Montgomery, Alabama. He went to report the news to the Creosoting Company headquarters about the managers in his city embezzling funds and selling poles through certain foreign consulates in Pensacola. However, a very confused and angry accountant drove back home with a pink slip in his front pocket in complete shock as to why the company boys would fire him after protecting their interest. What Mr. Jones didn't know was that they too were doing the same thing. Although, that didn't stop them from firing the boys down in Pensacola Creosoting Company.

Corruption permeated the American Dream and most common men were feeling it during the 1930s. A few days later, the San Carlos Hotel manager called Mr. Jones and offered him a job. Ironically, the job came with some interesting benefits. The manager asked him if he could meet with his associates at the hotel and told him that he could bring his family too. They would treat them to a dinner at the restaurant.

By the time Mr. Jones arrived and entered the restaurant with his wife and child, both of the Sullivan brothers had arranged for the Cadillac to be pulled around to the front entrance. They had a table already waiting except for them at this time it would be the Sullivan's closing the deal and not the hotel manager.

Byron and Tom where standing by the table and motioned for them to come over. They all exchanged introductions and the men let Mrs. Jones sit down first with her boy and get comfortable, then they all sat down. The Sullivan brothers were quite adept at entertaining their company and politely began to explain to Mr. Jones that they represented the interests of the hotel and many more businesses in Florida. Both of the brothers touched their rings simultaneously and Mr. Jones immediately noticed they had on the similar Masonic Apprentice rings like his. He quickly without meaning to, touched his ring and looked at it.

"We both work for a large corporate interest and we've noticed your honesty, and integrity sir. We are after all fraternal brothers, are we not?" Mrs. Jones didn't quite understand what they were saying but she was having a time getting her son Richard to stop fidgeting so much to notice. The waiter came to the table and Tom Sullivan asked him to bring his guest whatever they wanted it was already paid for. Both of the brothers winked simultaneously at the accountant and Mrs. Jones began to laugh. He was going to have a difficult time rejecting their offer and he was starting to realize it but was enjoying the lavishments too much to care. He was enjoying this as much as his wife.

When the dinner was over and the Jones had their egos stroked for the umpteenth time, it was time for the brothers to introduce the last bit, the proverbial cherry on the cake. They walked out of the hotel and presented the 1931 Cadillac automobile to Mr. Jones for coming to work for them. Mr. Jones immediately looked at them and asked what he was supposed to do with his other car. The brothers simply laughed. "Sell it, go hunting and fishing with it. Do what you want but this here car is yours with all the other details we mentioned if you come work for the hotel and us. We like your style, Mr. Jones. An honest and loyal accountant is worth all of this fuss, Sir." Remarked Byron Sullivan.

Mr. Jones couldn't believe it. His wife held on to her son's hand and walked over to the car. Both of the brothers walked over together and began to tell them that he could drive home in the car and give it a test ride around town before he made up his mind. Mr. Jones looked in the car and looked back and told him that would need to be done.

"We will have someone follow you in your other car while you drive your new one home tonight. If you don't mind?" said Byron Sullivan as he handed Mr. Jones the car keys. Mr. Jones was a veteran that enthusiastically enjoyed learning how to operate modern machinery. With his family somewhat secured, Mr. Jones jerked and jumped around the road at first, trying to get use to the gears. By the time he made it to East Hill he was coasting right along with a grin and confidence in his new vehicle. He never really said yes to the job offer but he wasn't going to say no either and he was, after all, driving home in the new fancy car.

The Families were mighty particular about claiming intelligent accountants and they were constantly looking for new talent. Before long Mr. Jones would be on his way to a political career and he didn't even know it. Talent and loyalty was a precious commodity that was extremely valuable in American politics and Mr. Jones had both.

Chapter 12

Ed opened his barber shop the next afternoon and began to cut hair and had already shaved six men before Mabel rang the dinner bell and called him to dinner. He was just finishing shaving his last customer when in walked Mr. Goldring. Ed couldn't stand being in the same room too long with Mr. Goldring because Saul had shot Gunny and killed him just a few months earlier. Mr. Goldring walked in and sat down on the church pew and began to read a newspaper when Ed's last customer got up, paid him and began to walk out of the shop.

"What can I do for you Saul? asked Ed as he counted his money. "So, we are on a first name basis now I see. Well that's alright Paul, said Mr. Goldring." "I've come to declare my terms for you. I simply can't have you holding the Gunny's death over me like some fucking school boy brat. This business is harsh and it's a cut throat, cold hard world. We do what we are told and we can't disobey our bosses. I had to fucking do what I was told, Paul. You will find yourself in the same situation one day and I hope you don't act this way again or you're going to find yourself in a new line of business. That's not a threat. It's a promise. Now let's shake hands and let bygones be bygones. What do you say, Paul?"

He gave a long hard look at Mr. Goldring, took a deep breath, and shrugged his shoulders in acquiescence. He walked over to Mr. Goldring and shook his hand. "I promise you there are no grudges, Saul." They shook hands and he helped him up from the church pew then walked him outside. "Is there anything the bosses need?" Mr. Goldring shook his head no. "Are you sure you can get over this?" Mr. Goldring asked. Once again, he reassured him that he was over it and would try to be more respectful. Mr. Goldring looked at him and nodded his head. "I hope so, Paul. I will see you tomorrow evening. Good night." Ed waved him good bye as Mr. Goldring drove off down U street. "Fucking Jews," replied Ed as he walked back up to his house for dinner.

He drove around the next day looking for the telephone lines on his work order to fix or mend to his satisfaction. It wasn't easy being a lineman for Bell South in those days, the pay wasn't that great and the job was dangerous. Not everyone could stomach the heights or deal with the incessant heat that was routinely delivered without much cover. Ed's fingers looked like rather thick sausages. With the type of work, he did his hands had become thick, strong and very rough. He had larger than normal hands to begin with and they only kept getting thicker.

The Sullivan's used to kid him about it and even Gunny and the Chief said his large hands probably made him a better swimmer. He always wished he could play a musical instrument but he knew that it would probably be difficult because of his larger than normal fingers. As long as he could choke the life out of his victims with his bare hands then it didn't matter no how, thought Ed, as he drove to each business and collected his payments after work.

He seemed to always be at work whether it was home, at work, or working for the Family bosses. Work was work and Ed was glad he had plenty. Every day that he drove home he could see unemployed men searching for work and wondering how they were going to make a living. He drove over to the newly built bridges and discovered that they were built fairly solid but it still felt strange to him. The modern era was a fascinating business and he was utterly loving the fear it created.

After the passing of the Chief and Gunny, the Sullivan's had to reshuffle the management on the beach. Mr. Ball chose a fellow from up north. The Sullivan's didn't really have any choice in the matter. Mr. Dupont would have his own guardian to the western gate of the Sunshine state and to no one's surprise, Mr. Ball chose another fellow that would be loyal to the Families. Mr. Charles Novak and his crew were originally from Philadelphia. Apparently, he and his boys had a few run-ins with General Butler back in 26 and they, too, were no longer welcomed in their home city. Now they worked for the Families. They remained respectful and everything so far was running smoothly. Men of similar interests made for much easier transitions in the racketeering and regulation businesses of the South.

The new Casino was going to out shine the old gambling structure. This time there would be a dance hall, bath houses, shops, a casino and even a luxurious restaurant with rooms and accommodations. The beach was open for business and all the players were ready to act out their parts. They even relocated the brothel down the beach some ways so the families could not see it. It was out of site and out of mind. Mr. Novak helped start new boxing events set every Tuesday night. The bookies were loving the action and even Pensacola's finest got a cut. The money flowed right up to the top and the bosses were happy. During a time when most people didn't have a dime to their name, Pensacola's deep-water port still remained active even if most of the contraband was off the books. If there wasn't money to pay a debt, then they would find another way. Bartering for other goods and services became the norm.

The celebrations for the grand opening of the newly built bridges and Casino were over and Ed needed to collect that month's payment from Mr. Novak. There were local boys scouring the beaches and dunes looking for garbage to clean up that was left behind by all the people from the ceremonies. He drove his trusty bread truck to the Casino and got out. Before he was able to walk over to the building, Mr. Bert walked out and greeted him. "Howdy, Mr. Paul." Ed tipped his hat and shook Mr. Bert's hand. "Looks like it was a pretty big shin-dig, Mr. Bert." Ed was at the festivities with his wife and kid but he was curious about Mr. Bert's own observations. Mr. Bert began to recite what they did as if he were reading a script. Ed looked at him and waited patiently until he was done.

"That's something else, Mr. Bert. I hope the accounting is all done and the ledgers are ready. Mr. Sullivan wants to see them sometime today." Mr. Bert looked at him and just stared, looking a bit dumbfounded but did not blink his eyes. "Today," was all he said. Ed shook his head in astonishment and began to walk toward the Casino, Mr. Bert began to stammer and walk with him up to the building. "Mr. Novak keeps the books now. He doesn't let anyone else see them except himself," replied Mr. Bert. Ed shook his head again, took off his hat and walked to the manager's office inside the casino.

"Good morning, gentlemen." He looked at Mr. Novak and his associate with a smile as he walked inside, sat down and lit a cigarette in the plush office. "What can I do for you, Paul?" Mr. Novak always spoke right to the point and Ed greatly appreciated his professional demeanor. "I need to bring the bosses their cut and our business ledgers for inspection." He blew out a puff of smoke from his cigarette. Mr. Novak looked at him, smiled, and told his associate to retrieve the books from the vault.

Mr. Novak smiled back at Ed and offered him a drink. "No, thank you, Mr. Novak. Can you tell me more about this concrete company you've decided to buy?" Mr. Novak looked surprised but came right to the point and was thorough but brief. It was all about money and disposal. Ed put out his smoke, gave him a smile and looked around the room. The new office looked nothing like the Chief and Gunny's old offices. He took a deep breath and said. "You mean to tell me that a concrete company is going to help you make money and dispose of certain people too? Well if that don't beat all. I guess you'll be purchasing one of them freight airplanes next?" Mr. Novak looked at him rather strangely and asked, "why he would say that particular thing." "To feed the sharks and fishies of course." Ed winked at Mr. Novak and they began to laugh together. Mr. Novak stood up when his associate walked back into the room and handed the books to his boss. He waited and watched as Mr. Novak counted the money and put the books into a large cotton sack along with the payout. "How do you like living out here on the beach?" replied Ed as he was handed the sack of cash and ledgers. "It's like being on vacation, Paul. I love it. Can't wait to use this new Navy patrol spot light that was given to us from the base. "Mr. Novak walked over and showed him a large spotlight perched on a tripod. "Apparently, we are supposed to start making a journal of everything we see off the coast here at regulated times."

Mr. Novak looked at him curiously. "I didn't know we were on the Navy's payroll." Ed smiled and told him not to worry. They were simply scratching each other's back. "They need us and we need them Mr. Novak. It's as simple as that." He got up and began to walk out. Mr. Novak replied, "I just hope they know that there are no military discounts at the whore house." He stepped through the door, looked over his shoulder and said, "There's never been any given that I know of, Mr. Novak." "Really?" Ed had never heard of such an absurdity before. "Everyone pays for pussy," he replied. "It appears that our newly minted Naval Officers think otherwise." They looked at each other. "Hmm, I'll say something to the Sullivan's about that, Mr. Nova Good day, Sir." He tipped his hat and headed back outside.

As he was walking through the casino, he noticed one of the coat check girls, and immediately recognized her. It was Clare Brightwood. He first met her at Essi's whore house several years earlier. She was currently cleaning the carpet with a push bissell. It didn't take him very long to make sure it was really her. Poor Clare was actually purchased by Ms. Essi herself from an orphanage overflowing with children back in twenty-five. She was only ten years old and Ms. Essi kept her untouched until the highest bid was placed on her virginity three years later.

He could not ever forget. The man that purchased her was a former deranged doctor that was kicked out of the Navy and had made his home in Pensacola. If it wasn't for Ed making his rounds collecting the dues one afternoon, he would have never heard the noises from the doctor's house that dreadful afternoon.

He remembered everything all too well. It was 1928 and he was still apprenticing with the telephone company. After work he made his rounds, except on that one particular afternoon he would learn about what night mares were born from and what a sadistic person was capable of doing. He was checking a telephone line distribution center along the rail line that his boss and he had worked on earlier that morning.

He had to collect a payment from a business owner near the rail line and he wanted to review his handy work as well. While he was walking back to his work truck, he heard a strange noise. The young and innocent Clare was moaning from the inside of an old carriage house behind a fancy Victorian home. So, he decided to investigate the noise when he noticed Dr. Spreager walking to the garage wearing an apron and black rubber gloves.

He waited until the doctor had closed the door and found a window in the back mostly covered in old newspapers. However, there was a tiny little place where he could look through. What he saw disgusted him to no end. Apparently, the doctor was a disturbed individual that liked to torture innocent young kids. Especially little girls. Clare was naked and suspended with hooks and wires from the rafters of the garage ceiling and the doctor was examining the incisions around the metal hooks.

Ed couldn't take any more of it. He ran back to his truck, retrieved his sawed off shot gun, wire cutters, and ran back to the garage locked and loaded. As soon as he opened the garage doors, a very surprised doctor jumped around the suspended Clare and tried to cut him with a surgical scalpel across his face. Ed threw the butt end of his gun up and deflected the blade. Then he jammed the end of his shot gun onto the doctor's face, busting his nose and upper lip. Blood splattered all over him and the doctor.

He kept hitting his face with the butt of his gun until the doctor fell on the floor and stopped moving. Ed could still hear Clare moan from the pain from every movement that she made. This was something too horrific for him to phantom. Thank goodness he had wire cutters in his truck. Without waiting another second, he began to cut Clare down using his tools and ropes to prevent her from falling. He then began to tie up the doctor so he couldn't get away. The thirteen-year-old kid was presently unconscious but still in a lot of pain.

When Clare finally came around she was lying in a bed in unfamiliar surroundings. She began to get up but everything hurt too bad. Ed walked into the room and removed his hat and set a leather bag down on the floor. He introduced himself and began to tell her what had happened. She only starred at him and held her hands together trying to stop them from trembling. Ed continued to speak softly but reassuringly as well. He came over while telling her that he needed to administer some ointment to her cuts and to cover them with bandages. He gave her what she needed and took out a bottle from Chrystal's Pharmacy that would help her with the pain. He told her what it was and encouraged her to take a few swigs.

He helped her with the ointment and bandages the best he could but Ed was no doctor or nurse. He began to tell her that the demented doctor was lying hog tied and gagged downstairs in the living room. He had also made a few phone calls and had discovered a few things about the perverted physician. Apparently, Dr. Spreager was a relatively new resident in Pensacola after he was dishonorably discharged from the Naval base for sexual misconduct towards various military dependents. Ed was always suspicious of new folks in his home town. Sometimes port cities in the South had a way of attracting people that were running from somewhere and somebody or just plain hiding from the law. Either way it usually wasn't for a good reason.

He encouraged her to take a few more swigs from the bottle and took it back from her. He could tell she was feeling a little bit better already. He looked all around the physician's home and found her clothes. By the time they were done with the first aid, he gave her back her clothes and asked her if she could walk. She got dressed slowly and got up but winced from the pain. He could tell it simply was too painful and the cuts began to bleed through the bandages anyway. Ah, hell, thought Ed as he scooped her up and told her he couldn't stand to watch any more. She simply held on to him as they headed out the door. As they were walking down the stairs, Clare looked over and saw a very bloody faced doctor starring back at her with hatred seething on his face. She began to tremble with the shock of seeing him. Ed could feel and sense her discomfort and began to whisper to her that everything was alright. He finished with; "What would you like me to do to him?" Clare stopped trembling and looked at him. "Hurt him. Kill him. Destroy him, please." Even in her state of shock she was polite and specific.

Ed never quiet understood why he had asked that specific question or the next one but he did and something twisted inside him began to unravel with a frightening clarity. "Do you want to help me?" She squeezed his coat sleeve and nodded her head affirmatively. He immediately took her to his truck and carefully sat her down in the passenger's side. It was already dark and there was a hunter's moon in the sky. He came back to his truck with the dazed physician and threw him into the back of his work truck and threw a cover over him. He got back in, gave Clare his best Cheshire grin and they all three drove off toward Bayou Texar. He carried Clare to the skiff he had hidden along the tall reeds along the bayou then came back with the physician and his tools. It didn't take long before they were beyond the bayou. He stopped rowing, took a deep breath and let out the sails. The moon was directly over them when he dropped the sails and turned the boat around.

He gave poor Clare another swig from the bottle and drank some himself. Sometime that night in the middle of Pensacola Bay, Clare Brightwood would embolden herself in vengeance with the power of life and death. Clare helped him saw the doctor's head off, over the side of the boat. The physician woke up and began to squirm and screamed the entire time while Clare held the doctor's hair and head straight so Ed could get a clean cut. He threw a towel over the blade and began to cut the front of the doctor's neck. Blood began to spray and soaked the towel as Clare told Dr. Spreager to go to hell right before he stopped screaming and his eyes rolled back into his head. The job was done and she had made her first kill. The blood on their hands proved the point. She was now blooded. Ed was almost afraid to look at her but he did. She looked rather relaxed and simply smiled back at him with a look of contentment and complete relief.

He and Clare never told anyone what happened but Ms. Essi suddenly had to pay a higher protection fee for her foolishness. Madam Essi eventually went out of business due to the fact that she suddenly disappeared that year. He knew Clare probably had something to do with her disappearance but never said a word

His memory of that event had come rushing back to him when he walked over and extended his hand to Clare as she was cleaning the carpets in the casino. She immediately recognized him and ran over to hug him. She still had visible scars on her face and arms.

"I haven't seen you in a whole month of Sundays. What have you been up to?" Clare was obviously elated upon seeing him. He took off his hat and began to tell her about his crew he had been assembling. He could already tell there was a twinkle in her eye and a deeper understanding of what he was about ask her.

"You want me to join your crew, Paul?" He smiled and winked at her. "Couldn't hurt to have a woman's touch, or a woman's perspective, "he declared in a hush tone and whisper. Clare Brightwood would eventually become one of his favorite knock-off-man or woman as he was quick to utilize. Clare was a fast learner and began to work for him that same week. She was quick to learn that his real name was Ed but to never call him by that name when he wasn't at his home. Instead, she learned to use his business name like she had always done after that unforgettable night.

Chapter 13

Clare and Giger drove Ed and Mabel to the Grand Masonic Ball the next week and that's when she began her apprenticeship. Mabel thought it amusing and sad that Clare wanted to be treated like a fellow but said nothing about it. Apparently, Clare liked other women too much to be a girly woman and she openly showed her taste in the same sex as well. Ed thought it all too amusing and welcomed her into his new crew like a father figure with a new child. She never disappointed him.

Zelica Grotto Hall was hopping with excitement as all the fancy cars drove up and the gentlemen walked their wives to the Ball. Clare drove their car up to the front door and Giger got out and opened the doors for Ed and his wife. Mabel was dressed in another evening gown that she purchased in St. Augustine but it was all too obvious that she was pregnant again with her third child. She must have done some serious alterations to the evening-gown, so she could fit in it. He told Clare and Giger what to do and they left and parked the car.

That night was a telling event for him. Mabel enjoyed all of the interesting food but was simply too tired and pregnant to dance that evening. With his wife's permission Ed danced with nearly all the women in the hall. Before too long he was able to distinguish which, fellow brother was in on the newest number's racket. The Sullivan's had warned him but he never really believed it until that night. He eventually found collaboration with Mr. Jones. The honest accountant candidly told him that it was a harmless game the pharmacist downtown played. He even had purchased a few numbers and got lucky on occasions.

A nickel or dime was an easy amount to gamble with anyway remarked Mr. Jones with a sheepish look that portrayed his guilt. Ed smiled and congratulated Mr. Jones on his apprenticeship. Mr. Jones introduced his wife to him and he graciously smiled and shook her extended, gloved hand. He liked straight forward women and she looked and acted just like one but had a quiet and submissive voice. However, he politely excused himself, walked back and told his wife they needed to go. The Telephone Man had some business to attend to, thought Ed, as he and Mabel left the ball.

He never shared with any of the fellows in his crew anything that had to do with the telephone business. They had their own jobs and most either worked on the Navy base or worked downtown for the Sullivan's in various businesses. He had to barter in order to miraculously convince his boss, Mr. Johnson, at the phone company to hire Clare as a linewoman. The title never existed before and Mr. Johnson laughed so hard he almost hurt himself. Even with Ed's suggestion that the Sullivan's wanted him to take a new apprentice his company boss still laughed and thought he was joking.

He continued to explain, Mr. Johnson began to listen to him, seriously. His boss didn't like it at all. Mr. Johnson thought it went against proper etiquette. Finally, Ed gave his boss something he had never done before. A discount on pussy. Ed's company boss was allowed one free night at Madam Mirabella's every month at no cost. Mr. Johnson repeated the sentence verbatim and shook his hand. Mr. Johnson smiled, put on his coat and began to tell him what a sour deal he had just made for himself. Ed just shook his head instead and said that he would learn to regret his words. Mr. Johnson couldn't stop laughing as he exited the office with a look that betrayed his lust.

From that day forward Clare would always use her middle name Betty. For some reason she preferred the name. Although Ed would always call her Fred because she acted too much like a boy.

During her first week training to climb telephone poles she nearly ripper her arms and legs to pieces sliding down various telephone poles. Kicking her spurs into the wooden pole was not an easy thing to do for a light weight person.

"Put your ass into it, Fred," yelled Ed from the back of his work truck. She was nearly in tears, bloody, and angry with herself as she looked back down the pole. She was only half way up but she was trembling with fear remembering what happened the last time she made it this far. He looked up, lit a cigarette and began to recount that night he found her in Dr. Spreager's garage.

Betty began to flush with anger as he began to yell at her to keep climbing. With determined frustration she kicked her heels in and began to climb the telephone pole. Before she realized it, she was all the way to the top. He threw his smoke down, walked over to the pole, wrapped his pole choker around the pole, and began to climb up to meet his new apprentice. She was elated but pissed. "Don't ever mention that night again, Sir." He looked over at Betty, winked at her and told her that he wouldn't. "Now fasten yourself so we can get some work done," replied the Telephone Man as he began to teach her about working on the lines.

The training continued and she began to learn everything he taught her. It was obvious that she was becoming his pet project and the fellows began to show their resentment. That was when he invited all his crew to the boxing match at the beach one Tuesday afternoon. What he did was unthinkable for any boss but for Ed it was nothing more than a simple demonstration of his skills.

After the boxing match was over and the bookies were making their payments, Ed stepped into the boxing ring and began to remove his shirt and tie. The announcer began to speak into the microphone and asked if there was anyone man enough to beat Mr. Goodwin in a three-round fight for fifty dollars. Even the other boxers took notice of this and each one began to step up to the challenge.

The first boxer stepped into the ring and never took off his gloves. The fight was over in less than thirty seconds. Ed's bare knuckles were no match for the young boxer. The second boxer stepped into the ring but took off his gloves. He lasted fifteen seconds longer than the other boxer. Finally, the third boxer stepped into the ring without any gloves on and watched in horror as Ed swung his leg up and swiped down on top of the boxer's thigh causing it to fracture. The third boxer couldn't even stand up as Ed beat his face with his bare fist.

The crowd was a bit shaken up but the bookies began to yell out the new odds and a betting frenzy began to take place. Charley Monk stepped into the ring and looked at his boss. He, too, became fodder for his boss's outrage. After he finished breaking Charley's arm. The other fellows began to get ready to step up to recover what little honor was left. He beat each and every one in his crew except Betty. She knew better and idolized her boss not only as a hero but as a savior and father figure.

Ed's bloody fist began to swell as he finally collapsed into the chair in his corner. The Brownsville Boys would never question their boss's opinion again. He had literally beaten them all into submission. After a few days, the swelling in his hands receded and he was back working his usual beat again. Betty and his wife began to become friends and pretty soon Betty was hanging out in the barber shop learning how to cut hair. Mabel thought Betty was charming and very polite but still didn't believe she was as he had described it to her in a nut shell. "Mabel, she's a rug-muncher from down south, she's queer as a three-dollar bill, Sweetheart." Not matter how he explained it to his wife, she simply saw what she wanted to see and that was alright by him. He wouldn't have it any

other way.

Chapter 14

The following morning came and soon they were both heading up to Atlanta on their next assignment. Driving through the country side in Alabama during the twilight period of the morning is a very beautiful experience, thought Betty, as she drove toward Atlanta. Ed slept next to her as they drove down the road. Or so she thought. "Don't drive so fucking fast Fred. I want to get there in one piece, please." replied Ed as he looked over and gave her his best meaningful look. She could tell the difference between an order and a request just by the way he looked at her and she immediately acquiesced.

Somewhere between Montgomery and Atlanta they pulled over, refueled the bread truck, and ate the lunch Mabel had made for them the night before. As they got back into the truck and began to drive to Atlanta, he explained what the bosses wanted. The plan was simple and straight forward. They were going to find out who ran the negro newspapers and start disseminating chaos and paranoia. Betty would soon find out that her job was more entertaining than she originally thought it would be. What she didn't know was that

Hercules and his associates were paid to scout ahead of them and find out which community was the loudest. Money always made jobs easier to pull off and he was, in no, way going to let down his bosses on this assignment. He needed to make sure Betty could work well with him and continue her trade or they would find a way to make sure she disappeared.

Hercules had arrived the day before and began to make his own personal contacts in Atlanta with his own crew from the Blocks. It didn't take him long to discover who the rabble-rousers were. William Alexander Scott II was a college graduate that had learned his distaste for whites at a negro college that gave him everything he needed to stir up emotions in the black communities of Atlanta.

In 1927 he created the first negro directory and soon discovered that American Blacks were hungry for more information about other black communities and businesses. He was soon printing out circulations that were sent out to various cities around the states. He had a following of other negro graduates that were devoted to him and their cause. It became abundantly clear that they were responsible for the print. Hercules was true to his word and quickly discovered which communities were behind the rebellion causing such a ruckus and where they were located. Ed met Hercules in downtown Atlanta and was given the information. Ed thanked him and told him to head back to Pensacola. Hercules did exactly what he was told.

Betty was finishing writing her notes on top of a telephone pole about a conversation that she found during her detective work and began to descend down the pole while Ed was stripping insulated wires in the back of his truck. She had what she needed and began to remove her tool belt as one of the main culprits walked out of the store across the street in front of them. She motioned for Ed to take notice and he nodded his head and told her to get in the truck. They cautiously watched the fellow as he got into a Buick and headed off down the road. They followed him to his house without being noticed and drove on by as their newest victim got out and walked into his parent's home.

That night, Betty would learn just how dirty and nasty Ed applied his trade. She would learn to become just as stoic and calculated as he was. Sometime early that night, the fellow that they had earlier spotted left the house and walked towards his car. As soon as he put his key in the car, Betty drove the truck by, stopped next to him. Ed jumped out of the back and hit the guy over the head and carried him to the back of the truck and closed the doors.

She drove to their next victim's house as Ed administered his knock out gas and tied up their victim. Three more times they repeated their performance and soon had the back of the truck filled with four fellows, bound and gagged, and ready for the torture that soon followed. In the early evening hours Betty drove the truck down an old dirt road that meandered along a river somewhere outside of Atlanta. Ed told her to find somewhere that she could pull over off the road and she soon found another dirt road and turned down it, then parked the truck and turned it off.

Ed lit a lantern, got out from the back of the truck and began to pull out his sliding. Betty was told to bring his suit case that hid his tools and together they began to set up a workable, makeshift surgery structure. Betty watched silently and did exactly as she was told and only asked a few questions as he prepared the first fellow on the table.

"What are we going to do, Paul?" she asked. "We are going to remove something very important that every man needs to be a man. Their balls, Darlin. You are going to learn how to remove and sew up a male's groin." She dropped open her mouth and raised her eyebrows. "Don't worry Fred, it's easier than it sounds. Now hand me those medical gloves and put on that other set." He picked up their first victim in the back of the truck, threw him over his left shoulder and carried him to the work bench that was covered with a sheet and lit from the lantern that hung from a rod that extended on the top of the bread truck.

After administering more ether to the victim, he had her remove the pants and spread the victim's legs apart for the surgery. "Go ahead, get the needle and thread ready. This won't take very long and we've got three more to do so get ready. Now watch closely, Fred, and pay attention. You see how much skin is connecting to the scrotum and his body. We are going to tighten it like this, cut it all the way across, and start sewing it up as soon as possible." She watched wide eyed and was amazed at the amount of blood that flowed out of his groin.

"That's a lot of blood, Paul." "It sure is. That's why we have to sew it up so fast. Now, hand me that soldering tool. This tool is electric and I've got it plugged into the battery inside. A touch here, here, and here is all that's needed. Now I want you to help on the next one and I'll show you again what to do. There ain't nothing to it." He had her pull up the pants and fasten them as he lifted their victim off the work bench and carried him back to the truck and got the next one ready for surgery.

After the second one was done she started to get the hang of it and pretty soon was picking up her pace. He was pleased with her quick learning and stoic disposition at all the blood and the smells of surgery. She wasn't squeamish a bit and took to it with ease. "Hey, Paul, will they ever be able to have sex again, I mean will they be able to get it up?" He looked at her and winked. "Probably but they ain't going to be having any young'uns, that's for sure and they ain't going to be real men either. We've made sure of that." Betty just shook her head in amazement. She began to wonder how much he knew and began to appreciate true raw power. She had physically emasculated four fellows and did it without becoming too nauseous or scared.

Within a few hours they finished their job, cleaned up, buried the left-over specimens, and headed back to Atlanta. During the late hours of the night, each of their victims was dropped off in front of their homes and together, he and Betty drove straight to Alexander William Scott's house, and waited. Ed rolled several cigarettes and they smoked them and quietly talked while they waited until their next victim walked out of his home to go to work early that morning.

They repeated what they had done earlier that night. Betty drove by Mr. Scott as he was opening the door to his car. Ed stepped out, knocked him out quickly, and put him into the back of the truck. It almost seemed too easy for him thought Betty. He had obvious done this work many times before and she could tell he was real professional that took his job seriously. They didn't head out of the city however, instead they drove around and found a quiet street that she could park the truck and together they continued their work.

Ed bound Mr. Scott and hung him from one of the hooks in the back of his truck, unbuttoned his shirt, removed it, and draped the same blood-soaked sheet around the man's waist without getting any blood on himself or his victim. Betty kept the truck running but got out and walked to the back and waited for Ed to tell her what they were going to do next. "As soon as he comes around we are going to have a little conversation and teach him some respect. Now I want you to watch and learn just like you did earlier." She nodded her head and watched as he threw water from a canteen into Mr. Scott's face. Mr. Scott started to come to and tried to yell and scream but wasn't successful because Ed had tied a cloth around his face and had him gagged and waiting.

"Mr. Scott, me and this fellow here are representatives of the America's Industrial Families." Betty smiled at being called a fellow. This is going to get interesting, she thought, as Ed continued to explain to Mr. Scott why he was there. "You see, Mr. Scott, they aren't too happy at what you've been doing. Now they really don't care about some negro publications or directories but they don't like it when you start stirring up the pot and sowing seeds of discontent and rebellious ideas of equality. You hear me, Boy?" Mr. Scott just starred at them and began to mutter something that sounded disrespectful so Ed told Betty to put on the medical gloves. They put their gloves on and he reached over behind her and brought out and opened up a little zipper case, pulled out a surgical knife, took one, handed it to Betty, and took another one out for himself.

"Apparently, you don't believe me, so I'm going to have teach you some respect. Now watch closely as I begin to fillet the skin and peel his left nipple off." Betty watched carefully as Mr. Scott began to scream into his gag, wail, and shake, trying to kick his bound legs and torso. "Yep, that ain't going to help, Mister. No sir, that ain't going to help at all." Blood began to pour down his waist and soak the sheet. "Now do I have your attention, Mr. Scott? I hope I do because we can continue doing this all day if we have to. There is a lot of skin on a person's body." Mr. Scott nodded his head up and down with vigor. "That's better. Now listen here, Boy. You are going to stop stirring the pot or we are going to take this party to your entire family and I guarantee we will find each and every one and teach them some respect too. That is right before we kill them and dispose of their bodies. You understand?"

Mr. Scott shook his head vigorously again and Ed smiled. "Now that's better but to make sure you really get it, I'm going to let this here fellow remove the other one." Mr. Scott began his screams again as Betty began to fillet the other nipple with Ed's careful directions and help. "Hey, that was pretty good. Yep, not too bad." Mr. Scott's eyes couldn't have gotten any bigger.

"Now I'm going to take you to work and I want you to have a talk with your partners about respect. They should understand what I'm talking about. You see, I gave them a little help in that particular department tonight and I think y'all are going to be all right and little bit more respectful, you understand? But remember this, Mr. Scott, if you don't stop poking the beast, then your families are going to suffer the consequences of y'all's actions." Mr. Scott was in dire pain as the blood began to soak the sheet and start to ooze out and drip on the floor.

"Well, would you look at that, now I can't have a mess like this. Hey, get me that soldering tool, will ya'?" Betty hooked it up to the battery and watched him burn the flesh to stop most of the blood flow. Mr. Scott screamed again until the pain reached a level where he simply passed out. "Ah, that's better. Now help me put the bandages on him and put his shirt back on." Betty did what he said but told him that the smell was horrible. "Yeah, I agree. Ain't like a roasted hog. People usually smell bad." Together, they cleaned up, got Mr. Scott ready to dispose of, and drove off. Betty lit them a cigarette and handed one over to her boss. "Thanks, Fred."

They pulled up in front of Mr. Scott's business, Ed kicked him out of the back of the truck and closed the doors as Betty took off down the street. They got out of Atlanta as fast as they could but he made sure she didn't drive too fast and bring any attention to themselves. Half way back to Pensacola she pulled into another gas station, fueled up the truck, and let him drive for a while. Right before they entered Pensacola, he told her how proud he was of her training. "Fred, you're doing good but don't get to cocky and remember this, never ever brag to anyone of your accomplishments. You hear me?" Betty nodded her head and answered with a "Yes Sir."

"Part of this job is absolute silence. No one is to ever find out about what we do, unless you want to find yourself on the opposite side of this operation. It's what keeps us safe and allows us to continue what we do unencumbered." Betty gave him another "Yes Sir," and kept quiet. "Good, I'm going to go help Mabel's uncle in the morning and I want you to go to work tomorrow and do what Mr. Johnson tells you, then collect the payments, and deliver them, and our report, to our bosses at the San Carlos. I'll be home tomorrow night and I want to know exactly what they say. And don't open the payout envelope they hand you or you will be sorry." "Yes Sir, Boss," replied Betty as he pulled up to his house and they began to unload his tools and clean up the truck.

Betty and Ed both eventually uncovered who was running the numbers racket in town and to his surprise it was an up in coming group of college boys from North Hill. Apparently, one of the boys had mastermind the whole affair after he was expelled from college for gambling. The boy's father was a pharmacist and owned his own store and the son had convinced his father that it was nothing more than a harmless numbers raffle.

Two years later and nearly the entire city was playing the game. Gambling was always illegal but as long as the police and the pharmacist got paid, they never said anything. This kid simply didn't understand whose territory he was encroaching on and the

Brownsville Boys were about to remind him. Betty was amazed and fascinated at how quickly they were able to find out who was running the numbers racket.

Her newly discovered methods of listening to the right conversation on the right telephone line gave her goose bumps as she notated what she heard on her special work phone that he had given her to use for just that reason. Being at the right place at the right time and listening to someone's private conversation gave her a feeling of power and disbelief as she contemplated how freely people talked over the telephone.

Giger and Charley rounded up the fellows one night as he sat down to eat dinner with his family. It was a hot summer night and the Gulf breeze felt soothing as Betty sat on top of a telephone pole near the corner of Barcelona and Jackson street as the guys arrived in a model A Ford in front of the pharmacist's house. Betty called the house phone and spoke to the son of the pharmacist. "Hello Gus, how's the number's racket been treating you lately?"

Betty was having the time of her life trying not to smile so hard. Gus Killigan was too stunned to respond. Betty beat him to the punch instead. "You're going to go on a little trip to remind you where you from and who is in control, Gus. I'd advise you to listen, learn, and behave yourself appropriately, Gus." Betty hung up her end of the phone and watched through her binoculars as the fellows walked into the house, grabbed the young man by his arms and pants, hauled him outside, and threw him into the back of the car. Two of the guys rode hanging off the side of the car as it sped away. It was right then and there when Betty decided they were going to need a truck if they were ever going to do anymore stunts like this. She called the boss and told him the news. Ed hung up his phone with a new sense of satisfaction. Betty was going to be very helpful indeed.

Sometime in the early hours of the next morning Gus came walking back to his house with two black eyes, scrapes and bruises from one end of his body to the next, and a look of defeat that spoke volumes. Pretty soon the number's racket in Pensacola would be making rather large payoffs to the Brownsville Boys and to the Sullivan brothers too. No one ever operated inside their city without paying their dues or getting permission from the bosses. It simply wasn't done.

Betty did everything Ed asked her to do with a good attitude and a pleasant disposition. She even had him give her a gentleman's haircut. She began to look more like a teen age boy. They made a good team but she still needed a lot more training. The Sullivan brothers were happy with the new arrangements and were hoping to send Ed and his novice protege on a new contract from Atlanta, Georgia. The payoff was good and the job seemed straight forward. All they needed to do was infiltrate certain Atlanta communities and bring some fear and respect to the rebel Negros so they would learn to do what was asked of them. It was another job that involved terror, fear, and, constant vigilance.

Ed was impressed by the fee he would be given. Betty however nearly hit the roof when he told her that afternoon. "You mean we're going to spy on Negros in Atlanta." Declared Betty as she paced around the barber shop that afternoon. "You'll get paid and do what I say, Fred." Betty looked at her boss and began to close up the shop with a disappointing look. Ed watched his wife serve them dinner and kept a close eye on Betty's mannerisms. He would not tolerate any form of rude behavior from his subordinates and he surely would not accept it at his dinner table either. After he said the prayer, Arthur began to tell his father about the vegetable garden that he and his mama were making in the back yard. Ed broke bread that evening but said nothing to Betty as he ate dinner and interacted with Arthur and Mabel. Betty ate and didn't say a word to any one during the entire meal.

The next day he introduced Betty to all the people he collected from. Every business, brothel, or gambling debt was thoroughly and carefully managed. Each and every collection was taken by Betty and he made it clear that he would be using her to collect the payments from now on. If anyone didn't respect this, they would soon discover the seriousness of their stupidity. No one argued with him. After they were done with the collections he took Betty to visit the Sullivan's.

"Good evening, Paul, do come in." "How are you doing, Saul?" asked Ed as he and Betty walked into the Sullivan's offices. Mr. Goldring introduced himself to Betty and then introduced Betty to the Sullivan's for him. "Sit down, sit down." Replied Byron Sullivan as he motioned for Mr. Goldring to get Ed a drink. Ed handed Tom the payments in a leather satchel and told Betty to start reading the notes she made that week on their surveillance work. She began to read. After she finished her report both the Sullivan brothers looked at each other and smiled. Byron looked at Ed and gave him a wink. "I see you've been doing well with her new training." Then turned his attention to her and asked her if she had ever used a gun before. "No sir," replied Betty with a wide eye look of surprise. Tom immediately turned to Ed and told him to start the next phase of her training. "I want you to make sure she gets the same military training you received. You know what I mean. Mr. Ball wants you both to be equally efficient in that respect. Which brings up the next topic of business. Speaking of equality, there has been a new development amongst the Negros in the South. Apparently, they think that they should be treated equally and without so much as an ounce of regard to our way of life. They actually think that they are as smart and cultured as Whites. Can you imagine that? Not to mention that they have a total disregard for proper manners and etiquette of a civilized people."

Betty was seething in her chair and it became all too obvious for the Sullivan's not to notice. "Something wrong, Dear?" asked Byron. Ed looked at her and shot her a look that could freeze the air she was breathing. "No sir. I'm just having a hard time believing that these niggers think they can get away with this audacity." Mr. Goldring cocked his eyebrow and looked over at Ed.

Both the Sullivan's began to laugh and applauded her with that statement. She stopped fidgeting and Tom continued to debrief them on their next assignment. "There is a negro directory being circulated from Atlanta and also a few newspaper circulations being sent out as well and they're the ones stirring up the hornet's nest so to speak. We want the man responsible for this on the payroll so we can control it. Stopping its print would only cause more to rise up. However, the Families would rather have them in their coat pockets instead. Makes for a cleaner solution to their needs. My brother and I happened to agree with that and believe you, two, would be perfect for the job."

Ed nodded his head and complied to their request. "I'll leave first thing in the morning." Mr. Goldring handed him the folder with all the information that he needed. He finished his drink in one gulp, got up with Betty, and headed out the door. As soon as they were in the truck heading off to finish their daily telephone work he looked over at Betty and began to quietly tell her that she was going to have to control her feelings and hide them better if she wanted to continue her trade. Betty was too afraid to disagree. She quickly gave him a Yes Sir and kept quiet for the rest of the day.

The day went by smoothly and he gave her the truck to finish collecting payments. She dropped him off at his house to prepare for their next assignment. He didn't bother opening the barbershop. He needed the time for reflection and to gather his tools of the trade.

During his preparations he kept thinking about the Gunny and Chief. He sorely missed them and had a hard time trying not to get choked up remembering them. Gunny deserved more than he got and one day Ed would make sure that he would be avenged.

Chapter 15

In the morning of August 16 1931 Ralph Fults was paroled from the Texas State Prison Board. Bonnie Parker was waiting to pick him up in a stolen 1930 Chevrolet Six Coup. Ralph was elated to be free and ran over to Bonnie and hugged her off the ground. "Well, bless my soul, I thought we might never see each other again." Ralph jumped into the passenger's side and Bonnie started up the car and they drove off heading east. "Looks like they may have to let Clyde out soon. Maybe even next year sometime," replied Ralph as he looked out the window. Bonnie's eyes became large and her smile widened. "Do you really think so, Ralphie." Ralph began to tell her about his parole and its circumstances with the Texas penal system. Texas prisons were simply overflowing. The warden even instituted and prison rodeo to raise funds.

Bonnie began to talk to him about getting the old gang back together as soon as possible. Breaking Clyde out of prison was still her plan but she needed money to complete it and Ralph was going to help her obtain it. "Why in hell did you swipe a Chevrolet, Ralphie?" asked Bonnie as they were heading to the next gas station to rob. "What's wrong with my car Bonnie? You don't like coupes?" "It's not the coupe part that bothers me, it just that it's not a Ford." Bonnie looked at Ralph and began to laugh, "You boys are mighty peculiar, you know that, Ralphie? Mighty peculiar."

They hit the next gas station, robbed it without hurting anyone, but skipped the rest as they drove over the Alabama state line. Ralph had been on the lookout for a good Model A Ford to steal for Bonnie and he was not disappointed when they drove by a late afternoon church service near Evergreen, Alabama. Ralph parked the car and Bonnie helped put their belongings and firearms into the Model A parked at the back of the church. Together, they switched cars and drove off in a newly stolen Model A Ford.

In prison, Clyde told Ralph that his Grandfather Barrow put his money, in silver coins, inside mason jars, buried behind their barn. Bonnie and Ralph decided they would help themselves to that stash in order to help break Clyde out of prison. It was not a very well thought out plan. Clyde's grandfather, James Barrow, and his wife, Lonnie, didn't take kindly to folks poking around the back of their barn especially considering that was where they kept their retirement. Bonnie and Ralph didn't have a chance. Clyde's grandparents had shot guns on them within minutes of their arrival and they were forced to leave at gun point. Usually most folks were not armed and dangerous but the Barrows were and they knew how to use guns too.

Ed had just finished installing an outdoor light at his Uncle Henry's gas station. He and Henry had both chugged down a fresh home brewed beer Henry made just for such an occasion. The cold beers were wonderful and Ed needed to relieve himself out back after the first few. That's when Bonnie and Ralph pulled in and decided to rob the place.

Bonnie was tired of being the getaway driver and convinced Ralph that she would handle the next hit. Ralph didn't like it but she was too stubborn to talk her out of it. Come hell or high water she was going to learn her trade one way or another. Ed suddenly heard loud noises from inside Henry's gas station. He concentrated on what was being said and was able to discern that his wife's uncle was being robbed.

He reached for his steel driving hammer in his tool belt and quietly walked into the back of the store. Sure enough, Henry was emptying his cash drawer. And apparently, a cute strawberry blond in a butternut dress was holding a rather larger shotgun on Henry and demanding that he give her every dime he had. Ed didn't was a waste a second. He took a deep breath and threw the hammer as hard as he could through the air, aiming for the back of her head.

Bonnie never saw it coming. The hammer hit her hard enough on the base of head to knock her out. She fell down faster than her gun hitting the ground. He immediately ran over and seized the weapon and looked down at the girl. He knew things were getting rough in the country but this was a little too much, thought Ed, as he looked outside and noticed the parked Model A still running.

Henry came over and began to get his money back. Ed looked at the shot gun, made sure it was loaded, and stepped outside to walk over to the car. As soon as the driver saw him, he immediately took off and Ed began to shoot the back of the car and blew out the back window. He got a few shots in but the rest of the shots only sprayed the car as Ralph drove off. He never would see that car or fellow again but the girl on the floor was another matter entirely. "Let me take her to the law, Henry. At least I can get some money for their stupidity." Henry looked over at his nephew and smiled. "Be my guest, Edward. I'm mighty glad you were here today. Damn kids just don't want to put in a hard day's work anymore.

"Damn shame." Henry was so pleased with Ed that he even helped him tie up Bonnie as well. As they were tying her up Ed began to notice a similarity to his wife and sisters. The strawberry blond hair, fair skin, and small frame was appealing to him. His drive back to Pensacola might take longer than he thought, he mused. Henry let him place a call to Mabel and he told her what happened at her uncle's gas station and that he would be late getting home. She was grateful that he was there to help her uncle and asked if he and her uncle were alright. Then she thanked him for taking care of her uncle and told him to be careful. Ed looked down at a bound Bonnie Parker and answered, "Sure thing, Honey. Don't wait up, I'll probably be late getting home."

He drove back to Pensacola with the sleeping robber in the back of his work truck and decided to take a detour just on the other side of the Florida state line. By the time he parked his bread truck out in the woods, next to Cold Water Creek it was late was already late in the day. After setting up camp near the fast running creek and building a fire, it didn't take him long to find a good spot where the trout were swimming.

He threw his cast-net in the creek and captured all the fish he saw. That wasn't exactly legal but the trout would sure taste good.

He stoked the camp fire, wound up his radio, turned it on and began cooking a meal. The Grand Ole Opry was playing and he began to whistle a tune to an old country song while he battered the fish. He had brought Bonnie out of the truck and laid her down by the fire on a quilted blanket earlier when he first arrived and administered the knock out gas to her so she would sleep a little longer. After a while she began to wake up. Bonnie eventually sat up and began to examine the back of her head with her right hand. He looked over and saw that she was awake. He grabbed a piece of paper from his shirt pocket and a soda pop from his cooler and walked over to her.

"My name is Paul and who might you be?" He knelt down beside her, popped the top off the soda and handed her the drink. Bonnie looked at the cola and looked back at him. "Bonnie, Bonnie Parker." He gave her his best lopsided grin. "You're not going to hide your identity? Proud huh?" Bonnie sneered at him and sat up straighter holding her shoulders further back.

"You better believe it, pal. You better not do anything you'll regret. I've got partners that will kill you as soon as look at you." Bonnie took a swig from the cola and spit in the fire. He began to laugh so hard he thought he might hurt himself. "You sure sound like one tough cookie, Little Girl. But your partner, if I'm not mistaken, has abandoned you, Sweetheart." He pulled something out from his shirt pocket and began to open a folded piece of paper as she spoke.

"Where am I?" Bonnie looked around the woods and noticed the creek shimmering in the late evening twilight. "You're in Florida, Darlin." He began to think that she was another one of those free spirits, like Betty, but this one seemed more like a wild cat than a trained professional. "Does your head hurt, Sweat-Pea?" Inquired Ed as she held the back of her neck. Bonnie nodded her head affirmatively. "Hand me your drink and I will pour a little of this headache powder in it and in a few minutes, you'll feel much better."

He reached for her drink. Bonnie pulled back and asked him if he was trying to pull a fast one on her. Ed simply stared back at her but did not move a muscle. "You're hurt and you're free to walk right on out of here whenever you want to but you look like one of them wild woman outlaws that likes to play dirty and run hard. Am I wrong?" He smiled at her and she gave him her drink. "What's in that powder, Mister?" He concentrated as he poured a little bit of the cocaine into her drink, handed it back to her and told her to shake it and drink it down. "It's a little bit of aspirin that my pharmacist makes for me." She acted like it was a dare and chugged the rest of the cola in the bottle. He told her to get more fire wood as he got back up and began to fix their dinner.

Apparently, she didn't like to take orders and stubbornly sat there and amused herself in front of the fire. He sighed a breath of discontent and continued cooking. Before long he had dinner prepared and the fire wood ready. Bonnie listened to the radio and hummed with the tune. Ed draped a white sheet over the fold out table, brought some wooden folding chairs from the back of his truck, and invited her to sit down to dine with him.

She looked stricken and surprised but played along, nonetheless. He adjusted the kerosene lantern and served fried fish, hush-puppies, and beer. It wasn't exactly elegant but the way she was acting, you would have thought he was a royal prince. There was something about this girl that attracted him and he wasn't quite sure what but danger and looks weren't the only thing. There was something in the back of his mind that tugged on his feelings whenever he looked at her. She would kill him in a minute and take his money if she wanted to and he knew that all too well. Perhaps that's what made her so appealing. Dangerous women always did captivate his attention. Or was it simply his lust. He didn't care. He just wanted to fuck her.

He told her a few funny stories about himself and she began to relax and open up a little more. Apparently, she was in love with a fellow in prison and she and her partner were going to break him out as soon as they had enough money. He wanted to laugh in her face but knew better and simply listened as best as he could. Her story was that and only that. How sad, thought Ed, as he contemplated what life would have been like if he had never met the Sullivan's. No thank you, thought Ed, as he began to take his shirt and pants off. "What are you doing, Paul?" asked Bonnie, as he removed his underwear and socks. He stood there completely nude. "I'm going to go swim in that cold creek over yonder and dance around this here fire as naked as a jay bird and holler at the moon." Bonnie began to laugh as Ed ran over to the creek and jumped in and disappeared.

She began to look around the campfire for his gun or a weapon of some sort. She looked in the front of the truck and began to look inside the back. She couldn't find a knife, a tool, gun, or anything useful when she heard him begin to wind the radio up and start dancing around the camp fire. She got out of the bread truck and he looked over at her. "Did you think I would leave anything dangerous for you to hurt me with, Sweetheart?"

He was still naked but looked serious and sober. Bonnie tried not to flush as she kept trying not to gaze at his nether regions. It was hard for her not to notice however. He sat down on the blanket by the fire and opened another piece of paper and dumped the rest of the powder on a little jewelry mirror that he brought from the truck. She sat down beside him and put her hand on his thigh. "Whatcha' doing there Paul?" He put a rolled-up dollar bill to his left nostril and sniffed a bit of the cocaine. He handed the straw to Bonnie and she repeated what he did but tried to consume everything too quickly and began to gag. "Hell, Girl, you better take it easy." He gave her the rest and stood up. Bonnie grabbed him between his legs and said, "Where do you think you're going, Big Boy," and pulled him back down on the blanket. He could tell she was aroused but heavily drugged. The radio played Al Bowlly's, "Got A Date with An Angel." as she began to undress.

They made love that night under the moon light by the rushing Cold Water Creek. The fire raged by them as they lost themselves in the rut. She bit him, scratched him and punched him but he never stopped. She was louder than most girls and way more intense than any other woman he'd ever been with. After they were done he picked her up and carried her to the creek and they plunged into the cold water. Bonnie gasped in disbelief. She had no idea that the water would be that cold in Florida. They walked back to the camp fire and began to dry themselves by the fire.

It wasn't long before they were going at it again. There was an animal attraction that they mutually shared. He couldn't help himself. She simply relished his effortless ease. He was mesmerized by her intensity and together they made a blissful mess and loved every minute of it.

The fire began to dwindle down to a few embers as they shared a cigarette. He decided to get up to throw more logs on the fire when they heard a truck driving down to the landing where they were camping. Before Ed had time to snatch his trousers from the hood of his truck bed there was a spot light on him from the truck that had stopped in front of their camp.

A Santa Rosa Game Warden stepped out of his truck and walked into their camp. "Whatcha doing out here so late at night, Folks?" Ed winked at the officer and began to tell him that they were just out there necking on the beach where no one would see them, hoping that the fellow would see that they weren't up to anything mischievous. Apparently, the officer's moral indignation made things slightly different and he began to ask them if there was anything in the truck that they were not supposed to have. "Are y'all holding onto any hooch, Boys and Girls." asked the Game Warden.

Ed looked at the Game Warden's name plate and just nodded his head. "Yes Sir, Officer Ramos, I have some homemade beer. He knew all too well that the beer he picked up from his wife's uncle was going to be confiscated and enjoyed by Officer Ramos and his friends. But what happened next completely surprised him even more.

"Sit down on the ground, Folks, with your hands in front of you so I can see them." Ed and Bonnie did as they were told. Ed watched as Officer Ramos began to look through his truck while they sat in front of the high beams of the Game Warden's truck. In a few minutes the Game Warden walked from the back of the bread truck to the front holding onto Ed's case of homemade beer and put it inside his own truck. Before he knew it, the officer grabbed Ed's wrist and began slapping on hand cuffs. He couldn't believe this fellow was going to actually arrest him. Bonnie began to protest when the Game Warden turned toward her and said, "You want to get arrested too, Little Darlin?" Bonnie didn't care and began to complain about how this wasn't fair.

Ed was hoisted up by the officer and brought back to Officer's Ramos's truck and locked to the back with a chain. Bonnie ran up to the officer's truck, screaming obscenities at the officer, but before she got close enough the officer back handed her so hard that she fell down to the ground and didn't move. Ed was furious and completely helpless as he tried in vain to release himself from the chains. Bonnie was kicked in the gut and picked up and thrown over the hood of the Game Warden's truck. Ed couldn't believe his eyes as he watched the man rape her without any hesitation or care in the world.

After the short violent violation of her body, Officer Ramos pulled his pants back up and walked to the back of his truck where Ed stared at him in complete disbelief. The officer began to laugh as he began to pull out a long Billy-Club from inside the truck. "Well Boy, that was some piece of ass you got there. Yes Sir, she was real tight," said Officer Ramos as he began to beat Ed with his Billy-Club.

A few hours later Ed awoke in severe pain as Bonnie helped him to the front of the fire. "Where's the son-of-a-bitchin Game Warden?" asked Ed as he felt the knots and bumps on his face and head. She handed him the envelope of powder and said, "I recon he's gone off to enjoy his beer, Paul." He opened the envelope and swallowed the rest of the cocaine. After drinking a large gulp of water from the jug of water Bonnie handed him, he got up and began to pack up the camp and they quietly drove away from Cold Water Creek.

Ed drove back to Pensacola with an intensity of vengeance laying heavily on his mind. Bonnie just stared out the window, not saying very much. He looked at her and could tell that she was traumatized. "Bonnie, I want you to know something right now. I like you and don't think you deserved what happened to you last night from that sorry son-of-a-bitch. I promise you that he's going to pay dearly for what he did and will never do it again to anyone else. You hear me, Bonnie? He ain't going to ever do another sorry thing in his life again if it's the last God damn thing I do. And that's a Bona Fide fact." She slowly produced a smile and asked him where he was going to take her. "Sweet heart, I'm going to take you to the bus station in town and buy you a ticket to anywhere you want to go. I got some business to attend to and one Game Warden to take care of. Besides, I figure you want to get back to finding a way to break out your beau back home."

"That would be real swell of you, Paul, and don't you worry about me none. I'll be alright. You just make sure you sock it to that bastard for me and let him know that Bonnie Parker sends her regards and hopes he enjoys the Hell he's about to go through. "Will you tell him that for me, Paul?" "You better believe it Ms. Bonnie. He'll know that right before I get done with him. Bonnie smiled and held his hand for a few seconds as he began to pull into the bus station. Something inside her told her that she knew he would do exactly what he said and her only regret was that she wished she could be there to witness Officer's Ramos's pain and terror that he was about to receive.

Chapter 16

After dropping Bonnie off Ed drove back home to U street to wash and change his clothes. When he arrived home, he showered, got dressed, and sat down for lunch that Mabel had provided for him. "What happened to you, Edward?" asked Mabel, as she looked at all the bruises and goose eggs on her husband's head. "Apparently, there is a Game Warden in Santa Rosa that doesn't like it when someone's carrying a case of your uncle's beer through the Blackwater Forest. His wife suddenly realized that her husband always got a free case of beer from her uncle whenever he did any telephone or electrical work for him. "Well for land's sakes alive, Edward. They did this all because of Uncle Henry's beer?" "You know the law, Mabel. That Volstead Act allows these Authority figures to act as badly as they please without any fear from the federal government, Sweetheart. It's the oldest damn game in the world. Give a man a gun and authority, with laws against vice, and they will use it for their own self-interest.

Mabel knew better than to keep asking her husband any more questions. He looked like a beat dog that was about to turn rabid and mad. She told him she had to finish the laundry and excused herself to the back porch where Arthur was playing with his dog. Ed got up when he was done eating and walked over to the telephone and rang up Mr. Johnson at the Telephone company. "Howdy, Mr. Johnston, I'm back from out in the country. Say, I was hoping that you could give old Fred a message for me. Tell her to come home as soon as she's done working. Mabel needs help with this dress she's making for her."

Mr. Johnston began to laugh loudly through the phone. "Mabel's going to make Fred wear a dress? Well if that don't beat all. I sure would love to see her wearing it though. Sounds kind of funny when you think about it. Betty really does act more like a Fred even if she's so dang cute." "Hey, don't tell her or she won't come home. Mabel's damned and determined to show her off at church in a proper dress." Mr. Johnston laughed again and told him not to worry. He hung up the phone and rang the operator again. Pretty soon Ed had called all the Brownsville Boys for a barbershop meeting that evening to parley his new instructions. That Goddamn Game Warden's going to pay for this, thought the Telephone Man, as he prepared and assembled his tools of war.

When all the men arrived, they couldn't believe what they saw. None of them had ever seen their boss in such a poor shape.

He began to tell them what happened and they all sat in silence and listened. When he was through telling them his story, Ed announced, "So, who is the first one to get a haircut. Hey, Fred, grab one of them chairs and let's cut together," said Ed as he threw her a sheet to drape over the men.

He and Betty began giving the fellows haircuts, he began to hatch out his plans for what he wanted them to do. By the time Betty and he were done with everyone, they were through discussing all the details. The boss wanted immediate retaliation and he was going to get it, quickly, without anyone's hesitation. The next morning, all the boys headed out to the Blackwater Forest with everything they needed.

He and Betty drove there in her newly purchased old Ford. She was prouder than a peacock in a field of peahens, of her car. When she showed it off to the boys, they all mocked her for the way it looked. Though, Betty could care less what they thought. It was all hers and she was awfully proud of her independence. Ed sat in the passenger's seat and couldn't stop thinking about how he got caught with his pants down and let himself become a victim of a no-body Game Warden.

He knew that if the Gunny and Chief were still alive they wouldn't ever let him forget how badly he had forgotten the lessons they had taught him. He looked over at Betty and began to tell her what mistakes he had made and how he had forgotten what he had learned. "Fred, all you have to do is practice what I've taught you and this will never happen. Always be ready for change even if it's at four o'clock in the morning. Steady nerves and quick thinking have kept many a poor boy alive. When the going gets tough, Sweetheart, the tough get going. And one more thing, never ever get caught. Always cover your tracks, Darling."

"Remember, what I've taught you. Your boss just got his ass handed to him because I failed to apply those simple rules." Betty nodded her head up in down acknowledging what he said but offered nothing in the way of conversation. She knew when he wasn't in the mood for discussion by watching Mabel. She just kept driving to their destination, answering her boss with as few words as possible.

When they all arrived at the creek where he had been beaten, he began to exercise their plan of action. The fellows got out of their car and began to find hiding spots in the woods surrounding the beach where he and Bonnie had frolicked the day before. Betty got out of her truck with a blanket under her arm and he moved over to the driver's side. He quickly drove back down the road to a telephone pole located in Munson and climbed it as fast as he could, hooked up his telephone to the right wire and placed a call to the operator.

"Operator, I need to place a call to the Game Warden's office about a poacher killing a bunch of deer over in the Black Water Forest." The operator patched him through without any delays and Ed discovered how easy it was recognizing Officer Ramos's voice over the phone. He quickly changed his voice to that of an old timer's rambling rant about young folks not respecting nature and how he was going to go get that whipper snapper if the officer didn't himself. "Them son's-of-bitches are even butchering the deer down at Dewey Landing." Officer Ramos took the bait. Without much delay the Game Warden was off on a hunt he would not come back from.

Ed waited impatiently in Betty's Ford truck at Munson while the boys did their work. Meanwhile, Betty had taken nearly all her clothes off except for her under wear and laid out on the blanket while she waited for Officer Ramos. Within a half an hour the Game

Warden pulled down the lane towards Coldwater Creek, were Betty sat sunbathing.

The Game Warden couldn't believe his eyes. This dumb girl was going to get a good licking today, thought the officer, as he got out of his truck and began to walk down to the creek. "Well, howdy, Little Girl. What's a cute little button like you doing out here alone in the woods? Aren't you afraid of the big bad wolf, Sweetheart?" Betty just cracked a smile and waited till the Game Warden was in close enough range. Officer Ramos let out a loud seductive whistle as he walked close enough for Betty to pull out her boss's sawed-off shot gun and fired it at the officer's legs. Within seconds the boys were coming out of the woods with guns drawn and watched as the Game Warden bent over in agony from all the shot in his legs and groin. Betty was on top of the man in seconds and quickly disarmed him.

The men hog tied the Game Warden, got into his truck, and drove back to Munson where their boss was waiting. As they pulled up beside him in the Game Warden's truck, he knew they had just bagged the bully. "Fred's waiting for you with the package, Boss." He nodded his head and told them they had done a good job. "Hell's fire, boss. Fred took him by herself with one shot to the legs and groin. Man, you should have seen her, Boss! She lit a cigarette up afterwards as cool as a cucumber and never broke a sweat."

He smiled and told them to dump the truck at the ship yard and tell the old man to send it overseas. "He knows the deal." The fellows tipped their hats and drove off down the road. Betty was showing more signs of maturity every week. If only he could get the rest of his crew to be as calculating she, they would all be all right, thought Ed, as he drove back down to the creek.

Betty was waiting with the Game Warden on the side of the dirt lane when he pulled up. With a great big smile, Ed told her how impressed he was with only one shot and her quick thinking. Betty tried her best to not show her appreciation for his compliment but it was hard for her to hide it. She would always crave his approval, as a child would their parents. She adored him as a father figure but kept her demeanor in check.

Ed knew differently and understood her dependence for approval. The Chief and Gunny had educated him quite well about the affairs of the mind. They understood each other. Without saying much, she helped him drag their newest victim onto the back of her truck and he covered Officer Ramos's head and mouth with a rag to gag him and used the knock gas to keep him sedated. Betty threw a nasty work blanket over him and Ed helped her place spools of telephone wire around him with some of her tools on top.

They drove back to Pensacola and he began to tell Betty more details about what Officer Ramos did to Bonnie Parker. By the time she pulled into the old garage they used as a warehouse, Betty was already filled with that old, not forgotten, rage created by the events of her own history. He told her all the details on purpose, knowing well that it would help him with what he was about to do to Game Warden.

Betty closed the garage doors while Ed pulled their victim down from the back of the truck. "Hey, Fred, go get a chair and bring it here." Betty found an old wooden chair from inside the mechanic's office and brought it to him. Together they untied the moaning officer, sat him down on the chair and bound him to it using the same ropes that had earlier kept him bound in the back of her truck.

The Game Warden was still sleeping when Betty sprayed him down with a water hose, waking him up in complete surprise. "Hey, Partner, remember me?" asked Ed as Officer Ramos starred widely around the garage. "Looks like you're about to have a little fun there, Bud. So, you don't like vice much, do you, Officer Ramos? Yet, you sure do like raping girls and beating their beaus, don't you?" The Game Warden just stared at him but didn't say anything. Betty had on her work gloves as she picked up her hammer and slammed in down onto the Game Warden's arm. Officer Ramos let out a scream that was muffled by the dirty rag that was stuffed into his mouth. "You'll speak when spoken to, you son-of-a-bitch. Do you understand me?" Said Betty, as she looked at the Game Warden. Officer Ramos's only sound was a pathetic whimper. Betty slammed the hammer down on top of her victim's knee cap as hard as she could and heard the snapping sound bone makes when it breaks.

Ed raised the hose from the floor and began to pour water over the Game Warden's mouth with the stuffed rag inside. Within a few seconds Officer Ramos began to choke and as he tried to relieve himself of the drowning sensation he was experiencing. After his eyes rolled back into his head and his body when limp, Ed put down the hose and told Betty to wake him up. She pulled the rag out of their victim's mouth and began to slap the Game Warden awake.

Once again Officer Ramos awoke to the terrifying reality of his situation. "We can do this all day and all night long if you want. I'm quite good at this, you know. Now I asked you before and I will ask you again. If you don't like vice so much then why did you rape

Bonnie?" Ed watched and waited as the Game Warden began to speak. "It was a punishment that you both deserved." Said the officer as Betty looked at him in disgust. "For exactly what, may I ask?" replied Ed as he cocked his head to the side with sincere confusion.

"Drinking and fornicating is a severe offense," was all that the officer was able to mumble through all the pain he was experiencing. Ed turned the hose back on and Betty stuffed the rag back into the officer's mouth. Once again, the Game Warden began to fight the feeling of drowning and began to jerk and tug at his restraints. Ed eventually turned off the hose and laid it back on the ground. "Did you enjoy that rape and beating, Ramos?" Betty pulled out the wet rag and the officer's wide eye look of sheer terror was all too obvious. He was in way over his head and didn't know how or what to say in reply to this question. Betty began to stuff the wet rag back into his mouth when he let out a string of words that were almost unrecognizable.

"Yes! You're all sinners!" Screamed the officer. Betty dropped the rag and began to hammer the other knee-cap as hard as she could. "Yep that's what I thought." Ed grabbed the wet rag and stuffed it back into the officer's mouth and poured water over his face with the hose until the Game Warden's eyes rolled back into his head and he passed out. "Hey, Fred, help me hang him on the wall to dry off until tonight when we can get rid of this piece of shit." Together they pulled the chair over to the wall with tools hanging on hooks. Ed untied the Game Warden from the chair, checked and made sure the feet and hands were still bound together, then hoisted him up and hooked the wrist restraints over the hook on the wall, purposely hanging Officer Ramos just a few inches off the ground.

"All right now, we need to get back to work and take care of this later tonight, Fred." Betty agreed but not before she picked up the hammer and broke a few of their victim's ribs. "He'll have a hard time breathing when he wakes up, Boss," she replied as Ed cocked an eye brow and shook his head. Betty was learning fast and he was always amused at her tenacity to follow through on a job that needed to be done. "Come on, Fred, let's get out of here."

Later that day, Ed studied the new plans that the telephone company had given him. Nothing was out of the ordinary but trying to figure out how the phone company engineers drew up the designs always seemed to baffle him. Why did they have to make things so complicated? Betty marked the areas where the new poles were going to be placed and Ed began to drop the spools of line in the areas that they needed. The crew that set the poles were a bit slow for Ed's taste so he decided to move things along a little faster for the boys. "Y'all are going too slow, Boys. If you want the company to hire some of them out of work Negros down in the Blocks, I'm sure they can find a way to replace you guys with cheaper labor." The pole setting crew didn't like hearing that at all and quickly increased their pace and began working harder and faster. The depression was hitting everyone hard financially and no white man wanted to be replaced by cheap black labor. By early that afternoon the crew had finished the job, Ed and Betty had strung their telephone lines, packed up their tools, and headed off to make their collections.

Mabel had just finished removing the clothes on her laundry lines when she heard a ruckus next door at the neighbor's house. Mabel's mother, Mrs. Bailey was inside tending to Mabel's youngest child, Charles and little Arthur, as her daughter decided to investigate what was going on with the neighbors. Mabel could hear screams, furniture crashing about, and a man's voice shouting obscenities. So, she walked over to the fence that separated the yards and leaned over to get a better look and listened closely to what was being said.

Apparently, the neighbors were fighting and she was able to see the husband slap and knock his wife across the kitchen room through the widows. Suddenly their young son came in and tried to stop his father from further hurting his mother. That's when the man turned around and began to hit the child and begin focusing his rage on the little boy.

Mabel couldn't stand it any longer, she put down her basket of clothes and immediately ran around the fence out the gate and ran into the house to confront the out of control father. She could tell he was drunk and full of rage. "You'd best leave Tom if you know what's best for ya' mister. My husband's going to be home any minute and he ain't going to take kindly to what you're up to, no Siree. You understand?" Mabel noticed that Arthur's playmate was curled up into a ball and covering his face with his hands. The irate father turned around and glared at Mabel. It was obvious that he was contemplating hitting her too but began to quickly think about what her husband would do to him if he laid a hand on Mabel.

Within seconds, Tom threw his hands over his head and yelled at them all. "For Christ sakes can't a man manage his own affairs without being told what to do from a woman?" "Leave Tom and go get sober. Think about what you've done and make things right or my husband and fellows will. You hear me Tom?" The angry father just stared at Mabel, then stomped off muttering more obscenities. Mabel helped the beaten wife and child get up and began directing them to clean up. Delores, Tom's wife was crying and tried her best to calm down but was black and blue from head to toe with a large black eye. She was shaking so bad that her bottom lip trembled like a leaf in the wind.

"What happened? Replied Mabel as she began to help clean up the mess. "He's been drinking lately and I told him I wanted a divorce because he's been seeing another woman at his work and has now gotten her pregnant. She came by yesterday and told me with a grin on her face and I nearly lost it this morning when I confronted him. Tom says that it's not his child but wants to take my little Timmy away and move back to South Florida close to where his parent's farm is and I told him over my dead body. So, he left and came back drunk. That's when he started in on me." Mabel comforted her as best as she could and helped little Timmy by ruffling his hair and asked if he'd like to eat dinner with Arthur that night. His mother told him it would be alright and told Mabel not to worry. She'd be fine as soon as she got things in order and asked Mabel if it was alright if she could let her son sleep over that night so she could make plans to move in with her parents until things blew over. "That would be fine darling, give me a call when you get settled and I'll make sure Timmy is alright tonight." Delores thanked her and began to weep again. Mabel took her son by his hand and walked him back to her house.

By the time Ed and Betty made it back home Mabel had dinner on the table. As soon as Ed saw both the boys sitting and waiting at the dinner table he knew something wasn't right and had Mabel tell him what happened. "So how long do you think it's going to be until the divorce?" Asked Ed. "Don't recon I can say but I figure she'll be gone by the end of the week I suspect." Replied his wife. Ed just shook his head and began to tell her that he and Betty had to do something important for the phone company that night. Ed told her that he and the company suspected that some of the pole crew were stealing copper wire from the phone yard and that he and Betty were going to see if they could catch the culprits that night. "How long are you going to be gone sweetheart?" Replied Mabel as Ed scratched the back of his head and said "I will probably be back before midnight I hope. Them thieves ain't too smart. I expect their going to hit the yard around ten o'clock." With that said she kissed him on the lips and told him to be safe. Ed kissed her back and yelled for Betty to come on and off they went. Little did his wife realize what he and Betty were going to really do that night but she was too distracted to notice Betty's anxiousness and Ed's need to leave as soon as he could.

The Game Warden was still hanging on the hook when Betty and Ed arrived back at the converted garage. Officer Ramos was limp but still alive. They kept him blind folded and gagged, took him down of the hook, and then threw him in the back of Betty's truck. The moon was high over their heads by the time they put him into the skiff. Ed rowed the boat while Betty steered the rudder. As soon as they were far enough out he let the sail down within a little while they were in the middle of Pensacola Bay. The Game Warden was awake and fidgeting. Ed had brought two cement blocks and some rope and began to tie Officer Ramos's feet to the cement blocks and then tied it around his shoulders as well. The Game Warden tried to kick and scream but to no avail. Betty simply hit him over the head with one of the oars and told him not to fight back or things would get worse. Little did he know what they had in store for him. As soon as they completed what they needed to do Ed threw over the cement blocks and held on the Game Warden under his arms so he wouldn't fall over just yet.

"Take off his blind fold and gag Betty." Betty ripped the fold and gag away and looked directly at the frightened man. His eyes began to furiously look around so he could tell what was going on and quickly surmised what was about to happen. "Ramos, I need to tell you something. That girl that you raped back in the forest, her name is Bonnie. She wanted me to let you know that she hopes you have fun in Hell. May you enjoy your stay at the bottom of the bay Sir." Ed let go of the Game Warden and watched and heard the man let out a very loud yell as his body jerked off the side of the boat and begin to plummet to the bottom of the bay. Betty washed her hands in the water and said, "good fucking riddance."

Chapter 17

The next morning, Ed and Betty began checking the phone lines close to downtown Pensacola looking for any mistakes that might have been made during their new installation of lines in the newly built homes of East Hill. They had done a thorough job and couldn't find any discrepancies. All the phone lines were working and he and Betty were satisfied with their work. By lunch time they had completed their assignments and Ed decided to have Betty go make the rounds of that day's collections.

"Hey Fred, I want to you to knock off work, go make the collections, then take the drop offs to the Sullivan's, and meet me back at the barbershop when you're done. I'll finish up here and clean up our work." "Yes Sir, boss." Betty took off her work belt, got back into her truck, and headed on down the road. Obtaining collections always seemed an easy business for her but on this day, she would learn just the opposite. On her third stop she drove up in front of one of Pensacola's drive in motor lodges located on Bayou Texar in what would eventually become Pensacola Heights. It operated as a cover for some of Pensacola's business men and politicians that happen to have mistresses and needed somewhere to take them that wasn't too far from where they lived.

Betty walked into the main office of the motor lodge, rang the bell on the counter and waited for the manager to come in from the back room where he was mending cast nets for some of his neighbors and customers. When the office manager heard the bell ring he stopped what he was doing and walked out to the front counter. He saw who it was and immediately began searching for something underneath the counter where he retrieved a small metal box that stored his money. Mr. Johansson was a fairly new client that Ed had just recently put on his list of pay outs. After finding out that the motor lodge sold booze and operated as a cover for local business men's get away rendezvous for women of the night, he decided to make the owner pay out.

Mr. Johansson didn't like it but was too scared to say no. However, it wasn't very long before his family became involved and decided that he wasn't going to make any more pay outs like he had just recently been making. Mr. Johansson was still a little intimidated by Ed and his crew so he relented by only giving her two silver dollars and acted like it was enough of a pay out to satisfy her. Betty looked at the dollars in her hand and said, "You've got to be kidding me, Pal. This is all of it?" The manager gave a nervous laugh. "I've gotten into a real fix, Darling. I have somewhat of a little problem with one of my relatives. I don't know how to say this but my patrons are not paying as much because they've found out that I'm over charging them, due to you and your boss, and recently, my uncle just came back from prison and has decided to become involved in helping manage the motor lodge. He doesn't like our family being taken advantage of neither," replied Mr. Johansson.

Betty laughed in his face. "You don't know the meaning of being squeezed, Partner." It was at this time that Mr. Johansson's uncle walked into the office and motioned toward Betty with his fore finger and the office manager nodded his head. "Hey, Sweetheart, this here business is under new management. If you got any problems I suggest that you talk to me. I'm his new associate. You may call be Bo, Little Darling." said Mr. Johansson's Uncle Bo. Betty let out a laugh and shook her head back and forth. She angled her body away from the fellow while clicking her tongue on the roof of her mouth.

"Well Mr. Bo, let me explain something." As she was talking she reached for a solid metal pipe hidden inside of her coat and swung it around aiming for the man's left jaw. As soon as it connected it made a rather loud cracking noise. Then she swung it on top of the fellow's head so fast that it even surprised Mr. Johansson. Blood began to pour down the man's face as Betty swung it repeatedly at his head. Bo fell down immediately and she quickly turned around and walked over, around the counter, and began to break Mr. Johansson' arm as he held them up trying to defend himself. It didn't work out to well for him. Betty was quick and as crazy as a wild cat with a blood lust that seemed not to be easily satiated. No sooner had she knocked them out cold did she begin to calm down, while panting loudly, trying to catch her breath.

She reached under the counter for the metal box, took the rest of the cash from inside it and walked out of the office while looking around to see if anyone noticed. She was angry but also a little elated at what she'd done. Betty started her truck up and then headed off to the other businesses that owed her boss money. When she eventually dropped off her collections to the Sullivan's at the San Carlos, she didn't tell them what had happened but acted like it was just another routine day for her. They'd eventually learn of what happened and were thoroughly shocked.

Apparently, the brothers had a running bet with their boss that Betty wouldn't last very much longer at her new role. Mr.

Dupont's man, Edward Ball thought differently after hearing the Sullivan's news about Betty becoming the Telephone Man's apprentice. Mr. Ball believed that she would make a valuable tool. The Sullivan's made a wager with Mr. Ball for a thousand dollars that Betty wouldn't last another year. Mr. Ball only laughed and agreed to the wager. What the Sullivan's didn't know at the time was that Edward Ball almost never, ever lost a bet. In fact, Mr. Ball could have been one the country's top handicappers but instead of applying his talents to the gaming world he worked for the Dupont family in Florida. Power was the profit in his world. Money just seemed like a byproduct. Power was far more important to him.

By the time Betty made it back to the barbershop, Ed was just finishing cutting a patron's hair and giving him a shave. She sat down on the church pew across from where her boss was working. When as the man paid and left, she briefed Ed as to what happened at the motor lodge. Ed let out a whistle and sat down in his barber chair. "Well hot-to-mighty damn girl. You never fail to surprise me sweetheart." After saying that, Ed scratched the back of his head and began to laugh.

"Yep, I believe you're ready for your new training," said Ed as he picked up his newspaper and began to read. Betty looked at him with a slack jaw. "What new training are you talking about, Boss?" Ed looked over his newspaper and simply said, "Sharp shooting, Sweetheart. I'll let the Fellows know what happened and tell them to manage it for us. Tomorrow you and I are going visit the Navy base. I have someone I want you to meet."

The next morning, they drove out to Pensacola's Naval Air Station. Staff Sergeant Hickum met them at the front gate. After getting their passes, Ed and Betty followed the Marine in his truck to an outdoor shooting range. When they got out of their vehicles Ed introduced Betty to Staff Sergeant Hickum. The Marine was short, thick, had a gravelly voice and began to ask Ed if she was ready. Betty cocked an eyebrow wondering why he had asked that question. Sergeant Hickum noticed her expression and quickly remarked to her that guns were for killing and that was a commitment that not everyone could make. Ed and Betty reassured him that she was willing and ready to make that decision.

The sergeant nodded his head and asked Ed if he could see his weapons. Ed climbed into the back of his truck and brought out two suit cases. Inside of the suit cases were two disassembled, bolt, action, long range rifles. Sergeant Hickum looked at Ed and asked him if he could touch them. Ed grinned to the sergeant and handed him the suit cases. The sergeant opened both the cases and immediately focused on one of the rifles. He reverently touched the shoulder piece, picked it up and read the initials and words carved into the wood.

Betty looked at the mesmerized Marine as he studied the broken-down gun parts like a man who had just found hidden treasure. Sergeant Hickum looked up at Betty and Ed then said, "What we have here is the famous Battle of Belleau Wood Twilight Sharp Shooter. I really didn't know the Gunny too well back then. Hell, I was only a Private but I was there, I remember the nightmare. If it wasn't for this gun and Gunny Fletcher them God dam Germans would've nearly had us." The sergeant began to tell them the story as he assembled the rifle with the ease and speed of a mechanized machine.

"Each piece of this gun was hand crafted by Gunny Fletcher himself. It was said that after serving in the Spanish American War he became obsessed with long range rifles. Apparently, the Gunny always seemed to get into trouble fighting other Marines and would get demoted time and time again. It was his talent for shooting and his history in Cuba that kept him from being booted out. Some of us figured that the brass wanted him out of the way and purposely put him on the front line."

The sergeant laughed at his own words after he said them. "Whatever their reason was, it kept us alive. Thank God." Sergeant Hickum began assembling the second rifle as he continued his story. "The Germans would slither around at night trying to get a wedge into our line to start sniping us in the earliest hours of the morning and the Gunny knew it. He would sneak around at night, himself, and choose the perfect killing nest. He never missed a target. It simply never happened. The Gunny's death toll was off the charts. The speed and skill of his marksmanship was phenomenal," replied Sergeant Hickum while studying both of the rifles that he'd assembled.

"Say whose rifle is this one?" Asked the sergeant. Ed immediately replied, "It's mine. The Gunny and I made it when he was instructing me in marksmanship. Said I needed to understand and know how it works before I could learn how to be good." The sergeant laughed at Ed's words. "Partner, you have no idea how truly fortunate you were to have that instruction." Ed put his hands in his pockets, held his shoulders back, and cocked his chin up. "Sir, I'm fully aware of that privilege and honor. Don't think for one minute that I don't miss that old son-of-a-bitch. The Gunny made me who I am today and I wouldn't trade it for the world," replied Ed with a proud smugness that portrayed his loyalties.

Sergeant Hickum smiled a rather large grin and stood up. "I appreciate that loyalty Paul. The Gunny was the savior of the 5th Marines and we will never forget him." Ed nodded his head and the Sergeant continued inspecting the gun. "Have her show up every Wednesday and Thursday morning at precisely 0700 across from the Cory Field front gate and I'll take her to the gun range for training. If there is a no show then consider the training over. I will not tolerate any tardiness. Understood?" said the Sergeant without any hint of expected rebuttal. Ed shot Betty a stare that told her to comply with an answer. "Yes Sir!" Quipped Betty with much enthusiasm. Sergeant Hickum, coolly reminded her to never call him sir. "You may simply refer to me as Sergeant or Sergeant Hickum. I'm not an officer." reminded the Sergeant.

Betty began her training the next morning. Sergeant Hickum picked her up in a large truck filled with young Marines sitting in the back. "Hop in the back, Sweetheart," said the Sergeant as he looked down at her from the driver's side of the truck. "Yes, Sergeant," Betty replied then climbed into the back. The other Marines looked at her as she climbed in. One of them snickered something under his breath. Betty ignored it and sat down as the Sergeant drove back onto the base.

They eventually drove to a firing range where everyone piled out and stood at attention in front of the Sergeant, including Betty. "This is not a child's game! You have been taught the fundamentals of rifle marksmanship! You will demonstrate what you have learned and I will be watching your aiming, your breath control, and your trigger control with prejudice. Understand?" declared the Sergeant with a loud, clear voice. Everyone immediately remarked, "Yes Sergeant," including Betty.

Betty was extremely nervous. She didn't know a thing about rifles or guns and felt the pressure descend on her like a ton of bricks. Four long boxes were removed from the back of the truck and brought to the firing range. Inside of the boxes where the rifles and ammunition. Each Marine was issued their weapon and ammunition then he stood back at attention. Betty was left standing empty handed.

The Sergeant called Betty over to him and introduced her to the other Marines. "This here is Ms. Brightwood. You will be responsible for her training. I will assign one man per week to teach her the fundamentals of rifle marksmanship and everything else that every Marine understands about his weapon. You will treat her with respect like you would any other Marine. Understood?" replied Sergeant Hickum. "Yes, Sergeant!" yelled the Marines.

"Lance Corporal Ingram, you will be the first to instruct Ms. Brightwood." The Marine responded, "Yes, Sergeant" and waited until Sergeant Hickum was done with his briefing then they all started to line up on the firing line. The lance corporal came over to Betty with his weapon and had her follow him to where he could teach her about each part of the rifle. By the end of the training she was shown how to assemble and break down the rifle.

Lance Corporal Ingram was methodical and very thorough with Betty. She learned quickly and appreciated the lack of condescension in the Marine's voice. She was being treated just like the other men. Over the course of a few months she would learn to respect each and every Marine that was assigned to her training. Sergeant Hickum treated Betty no different than his men. She was even forced to run for three miles with the other Marines while carrying her rifle. Betty never failed to do what she was asked. Much like her boss, she learned fast and always complied with the orders she was given.

Chapter 18

"Jeepers, Boss. You think they're going to allow them to name the beauty contest theme on the beach, "Make Whoopee," this year? asked Betty, as she drove them to their next pole they were setting. Ed looked over at Betty and said, "You know they're going to kill a few cylinders of that song during the contest. I'm sure the Sullivan's have already given Novak their consent. It's all about the money, Fred." answered her boss as she parked the truck and they got out.

"You mean to say "asked," boss." Replied Betty as she began to get her tools out. "Cylinders, records, it doesn't matter what they use to play that damn song. I'm tired of hearing it. If you want to go see them gals and hear that confounded song over and over again then I would appreciate it if you go and make the collection that night, Fred." said Ed with a tone that sounded like an order. Betty looked over and smiled, "Yes Sir boss."

Later in the day Ed gave Betty another job to do. "Fred, the Festival of Lanterns at Ferdinand Plaza is tonight. I want you and Giger to go down there while the Mayor is giving his speech and find out who's been pick pocketing the city folk during the festivals.

Apparently, the police haven't been able to catch the culprits and the Sullivan's are up my ass to fix it. Bring them idiots to the back of the courthouse and the police will be waiting." "Yes Sir, Boss." Answered Betty.

That night, in downtown Pensacola the sea breeze blowing off the bay was unusually cool and thick with a blanket of mist and fog. The Lantern Festival had an almost eerie feeling. The dappled light was filled with a thick bay mist combined with the smell of salt, paper whites, paraffin wax, and boiled peanuts. It was a perfect opportunity for the would be thieves in the pickpocket trade. Everyone there was in a jovial mood and they even had the runners up that would be picked to compete in the beauty contest on the beach later in the week.

Giger and Betty decided on their plan of action. Giger would climb on top of the government building with binoculars looking out of one of the office windows with a phone nearby. Betty would be stationed at the top of a telephone line with her phone connected and together they would be able to see the crowd below while they were on the phone together. Once they found the culprits they would descend from their look outs and take out the thieves.

It wasn't too long before the mayor stepped up to the stage in front of the government building to give his speech. While everyone's attention was focused on the mayor, the thieves began to walk through the crowd. Betty watched a young teenage boy, an older woman, and a middle-aged man walk through the crowd, accidentally bumping into people and apologizing. "Are you seeing what I'm seeing, Giger?" Asked Betty over the phone. "I sure am. How about we corner the older folks over towards Jefferson Street then get the kid later." suggested Giger to Betty as he watched and spoke into the mouth piece. "I'll go for the woman, you get the guy." responded Betty over the phone. Giger agreed and they hung up their phones.

They were down from their look outs within minutes and immersed amongst the crowd looking for their targets. Betty was eventually able to catch up with the woman. She pulled a wad of bills from her pants pocket and began to walk over to the woman. "Ma'am, you wouldn't happen to have any larger bills than these one dollar bills I just won in the raffle?" asked Betty as she approached the woman while counting her one-dollar bills.

The woman's eyes widened as Betty began to openly count her money. The eager woman looked around the plaza and quickly claimed that she indeed did have some larger bills that she would exchange. Betty nodded her appreciation of the woman's help. "Let's not do this here in front of everyone, Darling." Suggested in the older woman with a sparkle in her eyes. "I'm parked right down the road. Let's walk that way while we exchange money, Sweetie." Responded the woman. "Yes Ma'am," replied Betty as they began to walk down Jefferson Street.

As soon as they were a little way away from the crowd and she could see which car the woman was walking towards, Betty stepped back a few paces to let the older woman lead the way. Then Betty pulled out her metal pipe and quickly hit the woman over the head while she reached for her car door. Betty caught the woman's body as it began to fall over from the blunt blow to the back of her skull. Within a few minutes Betty had dragged the woman into the passenger's side of the car, tied her hands together then closed the door and acted like she was talking to her while the lady sat slumped over in the car.

A few minutes later the teenage boy came running down the side walk toward the car with a look of terror in his face. Betty began to speak up and laughed at something imaginary as the boy came closer to the car. "No Ma'am. I ain't never heard a tale like that one before. No Ma'am." said Betty as she looked over at the boy running up to the car. "Is this your son?" asked Betty as the boy got closer to the car. As soon as he got close enough, Betty jumped on top of the kid with a fierceness that surprised the young man. Betty quickly yanked the teenager's left arm behind his back as the confused and terrified boy began to scream and holler.

Betty immediately grabbed the back of the kid's hair, pulled his head back, then slammed it on the sidewalk concrete. "Say one more word, Kid, and I will crack your skull open like a hardboiled egg." whispered Betty to the boys bleeding face. The kid began to whimper and cry but didn't say another word. Within a few minutes Giger drove down Jefferson Street with the older man tied up in the trunk of his car. He saw Betty holding the boy down and pulled his car over to get the kid.

Betty looked over at Giger as he pulled his car over and got out. "What the hell took you so long, Giger? asked Betty as Giger began to tie the kid's hands behind his back. "The fellow got the jump on me, somehow, and ran for it. I chased that son-of-bitch for two damn blocks. He, thankfully, ran right towards where I parked my car. I had to tackle him on the daggum street and beat the tar out of him before I was able to get control of 'em." Replied Giger as he looked over and noticed the woman waking up in the car next to where he was parked. "Hey, that's the woman we're looking for, Betty." declared Giger. Betty began to explain how she had already got to her before the kid.

"Well, shit fire, and save the matches, Betty. That was well done, Girl. The fellows are going to get a kick out of this when I tell 'em." Laughed Giger as the boy and woman were forced into the back seat of Giger's car and tied up good. Betty looked around and noticed there were people that had been watching them from down the street. "Take them to the back of the courthouse, Giger. The police are already waiting." remarked Betty as she left Giger and headed back to her truck close to Ferdinand Plaza.

Most folks in the South were either too polite or too afraid to stick their nose into other people's business. So, when Betty walked by the people that had been watching her they turned their heads and acted like they hadn't seen a thing. Which was all the better for Betty. She decided to get some boiled peanuts that the concession stands were selling before she went home for the night. However, as she was waiting to buy the peanuts a large gaggle of young beauties from the pageant gathered around the concession stand and were all in high spirits giggling and talking amongst themselves.

As soon as Betty purchased her boiled peanuts, one of the girls walked by her and said "Excuse me, Sir," as she made her way to the peanut vendor. Betty tipped her hat and lowered her voice. "Ma'am." Said Betty as she stepped out of the way. However, one of the girls had been watching Betty and apparently must have seen that Betty was a female too and walked over to Betty and said, "You sure look like a pretty boy for such a polite and strangely dressed girl. Why do you dress like a man?" asked the strikingly beautiful girl.

All the girls stopped talking and immediately looked over at Betty. Betty wanted to say something, anything, but Betty was simply tongue tied. The girl that had asked the question was one of the prettiest girls that Betty had ever seen before and there was something mischievous in the girl's eyes that spoke to Betty in unheard tones of quiet comprehension. Betty simply stared and stared. Then one of the girls said, "Cat got your tongue, Missy?"

Betty doffed her hat once more and quickly headed back to her truck. She was covered in a thin layer of sweat by the time she started up her truck. She banged her fist on the stirring wheel and tried to regain her composure. What in the hell was all that about, thought Betty, as she began to drive off towards Brownsville. She had never felt that befuddled or smitten by a bunch of girls before much less tongue tied like that. Yet, as she drove off she looked out her window and noticed the pretty girl that had asked her the question was still watching as she waved good bye.

Betty felt her heart begin to race and her hands started to become clammy and sweaty on the stirring wheel. She simply couldn't focus her attention. Her thoughts began to race for the first time with feelings and emotions that she had never felt before. Betty waved back and tried her best to act natural as she drove away. She looked back out the window and noticed that the girl was still watching her. Holy Hell, thought Betty. If I can't act right in front of a pretty girl, then I'll never hear the end of it from the boss-man.

Later that week, Betty discovered that the beauty contest on the beach would be judged by not only the mayor himself but also the Freemasons from her boss's lodge. Apparently, the entire contest was rigged and thwarted by Pensacola's business elites that wanted their daughters to feel pretty and important. The Southern Beauty Ball on Pensacola Beach in 1931 was held after three knock out fights that would have the spectators hooting and hollering all night long. Violence and the hint of sex made for a very profitable night for Pensacola's businessmen and underbosses.

After the last bloody boxing fight, the spectators moved back to the Casino where the beauty contest was held. Betty was already inside and sitting with Mr. Novak and a few of his goons at a booth drinking and smoking like they owned the place. Everyone that worked for the Sullivan's liked and admired Betty. It was Mr. Novak that eventually introduced her, later that night, as Brownsville Betty, a name that she would forever be known by. Ironically, she not only laughed at the name, she also found it admiringly amusing.

Suddenly, they began to play George Olsen's "Makin Whoopee," and everybody began to clap as all the beauty contestants walked out on the stage. Wouldn't you know it, the same girl that made Betty so nervous walked out ahead of the rest of the girls. She topped at the end of the stage, looked directly at Betty's table, winked, and then spun around on her heels and curtsied for the audience while blowing everyone a kiss. Mr. Novak looked over at Betty and began to laugh.

Betty was three shades of red and couldn't, for the life of her, hide from anyone her blushing brightness. Novak knew that Betty was smitten but just lit a fresh cigarette then whispered across the table, "You'd better be careful with that one fellows. That's Mr. Merritt's daughter, Miss Mary Jane." As soon as Betty heard the name Merritt, she knew that it was one of Pensacola's wealthiest shipbrokers. "Yeah, apparently the old' fellow adopted Mary Jane when she was very young. Must have been one of them family issues that got swept under the rug. That vixen is more trouble than she's worth." Said Mr. Novak as everyone watched the other girls display themselves on the stage.

Betty couldn't help herself as she watched the ladies prance around and disappear behind the stage curtain. Ed was proven true to his word. By the time the competition had dwindled down to the last three contestants, they had played the song "Makin Whoopee," so much that everyone was beginning to hate it. When the runners-up were announced, they all came out on the stage and held hands. Mary Jane tried, inconspicuously, to look over at Betty but did her best not to be too obvious.

The Mobile Abba Temple Shriners and the Pensacola Zelica Grotto Prophets judged Miss Mary Jane as Pensacola's most beautiful lady. After Mary Jane's announcement was made she was told to sit on a throne that was turned into a carry- litter. The largest of Novak's goons picked her up and paraded her outside to be crowned. Everyone followed and watched as Pensacola's Freemasons orchestrated her coronation.

Eventually, things started to die down and soon one of the torch singers began to sing in the Casino. Betty was enjoying her dinner with Mr. Novak when Mary Jane walked over to their booth. They all stood up. Mr. Novak greeted Mary Jane as "Her Majesty," then introduced everyone there, including Betty. Mary Jane couldn't help but laugh when she heard Mr. Novak introduce Betty as Brownsville Betty. Even Betty couldn't help herself from laughing too, which helped calm her nerves tremendously.

"How did you get a name like that, Sugar?" asked Mary Jane as she sat down with everyone. Mr. Novak motioned for a waiter and told him to bring a chair and to bring a gin fizzie for the lady. "That's a good question." remarked Betty. She asked Mr. Novak how she was given the name. Mr. Novak winked at her and began to tell Mary Jane that Betty was the most dangerous woman in Pensacola and resided in Brownsville. "She doesn't look very dangerous." replied Mary Jane as she coolly looked at Betty with that same mischievousness she had when they first saw each other at the lantern festival.

"Looks are deceiving, my dear." replied Mr. Novak as he sat back and admired Mary Jane's beauty. Mary Jane picked up a pack of cigarettes from the table, pulled one out, and everyone including

Betty had their lighters out offering to light her cigarette. "My, what wonderful host you all are," replied Mary Jane as she accepted Betty's light. Mr. Novak cocked his left eyebrow up and sat back down.

"I sent Daddy's chauffeur back home so I may stay for dinner. I was hoping that I might get a ride home from a respectable person tonight. I hope you're not too dangerous." replied Mary Jane as she received her drink from the waiter. Mr. Novak calmly reassured her with, "I promise you, my dear, you will be safely escorted home befitting a Queen." Mary Jane gulped the gin fizzie down in no time and asked for another one. "Daddy only trusts other Freemasons and lady folk of course, but if I may, I'd rather be escorted home by a dangerous woman tonight, if you don't mind." replied Mary Jane as she snuffed her cigarette out and winked over at Betty.

All the guys began to laugh, making Betty awkwardly uncomfortable. Betty, too, put her cigarette out, stood up, and asked to be excused. One of Novak's fellows asked Betty which restroom she was going to use as she walked away. Betty ignored the comment. However, as Mary Jane was being given another drink. Mr. Novak replied, "Sweetheart, Betty drives an old truck. Wouldn't you rather drive home in a Cadillac?" Mary Jane laughed as she gulped down her second drink of the night. "That's perfect!" she exclaimed as she got up and swirled around then curtsied for them in front of the table. Mr. Novak just shook his head and lit anther cigarette.

As Betty was coming out of the woman's powder room, Mary Jane caught up with her and attached her arm through Betty's as she and Betty walked out of the Casino. Betty couldn't believe this girl. Her bubbliness, and daring attitude was voraciously addictive but also made her feel so damn nervous as well.

While they drove over the bridges back to Pensacola, Mary Jane told her all about her dreams of traveling the world in one of her father's ships but that he wanted her to get married and settle down instead. Betty was a very good listener that night. She couldn't help but feel insignificant to Mary Jane and that sort of upbringing. Mary Jane finally switched subjects and began to ask Betty who her parents were and where was she was raised. Betty remained quiet for a few seconds, then casually told Mary Jane that she was an orphan that was adopted by a whore house then was sold to the highest bidder but survived it all and became a telephone woman and trusted associate of the Sullivan's.

Mary Jane was stunned. Her mouth hung open and her eyes became wide as saucers. "Whoa!" She whispered as she sat further back into the front seat of the truck. Betty casually looked over in her direction. "Don't worry, sweetheart, I won't bite." replied Betty as her poise began to come back. Revealing herself, unashamedly, helped settle Betty's confidence as she knew she would never be able to relate to Mary Jane. However, that only made Mary Jane even more interested in Betty as she began to view her in a completely different light.

Mary Jane lived in North Hill but directed Betty to Paradise Point in East Hill Pensacola. As soon as Betty realized that Mary Jane was taken her where all the teenagers went to fool around overlooking Bayou Texar she pulled her truck over and stopped. "What are you doing?" asked Betty. Mary Jane tried her best to put on her little girl face and bat her eye lashes at Betty. "I was just hoping we could talk for a little while longer. I never get to meet anyone as interesting as you, Betty. Can't we just talk for a little while before you take me home?" asked Mary Jane as cutely as she could.

"All right, but first give me your address so I know where to take you later tonight." Quipped Betty. Mary Jane told Betty her address and giggled. Thankfully, there were no other cars or trucks parked at Paradise Point that night in East Hill. Mary Jane was no more interested in talking to Betty than she was in watching a fat man bathe in the Gulf. As soon as Betty parked her truck, Mary Jane sat real close to Betty and asked her if she'd ever kissed another girl before. Betty tried hard not to show her nervousness but it didn't matter. Mary Jane slowly began to show her that night exactly what Betty was secretly hopping. The windows were fogged up in no time at all.

Betty was completely mesmerized. She was kissing the most beautiful girl in all of Pensacola and loving it. However, she knew that if she didn't get Mary Jane back soon than there would be hell to pay. So, she tore herself away from Mary Jane and started up the truck. "Ah, come on now. Can't we stay a little longer?" asked Mary Jane. Betty looked over at her as she began to drive off, "How about we go see a movie sometime later this week and we can have more time for kissing later. My boss will have my ass if I don't get you back at a respectable time, Sweetie." said Betty as she drove back to North Hill.

"Okie Dokie, darlin!" Squeaked Mary Jane as she began to pull back and tend to her hair. Betty couldn't help herself from looking over at the first girl that she'd ever kissed. When Betty pulled up in front of Mary Jane's house, she was amazed at the size and beauty of the home. North Hill Pensacola in 1931 was where the city's elite lived. There were Victorian, Queen Ann, Tudor, and contemporary Art Deco homes scattered throughout the neighborhood with majestic old live oaks and ancient magnolia trees that gave the neighborhood a regal atmosphere. Mary Jane wrote down her parent's phone number and handed it to Betty.

"Daddy's got Iola watching from the kitchen window. That old black witch is on to me, I know it." Replied Mary Jane as she looked out the truck window. Betty put the peace of paper with the phone number in her pants pocket and asked Mary Jane, "Is Iola y'alls maid?" "Yes, and she knows." whispered Mary Jane. "Knows what?" asked Betty. "That I like girls, silly goose." replied Mary Jane as she leaned over and kissed Betty. The hair on the back of Betty's neck rose to attention.

Mary Jane got out of the truck and said, "Bully for her! I don't care, no how." Then she turned around and sauntered up the drive way to her house. Betty watched Mary Jane waive hello to Iola as she walked. Betty took a deep breath and began to wonder what in the world was she going to do now. Being love struck was not something that she had contemplated. Yet, she wasn't going to miss out on a delicious opportunity either. She began to wonder what her boss would think when he eventually learned.

Ed found out about Betty's adventure the very next day. While they were laying out more phone-lines to be attached, later on Ed said, "I hear you caught yourself a little Pensacola mullet last night." Betty jerked her head towards his direction. "How in the world did you hear that already?" asked the befuddled Betty. Ed replied, "Goldring called me earlier this morning. Looks like I'm going to have to go on a new assignment soon. He said Mr. Merritt's daughter won the beauty contest and got you to take her home last night." Ed couldn't help himself but grinned from ear to ear. Betty was trying her best to act like it wasn't any big deal. However, Betty's face betrayed her emotions. It was all too obvious.

"You might just get lucky with that one sweetheart. Enjoy yourself but be careful not to get caught doing anything in public. Remember this, discretion is key to your training and apprenticeship. We don't want any undue attention. Being unnoticed and blending in to the background is part and parcel to what you're becoming." Instructed Ed with a sincere tone of voice. "Yes Sir, boss," answered Betty with as much sincerity.

At the end of the day they were both exhausted and famished as they climbed finished climbing the stairs at the San Carlos. The Sullivan's wanted to speak to them before they went home. Mr. Goldring opened the door for them when they knocked. As they walked in Mr. Goldring took one smell of them and replied, "Good gracious, y'all smell to high heaven." Ed and Betty began to laugh. "Try working in this heat for several hours and see how you smell." answered Ed as he was handed a drink from Byron Sullivan.

Tom Sullivan sat down across from them and began to tell them about them knew assignments. "Paul, we need you to do some scout work for us up in Newport Kentucky. There's a hornet's nest of mobsters and mayhem going on in the eastern part of Kentucky, bordering Ohio. We want to know who all the players are and to whom they are connected to other than to the syndicate. We also want you to find out who and where the largest horse race breeders are located and find as much information on them as you can. We also need Betty to complete a job for Mr. Ball down in Miami. I know you both have been working together and Betty is still in training but we need various leads in two different areas of the country at about the same time and we can't think of any other way.

Ed immediately spoke up. "I want one of the Fellow's to be the point man for Betty if y'all don't mind."

Byron concurred with Ed. "This is a necessary job that needs to be done for the Families. Do whatever it takes to complete it. We have also enlisted Hercules for this job as well so use him and his associates as needed. He is already on his way to Miami as we speak." Betty quickly asked for Giger to work with her and they all agreed. Mr. Goldring handed them the folders with the information that they would need with their instructions as well. "Read these carefully and destroy them when you're done." said Mr. Goldring as he stepped as far away from them as he could. Ed was too tired to care. Together, he and Betty made their exit and drove back to Brownsville with their new assignments.

Chapter 19

It was just like any other morning in downtown Pensacola. The warm bright sunlight had just begun to burn off the early dew that had accumulated the night before. A horn from a Model T could be heard as it broke for a paper boy delivering the morning news on his bicycle. The smell of salt air and dust being kicked up from the store clerks that where busy cleaning off the front of their establishments could be heard and felt as the day's business rituals commenced. The Brownsville Boys had all met together at the converted filling station that the Sullivan's had purchased for them to do their covert activities discreetly.

All the fellows, including Betty, were present when their boss walked in and began issuing orders. "Giger, I want you to be the point man for Fred. She's going to do some scouting down in South Florida. You both will be leaving tomorrow morning with my truck, so be ready. Sheamus, you will be scouting with me up north so bring some warm clothes, we'll be leaving tomorrow afternoon. Eli and Bruno, you both will be making the collections and delivering them to Mr. Goldring at the San Carlos." Ed gave them each a list of whom they were to make their collections. "Remember fellows, we all have a boss to answer to one way or another. So, don't screw up or there will be Hell to pay. Understood?" Everyone responded, "Yes Sir."

Ed and Betty ate lunch together on the back of her truck, parked underneath a shade of oak trees. "Fred, I need to make some arrangements for my trip tomorrow afternoon. I need you to do the same yourself. I've already placed a call to Sergeant Hickum and told him you will be absent for an important job that needs to be done. Told him, you'd be gone for at least two weeks. I don't reckon your job will take more than a week though." Betty nodded her head in agreement as she began to roll a cigarette for herself and her boss. "Did he say anything about how I was doing, Boss?" replied Betty as she finished rolling the second cigarette.

"Said you were hanging in there doing just as good as the other Marines. I took that as a high compliment from the Sergeant." Betty lit her bosses smoke then her own, blew out a puff and began to grin. "Yep, I'll take that as a good sign." Ed grinned too and told her to keep up the hard work. "Say, have you and little Miss Beauty Queen gone out yet? Betty let out a long sigh. "Nope, she keeps asking though." Ed smiled, blew out a puff of smoke and said, "It'll happen soon enough sweetheart." He could tell that his young protege was more than a little nervous whenever he asked about her love life.

The next morning Betty and Giger headed off towards south Florida in their boss's converted bread truck. Ed had already made the arrangements at Corry Field for his and Sheamus's departure later that afternoon. He decided to visit Mirabella's and step in for a quickie before picking up Sheamus. Mirabella was always happy see Ed. It didn't take him very long to relieve himself. Miss Cecilia was the whore that helped him. Afterwards Ed decided to handsomely tip Cecilia. This wasn't something he ever did. He was just in a good mood that morning.

However, that made Miss Cecilia stick to him like glue as he headed back outside were she ostentatiously gave him a sloppy kiss on the front steps of Mirabella's establishment. Little did he know that Mabel and the next-door neighbor lady was driving by in a taxi heading to some attorney's office in the downtown. Everything went by in slow motion for Mabel as she watched her husband kiss a whore in front everyone in down town Pensacola. There really weren't any one looking but for Mabel, it felt like the whole entire world was watching.

Suddenly Mabel's world was thrown upside down. Her heart began to race. Her mind began to make excuses. She turned around and looked back out the window and watched the whore squeeze her husband's crotch as he released her and began to walk down the street. Mabel's anger began to boil. Delores Gainey sat next to Mabel and was so engrossed in her own affairs that she didn't notice Mabel's face redden and her fist begin to clench.

Ed's wife sat with her neighbor while she listened and learned about another woman's divorce procedures in an attorney's office twenty minutes later. Mabel tried her best to be patient with Delores but she couldn't help from being snappy with everyone. She just couldn't get the image of her husband's betrayal out of her mind. Her day passed by as if she were in a dream. Later that afternoon, she sat on the front porch shelling peas with a thousand-mile stare. Her mother, Sarah Bailey, could tell something was bothering her daughter something awfully bad.

"Go on, child. Get it off your chest sweetheart." Mabel's mother said, as she spit a tiny bit of tobacco juice into the front yard as she shelled peas too. Mabel took a deep breath and then began to tell her momma what happened earlier that day. "Dagnabbit! I knew that man would eventually show his true colors." Mabel was not in the mood to discuss it anymore. She felt sick to her stomach. She put her bowl of peas down and went back into the house. Mabel's mother kept shelling the rest while muttering obscenities under her breath. "That no good low-down son-of-a." Mrs. Bailey rocked in her chair while continually muttering.

Later that night over dinner Mrs. Bailey, decided it would be a good idea to offer an invitation to her daughter for them to stay a few nights on her husband's ranch in Beulah just outside of Pensacola. "It'll do you and your young'uns some good to get some good country air and vittles to help ya' settle your nerves." "Momma, what am I going to do about my garden or Arthur's dog?" "Don't worry about your garden, sweetie, and bring Bo-Peep along. I'm sure she'll love sniffing around the ranch." Mrs. Bailey reached over and put her hand on daughter's knee. "We're all leaving in the morn darlin." Mabel cracked a smile at her mother's tenaciousness and caring, then suddenly she burst out crying.

The next morning Mabel's step-father Orville Bailey picked them up in his motel T and drove them all, including Arthur's dog back to his ranch, the Diamond B. Everyone was quiet while Mr. Bailey drove. Mrs. Bailey packed her husband's pipe, lit it, took a couple of puffs, then handed it to her husband as he drove along.

When he looked over at his wife and thanked her, she just winked and grinned. Mr. Bailey winked back then began to ask little Arthur if he'd ever seen a horse race before. "No Sir," replied Arthur with a glint in his eyes. That's when his grandfather began to tell him all about horses. By the time he was done they had arrived at the ranch.

There were two large brick stacked columns with diamond shaped concrete blocks standing on top of each column. The letter B was placed directly inside them on either side of the entrance to the ranch. Mabel looked over at her mother and said, "Gee Ma, looks like y'all have been busy. I like your new entrance." Mrs. Bailey laughed and replied, "Sugar, you ain't seen nothing yet. Wait till you see the new barn and stables." Mr. Bailey quickly turned his head and asked his wife to let them change their clothes before they began to run around the ranch. "All right, Mr. Proper. I'll show them inside the house first but go ahead and saddle up one of the horses." Mabel placed her hand on her mother's shoulder from the back seat and thanked her. "Don't you stress none, Sweetheart. Everything's going to work out alright, just you see." Mabel wasn't quite sure what to make of that last statement but she was glad, nonetheless, for the distraction.

Mabel was able to put little Charles down to sleep in the back room where they would sleep together. After she and Arthur changed their clothes, they headed out to the front porch where her mother sat in a rocking chair beside two large tubs of corn. Arthur immediately ran over to his dog who was gnawing on a bone in the yard. "Don't go very far from the house Arthur and don't get too dirty. We'll be having dinner soon. Understand?" "Yes Ma'am, Momma," replied as he and Bo Peep began to walk towards the stables.

"Woowee, ain't those some fine looking riding clothes, darlin." "Thanks Ma, Ed got them for me when we went to St. Augustine." replied Mabel with a look of sadness. "Go on, sweetheart, Daddy is in the barn waiting for ya'. He'll have a horse ready and waiting." "Thanks again, Ma." said Mabel as she bent over and kissed her mother on the forehead.

By the time she got to the front of the stables, Mr. Bailey was walking out one of his favorite racing horses. "This here beauty be Blue-Sky Bruiser. He's the best of my stock and needs to be ridden daily." Mr. Bailey whispered something into the race horse's ear and immediately the horse began to whinny. Mabel slowly approached the horse and began to stroke the soft bluish-grey pelt while gently whispering to the horse.

"Be careful with her, Blue-Sky, and you too, Mabel. This is my prize stallion. He'll put the come hither on you if not careful, my dear." Mabel smiled down at her step-farther and gave him a wink. "We'll be careful, Pops. Thank you for letting us get away from the city for a little while." "Stay as long as you both like darling. Now, take Blue-Sky down to the creek and run him up to the Davis's farm. That's a good run and he needs the workout." "I haven't been that way since Hector left for school. Ok, sounds good. Thanks again." Mabel looked down at Arthur and Bo Peep and told them to be safe as she kicked her feet and rode off towards the back of her parents' ranch.

Blue-Sky was indeed a race horse. Mabel held on to the reins as the horse began to pick up speed. There was only one field left to ride before she reached the creek. Blue-Sky's gallop began to stretch out as sleekly as a bird's wing. As the wind rushed through Mabel's flaming red hair, her worries and concerns began to drift away. The speed of the horse was daunting yet exhilarating. Suddenly, she began thinking about her two little boys and as quickly as she could, she began to pull back on the reins just a little, letting Blue-Sky know to slow down as gently as he could. Without delay, Blue-Sky began to slow upon reaching the other side of the field, he knew exactly where to enter the creek.

Mabel relaxed and just let the horse make his way to the Davis's farm. It began to become obvious to her that Blue-Sky had traveled this way before and already knew the best way to get there. Before too long, an opening in the tree-line became clear and Blue-Sky headed toward the clearing. The Davis's farm was a rather large estate. There were cotton fields surrounding an old white Victorian two story farm house with corn silos and lots of other buildings behind the house. Blue-Sky headed directly to the old home.

Mabel wondered about her first true love, Hector Davis. They had grown up together and even went to primary school together. When she was little, her biological father used to work for the Davis's before he died. She and her brothers and sisters would become field hands for the Davis's when times got hard and the Davis's became like a second family to them. Hector was the first boy she had ever kissed and she was Hector's first kiss as well. However, Hector had college to attend and slowly over time, they had grown apart with separate lives.

Blue-Sky took her all the way to the Davis's stables where there were two mares eating oats in their respective stables. Mabel cracked a smile at this realization. Males were all the same thought Mabel as she turned Blue-Sky around to head back home. Mrs. Davis was just walking around the stables when she and Mabel ran into each other. "Well howdy, Ms. Mary, it's been forever in coon's age since we've seen you. How's your family?" asked Mrs. Davis. The Davis's had always called Mabel by her first name, Mary. She quickly got off her horse to hug the older woman. "We're doing just fine." "How's your family doing?" Together they began to walk towards the back screened-in porch of the old farm house where Mabel held her horse's reins. "Well, I cain't say it's been all sunshine and tulips considering that we're still in this here depression but us folks will endure. Say, did you know Hector was home?" asked Mrs. Davis as her son, Hector, stepped out the back-screen door of the farm house and greeted her. "Hello Mary. It's been a long time."

Chapter 20

Much like the European Aristocracy, the DuPont's in America were obsessed with breeding race horses. Alfred Dupont like many in his family saw himself as no different than the thorough-bred horse itself. Careful select breeding was what many of the moneyed families believed to be the reason behind their wealth and power and the DuPont's were no different than all the other industrialist. In the Spring of 1931, the Florida State Legislature passed a bill that would legalize horse and dog racing. In effect, would allow open gambling at tracks all across Florida. Governor Doyle Carlton vetoed the bill but it was overridden due to all the payouts to the state legislatures from the Dupont family. By late that summer, the bill was passed on the state floor and became law. Suddenly, all over Florida, all the underbosses wanted a piece of the action too. By December of 1931 newly built race tracks began to open up in the Sun Shine State. Other older race tracks got refurbished and reopened all across Florida as well. Gambling in Florida had finally become legitimized for racing horses and dogs.

Betty and Giger were traveling through the everglades on their way to Miami when Giger began to ask her about getting fresh with Pensacola's beauty Queen. Betty gave Giger a sneer and told him to mind his own business. "Hey, I'm on your side, Betty. All the fellows are too. Just say the word and we will help in any way possible." Betty relaxed her shoulders and simply said, "I got it under control. Just give me some space and tell the guys to mind their own business if they know what's best for them. Understood?" "Yes Sir, Betty. Yes Sir." That made her smile. She lit another cigarette and Giger simply rolled his eyes as they drove through Floridian humidity like a fish swimming through water. After hours of driving, they eventually arrived at their destination.

"Stop over there by them telephone poles, Giger." Betty went into to the back of the truck and began fastening her gear together. By the time the truck stopped she was already ready and heading outside of the truck towards one of the telephone poles. Within a minute she was up the pole reaching for her tools and placing a phone call to her contacts in Miami. Giger looked up and waited. He could see her shaking her head up and down while writing something down in her notebook. A few minutes later and she was back in the truck telling him that they would be staying the night in some golf club outside of Miami. "Hmmph, was all Giger said as she began giving him directions on where to drive.

An hour later and they were pulling up to the Miami Valley Golf Club. A very loudly dressed man approached their truck and introduced himself as the greenskeeper. "I have a two-bedroom bungalow waiting for you both. Follow me."

They watched the greenskeeper get into a flatbed truck and together they followed him to a single bungalow on the back side of one of the golf course greens. Inside the house were two rooms, a tiny kitchenette and a telephone.

Waiting for the phone to ring would be their next duty. It rang the next morning. It was a Mr. Randolph and he wanted to meet them at the golf club for breakfast within the hour. Betty and Giger complied. The dining hall at the golf club was both beautiful and elegant.

When they arrived, an attendant greeted them and escorted them through the club to the dining area, to Mr. Randolph, the club's new president. "Please have a seat. You both must be famished after such a long trip." Betty and Giger sat down and Betty introduced Giger and herself as she picked up a cup of freshly poured coffee. Mr. Randolph smiled as he listened to her introduction and chuckled a little under his breath. "Excuse me. I'm sorry. Is there something amusing, Mr. Randolph?" asked Betty as she set her coffee back down on the saucer. "No, no, Ms. Betty. Please forgive my rudeness. I just find it a little queer that Mr. Ball would trust a girl with such a delicate matter. Yet, Mr. Ball has never failed to deliver. So, I'm beginning to wonder just exactly what he has sent me, my dear. Amusing no, intrigued and curious, yes." Betty shrugged her shoulders and asked "What do you need done, Sir?"

"It's not what I need but rather what the Families want, my dear. What they want is for the Miami Jockey Club restoration to be completed on time. They want a certain property that's not for sale and they want certain politicians in their pockets. That's all. Nothing too difficult for you I'm sure." The sarcasm wasn't lost on Betty or Giger. Giger winked at Betty which made her smile. She looked directly at Mr. Randolph and replied, "That's why we were sent down here. If you don't mind, I would love some pancakes? How about you, Giger?" Giger nodded his head and said, "Yeah, sure. Pancakes sound nice."

Mr. Randolph simply smiled and told the waiter to make them some hot cakes for breakfast. During the meal he explained to Giger and Betty about each of the three jobs he needed done. He was actually very thorough which made Betty pay close attention.

After their breakfast, Betty and Giger excused themselves and went back to retrieve their truck. Their first stop would be at Colored Town, the Negro area of Miami.

They arrived at the Mary Elizabeth Hotel later that morning and parked the truck in the back. When they got out they were greeted by Hercules Green, smoking a cigar in a lavish three-piece suit. "Well, if it ain't old' Betty Boop and her trusty sidekick, Scoop." Giger turned his head from side to side looking for someone that wasn't there and said, "Who the fuck is Scoop?" Hercules shrugged his shoulders. "Just trying to sound smooth, Sir. No offense was intended." Betty shook Hercules hand and began to explain what they needed. After quietly listening to Betty, Hercules motioned for them to follow him.

They were escorted through the back entrance of the Mary Elizabeth Hotel, trying to remain as covert as possible was nearly impossible as all the staff at the hotel watched them with a peculiar stare as they ascended one of the staircases. "I ain't never in my life seen so many Negros's in one hotel." replied Betty as she followed Hercules. "Cain't say I've ever had to escort white folks into the back of a black hotel neither." Giger looked over at Hercules as they ascended the stairs and replied, "Say, why do we have to come in through the back entrance anyway?" Hercules looked directly at Giger. "It's because y'all are white, obviously." Giger just shook his head as Hercules finally came to a ladder that took them through a trap door that led them to the top of the hotel's roof. Betty took out a pair of binoculars and began scanning the landscape for telephone pole junctions near to the hotel.

Betty began to set up shop on the roof of the Mary Elizabeth Hotel. She made a working telephone connection by splicing one of her modified phones to a phone line attached to the top of the roof where other lines were connected. "Hercules, I want you and your associates to man this phone and others like it around the city. You will all need a pair of binoculars and a set of instructions. I want eyes and ears placed around these areas of the city." Giger unrolled a map and Betty pointed to exactly where in the city they would be working.

"How many men will I need?" asked Hercules as he took off his hat to wipe the sweat off his forehead. "As many as you can get. This should only take no more than a day or two to pull off. We are going to shock and surprise folks with the power of fear. There's no room for error Hercules. Make sure you choose the right people. Understood?" "Yes Ma'am." When Giger and Betty descended the ladder from the roof to the stair case they were immediately surrounded by well-dressed black men.

Hercules quickly introduced Giger and Betty as his associates which caused all of the men to relax. "We have a new job to do, gentlemen, so listen up. This here little lady is going to tell you what it is so pay attention." Betty began to explain her surveillance needs and what they were going to accomplish. She ended her briefing with "we will all get paid but mistakes and any failures will be punished. You are all in the big leagues now gentlemen. So, don't muck it up. Understood?" They all looked at Hercules who nodded his chin and agreed.

By the end of the day nearly half the city of Miami was under Betty's surveillance. Hercules had really impressed Betty with his style of recruitment. Almost every one of Hercules's crew were former military veterans from the great war. They were quiet, Black American veterans, that had tasted power in the war and now wanted more. Just what Hercules needed and acquired. Betty also found out that two of the veterans were talented sharpshooters. This was something she planned on using to her benefit. They had successfully placed men on roof tops with phones connected to lines all over Miami. Each one had a pair of binoculars and a set of mental notes telling them what to do. Giger and Hercules eventually discovered, later that night, who and where the targets were located.

In the early hours of the morning, subcontractors connected to the delays of the Miami Jockey Club restoration project would feel the power and wrath of America's industrial Families. At exactly seven fifty-nine o'clock, the phones began to ring simultaneously in two different construction offices. As each secretary answered the telephones, both Giger and Betty spoke to each secretary, clearly and confidently, that there would be no more delays in the reconstruction of the horse track. As soon as they hung up the phones, Betty gave the signal and watched through her binoculars at the events that began to unfold.

When the confused secretaries hung up their phones, two of Hercules's veteran sharp shooters successfully hit each phone with long range rifles shots from nearby roof tops. As each telephone exploded in front of the terrified secretaries, both the men quickly broke their rifles down, hid them under their janitor's overalls and smoothly exited without anyone noticing. They were simply negro janitors too scared to know what was going on. By the time the police were present at each business they were already gone. Betty was watching closely as Giger walked into each of the offices where he hand-delivered a letter to each proprietor. In the letter was a list of demands and threats that were backed by a promise of certain death and destruction if they were not met.

After the letters were delivered, Betty's team disbanded and she and Giger headed off to the next assignment: two of Miami's most prominent politicians and business men were the Sewell brothers. John Sewell originally worked for Henry Flagler at the Florida East Coast Railway and was a former mayor of Miami. His brother, Everest, had also been Miami's mayor but had just recently been voted out of office. The Families trusted them and also wanted them back in office. All Giger and Betty had to do was deliver a single letter from Mr. Rudolph at the golf club inviting both of the brothers to dinner at the club. Little did they know that they would be meeting Mr. Ball himself.

Three hours later Betty and Giger were heading toward Coconut Grove. It was already late in the afternoon when they found their next location and parked the truck. Betty and Giger changed their clothes in the back of the truck, disguising themselves as plumbers. When they were ready, Giger got into the driver's seat and drove back down the road and he turned into the driveway of a rather large water-front estate.

They got out of the truck and walked to the back door of the estate with tool boxes in their hands. Betty knocked on the door and waited while Giger walked around the front of the house and knocked on the front door. Eventually a black maid answered the back door and asked why they were there. "Excuse me, Ma'am, but we have been called to fix a plumbing problem in the upstairs water closet." replied Betty with an air of confidence. The maid shook her head and said, "Uh uh, there ain't no problems with the upstairs bather rooms." A tall balding man opened the front door and greeted Giger as he reached inside his tool box for a large crescent wrench and swung upside the tall man's head. Within seconds Giger had knocked the man out, pulled him back inside the foyer entrance and closed the door.

Betty apologized to the maid, turned around, and then stopped. She turned back around as the maid began to close the door and asked just one more question. "Excuse me, Ma'am, but do you know the address here?" The maid looked insulted. "Of course, I know what the address is. It's …." Before the woman was able to say another word, Giger came behind her in the kitchen and hit her over the head with his wrench. The maid hit the floor as quickly as he swung his weapon. Betty stepped inside the house and put her finger to her lips in front of Giger and pointed her index finger upstairs.

Betty quietly walked up the grand staircase as Giger tied up the man and the woman downstairs. "Leola, would you get me the violet dress. I just don't care for this emerald green." replied an older woman sitting in front of a mirrored dressing table. Betty knocked on the door and asked the lady if she knew which bathroom needed fixing. The woman looked surprised, she got up from the table and approached Betty while saying, "There's no problems that I'm aware of. Who are you, my dear?" Betty removed her cap and said, "I'm a plumber, Ma'am. We were called here to fix a toilet problem or something."

As the lady walked by Betty she yelled for her maid. Betty put her tool box down, reached inside it for a two-foot piece of rope with knots tied at either end. Then she jumped behind the woman and began strangling her till she went limp and unconscious. Betty quickly tied the woman's hands and feet as she heard an older woman's voice from one of the rooms down the hall. Betty got up and came to the door where she heard the voice. As she opened the door slightly to view inside, she saw an old lady that couldn't get out of bed and was trying to ring the servants bell but couldn't. After making sure that there were no else in the rest of the upstairs rooms, Betty closed the door as quietly as she could and returned downstairs

"Is there anyone else on the property?" asked Betty as Giger reentered the kitchen from the back of the house. "Just an old black man in the garage but he's been taken care of. He's sleeping sound with a new knot on the back of his head." "Good. Go get the lady upstairs that's tied up, bring her back down and sit her on the couch in the parlor. Giger went and retrieved the woman that was just starting the wake up. Betty went into the kitchen and dragged the maid to the parlor.

By the time Betty and Giger placed the man and the woman on the couch facing them in the parlor, all three had awakened and were obviously terrified. The maid was placed in a chair directly across from the man and woman. Betty placed gags in each of their mouths so they couldn't yell or scream. "Apparently, you Sir, have been offered a great deal of money to sell this property but you have consistently refused these offers." The woman looked directly at the man and began to mumble something through her gag. Betty slapped the woman across her face and told her to shut up. "Sir, we've been sent here because of your stubbornness. Because you and your significant other here don't seem to understand the seriousness of this situation, I am going to have to teach you both a lesson. While Betty was talking, Giger tied the maid's hand on top of her dress to her thighs.

"After tonight, you all are going to leave this property and never return. You, Sir, are going to sell it within the week or we will be back again at some unknown time. It doesn't matter where you go or how far you run. We will find you both and we remove you from this world. Understood?" asked Betty with as little emotion as possible. Both the man and woman began to mumble something. Betty motioned for Giger to hand her something from the tool box. Giger opened his tool box and handed Betty a bolt cutter. "Just to make sure you fine folks understand that we mean businesses, we're going to give y'all a little demonstration of what is going to happen to those you love the most, starting with your maid here.

Giger reached down and held the right thumb of the maid up as Betty placed the bolt cutters around the thumb. Betty easily cut off the right thumb as the muffled screams of the maid could be heard throughout the room. Giger held up the other thumb and Betty cut that one off as well. Blood began to gush out of the terrified maid's nubs as both the man and woman began to scream. Betty placed a thumb onto the laps of each of her victims. "This is just a little taste of what's to come if you don't sale the house." The maid was wailing and swaying back in forth within the bounds of her chair, completely hysterical as she looked down at the all the blood gushing out of her severed thumbs.

Betty and Giger picked up all their tools and quietly exited the house, leaving behind the sounds of their victim's muffled outrage. They drove away from Coral Gables in the late afternoon as if it were just another day on the job. Betty lit two cigarettes, then handed one to Giger as they drove back in silence. Within a few minutes, they broke out laughing at the exact same time, "You know something Giger? I could get used to this way of life." Giger looked over at Betty and winked at her. "Me too kiddo, me too." They drove back to the Miami Valley Golf Club that evening completely elated and confident of their mission.

By the time Betty and Giger had showered and changed from their work clothes, the phone rang in their little bungalow. She answered the phone and was surprised to hear a very happy Mr. Randolph from the club, congratulate her for a job well done. Betty acted like it was nothing but graciously accepted his invitation to dine with him that night at the club.

Within the hour, Giger and Betty were following the head waiter through the dining room. to the table where Mr. Randolph introduced them to a Mr. Ball and a Mr. Widener. They all sat down as Mr. Widener began to tell everyone about the Miami Jockey Club's new restoration project. "We are going to rename the club, Hialeah Park and turn it into one of the world's most premier race tracks with the most beautiful gardens and grandstand that Florida has ever seen." Mr. Widener was obviously very excited and quite proud of his park. He continued on and on as they were served dinner by candle-light in the opulent dining room.

Betty and Giger were uncharacteristically quiet during the dinner until a waiter came up to Mr. Ball and whispered something into his ear and left. Mr. Ball interrupted Mr. Widener's lecture concerning the proper horticultural needs of a large garden and explained to everyone that he had to be elsewhere for business reasons. He graciously excused himself, stood up, and asked for Betty to accompany him as he left. Betty excused herself as well and motioned for Giger to stay at the table as she got up and walked with Mr. Ball out of the golf club.

"I hear from the Sullivan's that folks are calling you Brownsville Betty back in Pensacola," Mr. Ball said as he lit a fresh cigar. Betty laughed nervously and said that she had nothing to do with that. Mr. Ball smiled and removed a large envelope from inside a brief case that had been handed to him by the coat lady at the entrance to the club and gave it to Betty. "Don't open that until you get back to the bungalow. It's everyone's payout including your bosses so don't lose any of it." "Thank you, Sir. Uh, Mr. Ball."

Mr. Ball waited to be picked up by his chauffeur as he began to tell Betty about who the Sullivan's worked for and why her role was important to the Families. "Keep your self disciplined, listen, learn, and you will do well, Betty. They are watching you and want you to succeed." Betty lit up with a bright smile. "Yes Sir, Mr. Ball. Yes Sir." A long four door baby blue Cadillac pulled up and the driver got out to opened the back door. Before Mr. Ball got into the car he placed his left hand onto the canvas of the roof and turned around toward Betty. "Keep up the good work darling. I've got a date with two politician brothers, thanks to you and your partner, and a whole lot of fear that was spread around." With that he winked at Betty and jumped into the car. Betty just smiled and waved him goodbye.

Later that night, Betty and Giger opened the envelope and found three more envelopes. One had their names on it. Another had Hercules name on it, and the last one had the name Sullivan's written on it. Betty opened their envelope and discovered that there was three thousand dollars in cash inside the envelope with a note telling her that they would get fifteen hundred each. Giger grabbed Hercules's envelope and started to open it.

However, Betty jerked it out of his hands and gave Giger a stare that spoken volumes. "Ah, come on, Betty, that Negro won't ever know how much he was given." Betty shook her head. "It ain't right. We do what the bosses tell us or else they will find out. Don't think for one-minute, Giger, that those that pay us aren't paying attention and watching our every move." Betty responded with an air of supreme confidence. Giger's face began to drain of color as he looked around him for some unknown boogey man. "Relax, Giger. Just remember the rules and maintain yourself, partner. Let's go ahead and get on the road back to Pensacola. I don't want to spend another day in this mosquito ridden swamp."

Chapter 21

Mabel froze when she recognized Hector standing on the front porch. "Has Orville conscripted you into training Blue-Sky?" Mary looked at Mrs. Davis. "Uh, no Ma'am. I was just visiting Momma and needed to get some fresh air. Daddy told me to take Blue-Sky over here and run him back for some needed exercise." Mabel couldn't keep her eyes away from Hector as he walked down the porch steps over towards them. As soon as Hector reached her standing next to his mother, he leaned over and hugged Mabel. "It's good to see you Mary." Mary Mabel was her first and middle name but the Davis's had always called her Mary ever since she was a little girl. Mabel was what Ed always preferred and after her marriage, she simply adopted it. That is except for the Davis's.

"Hello Hector." Mrs. Davis proudly put her hand on her son's shoulder. "Doctor Davis has just finished veterinary school." Mabel gave them a large smile and congratulated Hector on his graduation. "Thank you, Mary. Would you like to stay for dinner tonight?" asked Hector. Mabel politely told them that she was expected back at her mother's where her two children, Arthur and Charles were waiting for her. Hector raised his right eyebrow. "Two children huh?" Mrs.

Davis put her arm around Mabel and hugged her while saying, "Well, it's good that you've come back for a visit. You better take old' Blue-Sky back before Orville gets too worried. That feller has a real thoroughbred horse right here." Hector began to pet Blue-Sky as he began to explain how he and her step-father were breeding thoroughbreds for the new horse racing venues in Florida.

Mabel got back onto Blue-Sky and looked down at Hector and his mother. "It's good to be back home." Hector held on to the horse's bridle as he looked up at Mabel. "Perhaps I'll see you sometime later this week?" Mabel smiled at him but didn't give him any promises. All she said was "Maybe," as she pulled back on the reins, made a clicking noise, and kicked her feet into the horse's flanks. Blue-Sky immediately turned around and bolted back towards his home. The speed in which Blue-Sky ran scarred, yet exhilarated her as the horse made his way back to the Diamond B ranch.

Orville helped Mabel feed, brush, and wash Blue-Sky down before he was led into his stall. That night over dinner Mabel would learn just how close her step-father had placed himself with Hector. Apparently, her step-father had recently inherited his great uncle's estate in his home town of Dublin, Ireland. Orville's great uncle had been a successful and respected, "Togalai Capall." Orville explained to everyone at the table that night how horse breeding was first brought to the Gaelic Isles by the Romans. Mabel and Arthur were mesmerized by his lecture, Oville's wife was not. "Get ón with the story Orville."

Orville ignored her. "Anyhow, what happend is, that I've had the last of Uncle Henry's stock sent to Pensacola. I was in Dublin for over six months last year settling the estate with the solicitors." Mabel looked over at her mother. "Why didn't you go too? You never said a word of any of this." Mabel's mother just shrugged her shoulders. "I ain't traveling in no ship to some cold and dank old country. I'm fine right here and besides we don't have that kind of money, darlin. Still don't, Orville and I are still just barely making a living. Orville interrupted his wife. "Hector and I have made a partnership. We're going to breed race horses." Mabel could see the glint in her step-father's eye as he said it.

"Hector is going to open a practice in Pensacola and he's going to help me with my breeding program. I'll soon have three thoroughbred mares and one more fine stallion any day now. They're due in this weekend at the port. I was able to afford to bring back Blue-Sky but the others had to wait. There wouldn't be any chance you'd come help me and Hector with the horses?" Mabel was intrigued to say the least and immediately volunteered. "Oh, that would be delightful, my dear, splendedly delightful." Orville looked over at his wife and she gave him a wink as they finished their meal.

The next morning everyone was up bright and early. Mrs. Bailey was starting a load of laundry on the back porch. Arthur was chasing the chickens around in the back yard with his dog and Mabel was just finishing feeding Charles. In his back work shed, Mr. Baily was preparing his truck for a hitch. Hector suddenly appeared, driving his family's tracktor and towing a long trailer. Hector stopped the trackor next to the stables, jumped down, and walked around to the back where Orville had his makeshift work shop.

"What in the world are you doing, Mr. Baily? Orville looked up from what he was doing and was completely red in the face. "I can't for the life of me, figure out how this blasted welding works? I'm a retired school teacher for, Christ sakes, not a bloody machinst. How about we take this over to Mr. Collier's. He knows how to work that thing," supported Hector. Orville looked down at his contraption. "Alright, let's get this done as soon as possible. These horses are coming in tomorrow morning.

That next day was an eventful and exciting time for the Diamond B Ranch. Mabel, Hector, and Orville were in awe at the size of the ship that came into the port that morning. The stevedores were able to hoist each horse from the freighter without any problems at all. The three mares and stallion were obviously pleased to be leaving the confines of the ship and they could feel the Florida sunshine on their bodies. Hector quickly examined each horse with the newly acquired tools of his trade and was exstatic at their health after such a long sea voyage. They were loaded into the trailer easily as if they knew they would be heading off to brighter pastures. Hector even made the comment that it seemed as if they wanted to be trucked away from the ship.

Sometime later that afternoon after they all had finished tending to the horses. Mabel was able to take Blue-Sky out for another ride. This time she decided to ride past the Davis's farm, out to where the cotton fields stretched for miles and miles. Blue-Sky was indeed a bruiser. He rode hard and fast with a fierceness that displayed his intense stamina. Mabel was able to eventually slow him down near a creek where he could get something to drink and she could rest for few minutes under the shade of trees.

After drinking his fill of creek water, Mabel noticed a clearing on the other side of the creek where a field lay abandoned but was completely covered in flowers. The wild flowers and grass had grown up and taken over the entire field. Mabel and Blue-Sky rode across the creek and she and her horse immediately smelled the scent of lavender. The field was completely in bloom. Mabel decided to let her horse graze while she rested under a large tree next to the field. She closed her eyes for a few minutes or so she thought. When she opened her eyes, she noticed how the sun had moved in the sky.

Rubbing her eyes, she heard the noise of a person whistling. As she stood, Hector walked up, holding both his horse and Blue-Sky's reins. "Did you jump down the rabbit hole, Alice?" Mabel looked at Hector and stared. It was obvious that she didn't understand what he was saying. "Did you fall asleep, Mary?" "Uh, yeah. I guess I did," she said with a smile. Hector handed her Blue-Sky's reins and a little bouquet of lavender flowers from the tree where she was sleeping. She smelled the bouquet and asked Hector what they were.

Hector began to explain to her about that particular species of tree as he helped her get up on Blue-Sky. As they trotted across the creek, Hector changed the subject and began to ask about her new family. She immediately told him about her children. After a little while, Hector asked about her new husband. It had been more than five years that she was married, and to her, it had felt like an entire lifetime. Mabel felt guilty for even being there with Hector. Hector sensed she was uneasy and began to tell her about the mares and stallion that he and Mr. Bailey had just brought in to Diamond B. Mabel cracked a smile at hearing him describe her parents' homestead.

"Mr. Bailey wants me to call him Orville now that we're partners but I can't quite for the life of me call a retired teacher by his first name. It just ain't right. He used to be my own teacher." Mabel smiled at Hector and picked up Blue-Sky's pace. "Did you ever see yourself coming back to live in Pensacola?" Hector was a little surprised at her question. "I never planned otherwise, Mary. I was hoping that you'd still be here but I'm not surprised that you've moved on and got married." His words made her blush. She picked up the pace even more.

Hector caught up with her quickly. His horse was fast as well. "Have you ever ridden a thoroughbred racehorse before?" Mabel slowed down a little and replied that she hadn't. "Allow me to introduce to you Blue-Sky's half-brother, Cedar Spear." Hector reached over and petted his horse's mane. "They are beautiful horses, Hector. I know Daddy is over the moon. How soon are they going to be ready to race?" Hector was a little surprised at that question. "I'm fairly confident that Blue-Sky Bruiser and Cedar Spear are healthy and ready to race now. We're going over to the beach tomorrow morning to stretch their muscles. Would you like to come?"

"That sounds wonderful. Let me see if Momma will watch the children." Hector smiled at her and said, "Then it's a date." Before Mabel was able to respond, Hector challenged her to a race and took off with Cedar Spear, leaving her in his dust. She, too, kicked her feet and took off like a bolt of lightning. Mabel was eventually able to catch up by the creek that led them to the Diamond B Ranch. The water slowed Hector down. Instead of running her horse through the creed, Mabel raced Blue-Sky along the creek's side, making it appear that her horse was running across the water instead of through it.

Blue-Sky raced by them like a bolt of electricity. Hector was completely amazed at the speed of the horse. By the time he was able to reach her, she was already at the stables. "My God, Mary, that horse is incredible." Mabel got down from her horse and walked him towards the stables. "I know. He's absolutely wonderful." Mr. Bailey came out from the stables and helped them wash and clean the horses before they were stabled and fed.

That night over dinner Mrs. Bailey told Mabel that she should help Orville and Hector with the horses the next day. She would take care of the children while they were training the horses. Mabel was pleased but a little apprehensive about her mother's willingness. Yet, she was also very excited at working with the horses and Hector as well. That night, Mabel couldn't stop thinking about Ed. When she woke the next morning, she was in a foul mood. She had dreamt of her husband fooling around with all sorts of women and was again angry.

By the time Mabel ate her breakfast, fed her youngest child, and changed into her riding clothes her mood had completely changed. As her step-father, Hector, and she were on their way to the beach with the horses, Mabel had brightened up. They had only taken Matilda Fear, their only dam, and her son Blue-Sky Bruiser, and his brother Cedar Spear. The two other mares left back home were Matilda's sisters which like her, were only going to be used as brood mares for the ranch.

It didn't take them long before they reached the shore of Pensacola Bay. Waiting for them was a tugboat that was connected to a flat barge sitting near the shore with a loading ramp extended on the beach. The horses were a little skittish about walking onto the deck of the barge but managed without much trouble. Within a few minutes, they were backing out, turning around, and heading across the bay. The horses were tied to the front of the barge with their backs toward the front, so they couldn't see the water in front of them.

Mabel tucked her hair behind her ears and petted Blue-Sky. "Are we going to run the horses on the beach?" Hector and Orville began to laugh. Hector began to unbutton his shirt and pants. Then he removed them while explaining to her that the horses were about to go for a swim. Mabel's eyes widened. "You're kidding me?" Hector shook his head as he removed his shoes and socks. "No Ma'am, I ain't a kidding you." She was trying her best, not to stare at Hector in his drawers but she couldn't help it. His physique was tall, thick, and very lean. Orville reached over and began to untie the horses as the tug boat began to stop and turn.

As soon as the barge stopped, Hector and Orville put a bridle onto Matilda Fear, then turned her around. Orville helped Hector onto the dam's back and Hector looked down at Mabel. "You and Mr. Bailey are going to stay on the boat and coax Matilda and her boys along on the way back." Both Mabel and Orville nodded their heads in agreement. Mabel's heart was racing. "Daddy, I'm awfully nervous." "Now don't put the come-hithers on me, darlin. I'm just as nervous." Hector gave him his widest smile. "It's going to be alright. Just make sure the boys follow. You hear?"

With that, Hector signaled to the boat captain, who started up the boat, put it in reverse and began to pull away. Hector let out a loud shout, kicked his heels into Matilda and took off. It was too late for Matilda to realize that there were only a few feet of boat to run. She jumped into the water as naturally as a mullet jumping in the bayou. Orville and Mabel slapped the hinds of the other horses and they simply followed their mother and jumped as well. Hector was holding on to the reins while kicking his legs like a bull frog. Mabel began to laugh at the site as the tug boat pushed the barge slowly past the swimming horses.

Watching the horses and Hector swim was completely mesmerizing to Mabel. Orville was jumping all over the place yelling and coaxing the horses along. It was obvious how much he cared about his new beauties. Something began to change for Mabel's as she watched Hector and the horses swim beside the boat. She began to wonder about the possibility of a new life and new family that didn't include Ed but rather Hector instead. It was a fleeting thought but would remain in the back of her mind. They reached the shore before too long and the horses were able to simply walk out of the water. Orville and Mabel were there to welcome and manage the horses as they came ashore.

"That was amazing, Hector." Orville was beside himself with joy that nothing bad had happened to the horses. "They really were amazing. Their running gait became a swimming gait which I believe stretches their muscles while strengthening them at the same time. Most of their weight is removed in the water, as you can see for yourselves. Horses do naturally swim." replied Hector with an air of confidence. Orville let out a loud hoot. "Ms. Sarah' tis never going to believe it. She wouldn't come on the count that she didn't believe horses could swim. She nearly had me worried to death last night with all her damn rantings. Hmph. She'll get an ear full tonight."

With that, Orville gave them all a wink as they began to reload the horses into the truck's trailer.

That afternoon as they were finishing with the horses, Hector got in his truck to head back to his house. Before he left, he stopped in front of the stables, rolled down his window and waited for Mabel to walk past. Orville had already gone inside, leaving Mabel to lock the stables before she came inside. As she walked around the barn, she saw Hector waiting in his truck. "You need something, Hector?" asked Mabel as she approached the truck. Hector extended his arm and handed her a fresh bouquet of lavender flowers. Mabel was a little surprised but simply smiled and took them from him. "What are these for?" "Oh, I just thought you might like them. They're are in full bloom all over the place." "Thanks Hector." He tilted his hat, gave her a smile and drove off. Mabel shook her head, smiled and walked back to the house.

What none of them were aware of was the Sullivan's had been watching them with their binoculars from down the road. They wanted in on the racing racket and the best horses in Pensacola had just arrived at the port just a few days earlier. Nothing ever came into the Port of Pensacola without the stevedores notifying them of what was being unloaded. It wouldn't take them long to begin moving in on the Diamond B Ranch. Having Paul out of town on a mission would make their job a lot easier so they decided to move fast before things got too messy.

That night Mabel would have pleasant dreams of her and Hector, where he swiped her off her feet and made love to her. She woke up with a smile and a pleasant demeanor. That morning there were visitors at the Diamond B Ranch. The Sullivan's had stopped by for a visit and were already in the stables, discussing their proposition to Hector and Orville by the time Mabel walked in. "All we're saying is, you find us a worthy stallion, and we might just let you in. Until you can produce something other than money, there is no business to be made. We don't need your help, Sirs." Orville knew the Sullivan's and was simply too frightened to say a word, so was Mabel. The Sullivan's looked at Hector as if he were a dangerous man.

"Let us purchase one of your stallions and we will have our stallion that you'll need." Hector laughed at his words. "Why on God's green earth would we ever do such a stupid thing like that. Excuse us, gentlemen, but we have a ranch to run and our business here is done." The Sullivan's were astonished by his words. Either he was extremely arrogant or he was simply very ignorant of who they were. It was obvious though, that Mabel and her father did know who they were. Byron looked over at his brother and gave him a wink. "We'll give you a day to reconsider." Tom and Byron tipped their hats and excused themselves as they got into their car and left the ranch.

Orville and Mabel immediately began to explain to Hector, exactly what and who they were in Pensacola. "I don't give a damn who they are. We are not going to be bullied like that. Not here, not anywhere." Mabel looked over at her step-father and cringed. Orville looked up at the sky and turned white as a ghost. Ominous clouds were forming overhead, darkening the sky, as the wind picked up, hinting at a nasty storm. It was hard not to feel as if an omen had just fallen upon them that morning. The rain came and continued throughout the entire day and night. It didn't look like things were going to end well.

Chapter 22

Ed had assembled a four-person team. Two men from his crew and one from part of Hercules men from the Blocks. Miguel, Sheamus, and Ed sat in relative comfort as the plane landed in a grassy air field. Hercules man, Leonard, was not happy. He had to sit in the back of the plane on top of their equipment and the felt each and every bump along the way. Thankfully, Captain Riley's touchdown was another smooth and effortless landing. As soon as Leonard departed the plane, he bent over and began to wretch. Miguel and Sheamus just laughed at him as they began to unload the plane. Within a few minutes a couple of trucks drove up and parked. Two men got out of the vehicles and walked over to Ed. Captain Riley walked around the side of the plane and began talking to the airfield crew that was refueling the plane.

One of the truck drivers must have recognized Ed and began to speak to him. How the fellow knew that he was the correct person to talk to, made Ed raise an eyebrow. "Mr. Ball wants you to relay your report somewhere else when you're done. You're to come back here and another plane will take you to where you are supposed to go to next. That's all I was told." Ed nodded his head in comprehension, then was given a set of keys. "Come on, Sheamus, let's load up the trucks and get out of here."

Cincinnati, Ohio, was just like any other bustling city in America. Everything was segregated, ethnically divided, and economically depressed. That is, except for the world of vice. Within two days the newly assembled crew figured out where the best places to scout, in both Cincinnati and Newport, Kentucky. Ed made Sheamus rent a boarding room in a poor Irish neighborhood in Cincinnati, Leonard would be renting a room in the colored section of town and Miguel would stay and sleep in one of the trucks in and around Newport. Ed on the other hand would be staying somewhere else, yet unknown, and their first assignment would start at the Arrowhead Inn. Sheamus and Miguel must not be seen with Ed but always remain in contact with him and Leonard. After everyone had made their arrangements, they all met back together somewhere outside of Cincinnati. Miguel and Ed were assembling some interesting equipment in the back of one of the covered cargo trucks.

"Check this out, Sheamus. Have you ever heard of a two-way radio?" Ed handed Sheamus a headset and told him to put it on. "How do I do that, Boss?" "On your head, Sheamus. Just put those two phone speakers over your ears like this." Ed grabbed another pair and demonstrated for the fellows. Sheamus did as he was told and he was told to sit down and listen. If he could hear anything, he was supposed to reply by speaking into the microphone sitting on top of the equipment. After demonstrating what to do, he and Leonard jumped out of the back of the truck, walked a few yards down the road and got into the truck. Ed plugged his ear phones into a large apparatus that matched the one that Sheamus was plugged into and flipped a switch. "Sheamus, do you hear me? Sheamus, do you hear me?" Repeated Ed into the microphone.

"Hot damn! Do you hear that, Miguel?" Miguel nodded his head and handed the microphone to Sheamus and flipped the switch. "Yes Sir, boss. I hear you. It's a little scratchy but I'm hearing you." It took them a few hours to figure out the new radio system but, in the end, they managed to learn how to fine tune the reception. By nightfall they all headed to their new post and waited for instructions. Ed dressed in his suit and tie in the back of one of the trucks then was dropped off in downtown Cincinnati at a diner.

Ed walked inside, sat his suitcase down and ordered a cup of coffee. "Excuse me, Ma'am, is there a phone around here? I need to call a cab." The waitress looked at him and asked, "Where you going, I'll call Joe for you on the office phone." "Thanks, darlin, I'm heading over to the Arrowhead Inn. You know where that's at?" The waitress smiled and gave him a wink. "Sure thing, mister. I know where that's at." With a twist of her hips she pivoted around and headed back behind the counter. Ed couldn't help from admiring her behind as she walked off.

Within a few minutes a taxi cab arrived and took Ed to Branch Hill, east of the town. As soon as he checked his coat, hat, and suitcase in at the front entrance, a lovely looking woman in a scantily clad cocktail uniform approached him, carrying a concession serving tray in front of her. "How many chips would you like, Sir?" Ed reached for his wallet and pulled out some cash. "I'll take twenty dollars' worth, darling." The cocktail waitress smiled, took the money and handed him a box full of chips. After explaining to him what each chip was worth, she smiled, curtsied, and showed him the way into the gambling area.

Someone had obviously paid off the police. There were blackjack tables, roulette wheels, poker tables, slot machines, and dice games. Not to mention the amount of illegal alcohol that was freely flowing throughout the place. The busters, stickmen, pit bosses, and security were all over the place, keeping an eye on everyone and everything. Which was exactly what Ed hoped there would be. It was a smorgasbord of vice, booze, heavy muscles and a lot of loose women. Ed's smile stretched from ear to ear. He truly loved his job.

While walking around and studying which venue he wanted to take part in, he eventually decided to play at the poker table in one of the backrooms. It was the highest paying table in the joint and Ed wanted to get some attention. An hour later, Ed's chips were piling up faster than the management liked. "Your awfully lucky tonight, mister." Ed looked up from behind his cards. "Yes Sir, I am lucky tonight. Would you care to have a seat? I'm on a roll right now, I'll take anyone's money tonight." Ed let out a heavy-hearted chuckle then placed another chip on the pile in front of him. "I'll see your five and raise it another fiver."

The porker game was not going well for the Arrowhead Inn management. Having the pit bosses hang over the table just made the game even more intense. Everyone looked at the last man that called it. He was a balding, middle-class gentleman that looked like he had his very last dime riding on that hand. After the man turned his cards over and pronounced that he had a flush, Ed laid his cards down and showed everyone his full-house. The management quickly motioned for the pit boss to replace the dealer.

The new dealer opened a fresh pack of cards, shuffled them, and began passing them out for the new hand. "You're a little too lucky, if you ask me." Ed looked over at the pit boss that had his arms folded in front of him and while starring a hole through him as he was being addressed by the dealer. "Nah, not really. It's just that fortune rarely spreads her legs for me but when she does, I don't want to miss out on the opportunity to give Lady Luck a real good fucking. She asked for it and I aim to give it to her as hard as Hell."

The management didn't like this fellow at all. Ed began to lose. It was obvious that they were cheating him so he decided to call it quits. After losing half of what he had gained it was clear that they wanted their money back which was exactly what he was hoping for. He folded his last hand, got up, and excused himself. While walking back to the front with all his chips, a buster came up to him and escorted him to the payout window, where he cashed in his chips. "Say, you wouldn't know where I can find a place to sleep tonight?" A rather sharply dressed man approached him while the female clerk handed him the money through the window. "There's a new hotel that has just opened up over in Newport, Kentucky, that I think you will absolutely love." "That'd be fine, say could y'all call me a cabby, please?" "We can do even better than that. I'll give you a ride there myself. "My name is Peter Schmidt and who might you be?"

"Paul Godwin." Ed shook Mr. Schmidt's hand and was led back to the coat check girl to retrieve his belongings. "It's nice to meet you, Mr. Godwin. If you like this place just wait till you see my new hotel." "You own the hotel?" "Sure do, I even named it after my son, Glenn. It's got real swank and prettier women than this joint." Mr. Schmidt's car was brought to the front entrance of the Arrowhead Inn by the valet attendant. It was a new black and red Cadillac Roadster. "Is this the new Cadillac?"

Mr. Schmidt and Ed got into the vehicle and took off. "Yep, it's a 1932 edition, fresh off the assembly line." Ed loved the smell of new cars and this one smelled especially nice.

"You won an awful lot of money back there Paul. You know that folks around here usually don't get to walk away that easily?" Ed smiled and put a cigarette in his mouth, lit it, and blew smoke in Mr. Schmidt's direction without saying a word. "You've got some brass balls, Paul. I'll give you that but what makes you think them fellows back there are going to let you off the hook?" Ed took a drag and blew the smoke in Mr. Schmidt's face again without saying a word. "Son, you've come to the wrong neck of the woods but that's alright. You'll soon learn." Two other vehicles had been following them the entire time. Eventually, the cars caught up to the roadster and boxed it in. Mr. Schmidt pulled his Cadillac over and got of the car.

Five men got out of the two cars surrounding the roadster and began to approach it with pistols drawn. Ed remained as calm as a cucumber. Both of the doors were simultaneously opened and two pointed their guns at Ed and told him to get out. He remained seated. The man closest to Ed reached in and grabbed his arm to pull him out. Ed grabbed the man with the same arm that was reaching for him, pulled it with all his strength and twisted. He was able to slit the man's throat in two moves and held onto the dying man tightly as he used him as a shield as the man on the other side of the car began to shoot.

What the other goons didn't notice until it was way too late was the two covered cargo trucks that were racing down the road and screeched to a halt in front them all. Within seconds, Sheamus and Miguel had put holes into everyone except for Mr. Schmidt who was trying his best to get across a muddy ditch to make a run for it into the woods. Ed got out of the roadster, wiped his shaving razor on the dead man's clothing and yelled for Miguel to go get Mr. Schmidt that was trying to run. "Holy freaking Hell. Load up the bodies, clean the cars, and bring Mr. Schmidt to the back of Miguel's truck. Let's get out of here now." All the fellows complied. Ed got into the Cadillac Roadster and smiled. Within a few minutes, they were following their boss in the roadster down the road leaving the abandoned vehicles on the side of the road and a single note attached to one of the driver's wheel.

They drove over to the outskirts of Newport, Kentucky, and found a secluded run down old farm. Ed got out of his car, walked up, and knocked on the door of the old farm house. Eventually, a man holding a double barrel shot gun opened the door and pointed it at him. Ed took off his hat and introduced himself using the same name that he'd given Mr. Schmidt. "Pardon the intrusion Sir. Me and some fellows have a whole lot of liquor to move and we need to hide it for just one night. I've got forty dollars for you, if we can lay low here for just tonight. Ed was taking a chance with the lie, hoping that he didn't have to hurt the farmer.

The old farmer put his gun down and extended his left hand out. Ed gave him eight five-dollar bills. "You bootleggers are going to have to hide behind that pasture over there behind that hill." The farmer pointed to where he was describing. "Let me go open the gate and let you through the pasture. Make sure y'all are gone in the morning." The farmer was examining his money before he stuffed it into his overalls and walked across his yard to open the pasture gate. Ed got back into the roadster and motioned for the fellows to follow him.

The most notable observation Ed and the fellows had made when they arrived in Cincinnati was the number of operating stills. It seemed that everybody and his brother was brewing something or other in their back yards, garages, basements, barns, and anywhere else that they could use as a cover to make money off the prohibition. Kentucky farmers were no different. The ones that had fallen on tough times were even more sympathetic to the bootleggers all across America.

During the late hours of the night, Peter Schmidt would come to learn about the kind of things that give men nightmares. "Go get the Warf-rat box." "Yes Sir, boss." Leonard jumped into the back of one of the cargo trucks, grabbed a box, then walked back over and sat down a green footlocker with a small sliding door on the top of it. Ed kicked the box with his left boot until he heard a noise from the box. "Yep, she's alive and hungry alright." Peter Schmidt was sitting on the ground with his hands tied together in front of him. All the fellows were sitting around a small camp fire and were drinking coffee from tin cups.

Ed picked up the footlocker and brought it over and sat it down in front of Mr. Schmidt. He pulled out a soft leather-bound note book from his back pocket. "Peter. May I call you Peter? No, never mind. What I need from you, Sir, is the names of everyone that you know. That is, everyone that's in this new so-called Syndicate and any other syndicates. You know, like underbosses. I need their names, where they operate, and about how many men they manage?" Peter looked at Ed as if he were a mad man and began laughing. "Hmm. I see. This here box contains Priscilla, our little club's new mascot. She's always hungry and always gets to the truth. Do you know what a wharf-rat is, Peter? They are really quite nasty creatures." Mr. Schmidt's eyes bulged.

"Alright fellows, hold his hand out for me, would ya'?" Sheamus and Miguel got up, walked over and grabbed Mr. Schmidt's left arm and placed it over the sliding door on the box. Ed slid the door open and watched what happened. Right before Mr. Schmidt began to scream, Leonard came up from behind and gagged him. Mr. Schmidt tried his best to pull his arm away from the box but the men held him down without a problem. They all could hear Priscilla biting and ripping apart the area of flesh that was exposed to her.

"That's enough, gentlemen." Peter's arm was removed and Ed closed the door quickly. There were bite marks and chunks of skin and muscle removed from the inside of his arm. Blood was oozing out of the bite. Mr. Schmidt was wailing and crying at the sight of his wound. "Well, Mr. Schmidt, are you ready to talk or do you need another demonstration on the other arm? Priscilla really prefers the inner thigh mostly but she'll eat anything that's flesh and blood, including your old Taliwhacker. If you know what I mean. Sheamus let out a chuckle. "Priscilla loves peckers. Ain't that right, fellows?" The other guys nodded their heads in agreement.

Peter began to talk. Ed started taking notes. After a few hours of interrogation, they were able to squeeze everything that the man knew. Even including who he worked for. Apparently, Mr. Schmidt was directly connected to George Remus, whom he believed gave him the needed protection to operate outside of the new Syndicates. What Mr. Lansky had failed to inform the Families was that in truth there really was no actual syndicates yet but there were, three organized factions that were forming at about the same time and a whole lot of wildcards on the table in the way of freelance crazies like George Remus and Dutch Shultz.

These were names that Ed remembered from Mr. Goldring's report. So, it didn't surprise him to learn whom and what these Northern goons were up to. Ed motioned for Leonard to bandage up Peter's arm. Ed sat down beside him and began to explain what he was doing. "Peter, I am sorry this had to happen this way. You see, we here work for the American Families of Industry. They are a very old and powerful group of people that like to know what's going on in their country. If and when they want to remove someone from this life, it is done, and no one can do anything about it. They know all and they control everyone's life in this country. Do you understand, Peter?

"What, what do you mean Families of Industry?" Ed looked straight at Peter Schmidt. "Go ahead, name me a few people that you know that are leaders of industry in America?" Peter looked baffled, "Rockefeller." Ed nodded his head in acknowledgment. "Keep going." Peter's brow began to furrow, "Mellon, Carnegie?" Ed nodded his head in acknowledgment again. "Don't forget Vanderbilt, Morgan, or Dupont to name just a few." Peter scratched his head. "Paul, are you telling me that these highfalutin Robber Barons want to know who's running the gamblers, bootleggers, and pimps in these parts?" Ed stood up, poured coffee in a tin cup and handed it to Peter Schmidt. "Yes, Sir." "So, I guess that makes you their apostle?"

"Yep, they all are the ones that really run this country, not some fat politician, or any of those hoodlums you like to work with either. The American Families of Industry keep this country together and right now, they want information and yeah, I'm their Apostle." Peter took a sip of his coffee and winced at the pain from his arm. "You could have told me this first, Paul!" Ed smiled and looked straight at Mr. Schmidt. "Where would the fun be in that. Besides, I owe you for that little fiasco on the road earlier. I know you were doing your job, Peter, but that was just down right stupid." Peter looked at Ed and grunted.

Late in the morning of the following day, Peter and Paul drove to the Glenn Rendezvous in downtown Newport, Kentucky. Ed was given a nice room while Peter tended to his wound in his upstairs office. After shaving, washing up, and changing his clothes Ed left the hotel and walked down the street to where Peter Schmidt told him there was a horse-bookie operation in the back of a barbershop. Ed walked in and was greeted by the two barbers tending to customers. "Have a seat, mister. One of us will be right with you shortly." "No thank you. I've got a hot tip on a certain horse." Both the barbers tilted their heads in the direction of a door at the end of the shop. "Thank you, fellows." "What's the name of the horse?" Ed took his hat off and gave them a wink while opening the door. "That's a secret a birdie told me." Both the barbers just grinned at each other, knowing full well that they would discover his tip soon enough.

Ed was greeted by a man behind a glass window, so he took out four five-dollar bills and placed a bet on Gallant Sir. He had no idea whether the horse would actually win but he'd been told that particular horse was of interest to the bosses. The man behind the window took his money and handed him a piece of paper with some numbers on it. Ed left the shop and headed back to the hotel. He spotted one of the cargo trucks. Ed stopped and tied one of his shoes near the curb of a soda shop, then stood up and smoked a cigarette. After he was done with his smoke he flicked it aside, walked into the soda shop and sat down.

Leonard and Miguel were stationed outside the hotel in the covered trucks down the street some ways when they spotted their boss, walking into the soda shop. Earlier, when Ed made his wager on the horse, Sheamus had found a nearby telephone pole that was out of site down a back alley. It didn't take him very long to climb it, set up his boss's work phone and wait while scanning the city with his binoculars. As soon as he spotted his boss and the shop that he went into, Sheamus placed a call to the local operator and asked to speak to Paul at the soda shop.

The phone rang and a young soda jerk picked up the phone. After listening to the operator, the soda jerk put the phone down and asked the man seating at the bar if he was Paul. "Sure am." "You have a phone call, mister." Ed walked over and was handed the receiver. "It's Sheamus." "Are the boys listening on the radios?" "Yes Sir." "Good, then I'll see y'all later tonight." "Yes Sir."

Ed handed the receiver back to the boy and tipped him a quarter for his trouble. The young soda-jerk grinned real wide and profusely thanked him as Ed left the soda shop. He headed back to the Glenn Rendezvous Hotel / Casino / Brothel, and amused himself while he waited for more of the syndicate's men to arrive. Mr. Ball had told Ed before his trip that he wanted all the underbosses to recognize and fear his brother and all the other captains of industry. He wanted Ed and his men to instill that fear and he wanted them to be ruthless. It was a perfect job for the Telephone Man and his associates and Ed relished the sense of power and its authority over life and death.

After spotting several busters, point girls, and the obvious management, Ed sat down at another backroom poker table in the hidden casino in the back. It wasn't very long before Peter showed up and invited him to dinner. By the size and look of Ed's chip pile, it was obvious that the house didn't want him to play anymore. Peter escorted him to the dining room and they sat down. Peter lit another cigarette while Ed inspected the silverware.

"What in the holy hell are you doing, Paul?" "Having a little fun and making a little dough." "What else?" "They are on their way, Paul. I suggest you leave before things get real nasty." Ed smiled and sat back in his chair as he studied the menu. "I think I'll have a steak and a bottle of the best red wine. That is if you have any. You did say this was a swanky joint. Right?" "You're not listening, Paul. There's a whole lot of muscle getting ready to come in here and take you somewhere nasty so they can do very horrible things to you. I don't want a fucking blood bath in my establishment!" "Relax, Peter. I don't plan on doing anything violent in your establishment. I promise."

The waiter arrived and took Ed's order. Peter simply ordered a drink and kept smoking his cigarette. "I need some information about the horse farms in your state, Peter?" "What do you mean?" "Thoroughbred horse breeders. I need to know who the top contenders are and where they are located." Peter Schmidt looked confused. "Why hell, everyone knows that's got to be old' Col. Bradley's place, the baking soda king's Calumet Farm, and Mr. Hancock's farm. I forget what his place is called." Those three have some of the largest investments in the horse racing business. All the horse-bookies keep watch on them like hawks watching their prey." A little while later as Peter discussed the horse farms with Ed, the food and wine was brought out and served.

Ed was enjoying his meal as Peter talked. He was just finishing his dinner when in walked a herd of goons, led by a small thin set man in a three-piece suit. Within a minute, they were surrounded by the herd. "Where are my men, Peter?" Peter pointed toward Ed. "Ask Paul." The man took out a cigarette, sat down, lit it, and motioned for him to explain. Ed pushed his plate aside. "They are all dead, buried, and disposed of, mister. I recon they planned to do me harm. That's what happens to those who wish ill of me. Kind of rather ironic. Don't you think?"

"Buddy, you've got some brass balls. Who do you work with?" "I'm a representative of a very old American cartel. Your bosses all work for them. You work for them. We all work for them. Only some of us know the truth and some do not." The man put his cigarette out and stood up. " Take him to the castle." Peter wiped the sweat from his forehead with his handkerchief. Ed simply got up and let the men escort him out of the hotel and into the car parked out front. Sheamus and the boys were already waiting and watching when their boss was led outside and driven away.

A half hour later they were pulling up to a large building on the out skirts of Newport, Kentucky, called the Old Kaintuck Castle. It was just another gambling den for bootleggers and pimps. They pulled into the back of the place, parked the car, blindfolded Ed, and took him to the basement. What puzzled Ed was that he could tell that he was in a basement. Then he was led into another sub-basement that smelled fouler than the first one. He eventually sat down and his blind fold was removed.

Ed looked around the dark, dank room, his eyes were just beginning to adjust when he heard, the first gun fire upstairs. The sound of machine guns could be heard firing away in short quick blasts with people screaming. The men that were surrounding him ran upstairs and began firing their weapons, followed by the sounds of more machine gun fire. Ed sat still and inspected the ropes that bound him to the chair. A few minutes later there was more machine gun fire, then Leonard came walking down the stairs with his Tommy-gun in front of him and his trigger finger ever ready. It didn't take him very long to discover his boss, bound and waiting for him to release him from the chair.

"What's the damage?" "It ain't good. Maybe just a hand full of folks made it. Whatcha want us to do, boss?" "Let the people leave. Tell them to go or they'll all be killed. Then we're going to round up all the goons and bury them where we put their friends from the high way." Leonard took off his hat and wiped his forehead. "Yes Sir."

Apparently, Sheamus had sniped the front guards from a distance when Miguel and Leonard stormed the Old Kaintuck Castle with their Tommy-guns. They indiscriminately killed anyone that had a gun and didn't run away. There were bodies all over the place. Sheamus backed one of the trucks up to the front doors and together, they all four loaded up the bodies of the goons that had their guns drawn. They left everyone else lying were they were killed. A few hours later and they had disposed of the bodies and were on their way to some farm that there boss had named. Apparently, their boss had a tip on where the next part of their assignment would lead them and he also wanted to put some distance between them and Newport, Kentucky, as well.

Chapter 23

Sergeant Hickum took over during the end of Betty's training. "What makes you think that you're equal to your principle or your subordinates?" "I'm not their equal, Sergeant, I'm just saying that I think most men don't see the potential in some girls." "That may be true, sugar-pants but it doesn't excuse you from your training." "That's my point, Sergeant, and my pants ain't made out of sugar." Betty took a deep breath, concentrated on her target, and pulled the trigger. Sergeant Hickum was watching the target with his binoculars and witnessed Betty hit left of the middle circle with her shot.

Sergeant Hickum kicked Betty's feet apart with his left and right boot. "Keep your legs spread further apart if you want to hit your target." Betty grimaced but didn't make any remarks. She knew this was just a part of the sergeant's training and she dared not try to push him. The Marines never cared one way or another if she completed her training. Some of them even had money wagered that she'd quit before it got too tough. They didn't know Betty very well.

Her training was going well but it was becoming harder and more demanding as Sergeant Hickum increased her drills. Betty was not used to staying at the Goodwin's house by herself. Lately, Mabel and her children were staying at her momma's place and Betty was left to house-sit while her boss was still away somewhere up north. When Betty first got back to Pensacola she had to debrief the Sullivan's. That went well but they seemed more preoccupied with something and were only interested in hearing about Hialeah Park.

They wanted her to continue making the collections but they also wanted her to send someone to monitor her boss's in-law's place. That didn't exactly sit well with Betty. So, she simply asked. "What are y'all looking for at the Diamond B Ranch?" "Mr. Bailey has just acquired a couple of brood mares from overseas and our boss is interested in purchasing one of them. This is a delicate matter Betty, and we need your utmost discretion. Betty had never heard of the word discretion but she surmised the meaning. Everything they ever did required a certain amount of it.

"Ed ain't going to be happy if he hears about this." "That's why we want you, Betty. There is this fellow named Hector Davis that has partnered with Mr. Bailey and he doesn't want to sell the brood mare. We regret that this has to happen but it's coming down from the top. One way or another that horse is not going to stay in Pensacola for very long. That's why we have to handle this situation carefully, Betty." "Jesus Christ on a bicycle. I hope to hell; this Hector Davis doesn't give us any trouble." Betty looked worried but relented and promised the Sullivan's to carry out their wishes.

Sergeant Hickum watched as Betty broke her gun down, reassembled it, then handed it to him for inspection. The Sergeant was methodical and precise. "Passed. You're done for today. There is only three more weeks of training. See to it that you don't miss any more." Betty saluted and replied, "yes Sergeant" as she was dismissed from that day's training. The Sergeant shook his head. Betty drove back to her empty boss's home wondering just how she was going to deliver on her promise to the Sullivan's.

The next morning Mabel and Hector raced Blue-Sky Bruiser and his dam, Matilda Fear, from one farm to another. Together they raced along the side of the cotton fields that separated the farms. They eventually made it to the fallow field that was covered in wild flowers just across the creek. Mabel's horse, Blue-Sky Bruiser out distanced Hector and Matilda Fear with a marginal distance that showed off his talents. It was another exhilarating and exciting experience for them. By the time Hector and Matilda Fear made it across the creek, Mabel had already dismounted and was sitting under the tree in the shade.

"Damn that horse is fast." Mabel looked up at Hector as he jumped off his horse and led Matilda to the field where her son was grazing. He returned and sat down next to her. "Penny for your thoughts?" Mabel smiled at Hector but didn't say anything. She just closed her eyes and rested her head up against the tree as she listened to the crickets' chirp and the birds sing. She suddenly felt warm lips on her as she opened her eyes and saw Hector leaning over to give a kiss. Mabel suddenly pushed him away and got up.

"What the hell, Hector?" "I'm sorry, Mary. I just thought, that you were, that you wanted, I'm so sorry, Mary." Mabel wiped her mouth and looked down at Hector. "Don't worry about it. I wasn't expecting it. You know I'm married now Hector. Married." Hector's face was bright red. He began to stumble over his words, which made Mabel laugh. "Come on, Mary, now you're just being mean." Mabel's heart began to race and she too started to flush so she turned around and went to retrieve the horses. The kiss shocked her, she wasn't prepared for it and she wasn't expecting it. Yet, she felt something and it terrified her but also exhilarated her at the same time.

Mabel still had feelings for Hector. She had just recently discovered her husband cheating on her and now she was thinking about doing the very same thing. Perhaps it was the need to seek revenge or perhaps she secretly always desired Hector since she was a little girl. Right now, Mabel's mind was reeling with thoughts and emotions that she couldn't quite understand so she remained as quiet as she could on the way back to the stables.

Betty was waiting at the stables when they arrived. "Howdy, Miss Mabel. That sure is a beautiful horse." Hector and Mabel dismounted and led the horses to be washed down and groomed. "He sure is, Betty. How long have you been back in town?" Betty lit a cigarette and said, "about a couple of days now." Mr. Bailey came over to help clean the horses. "Have you heard anything from Ed yet?" Mabel looked at Betty and handed her brush to Mr. Bailey. "I haven't heard a word. I was hoping you'd know when he'd get back, Betty." Betty scratched the back of her neck. "Nope, I haven't heard anything either. He said it would probably take him at least two maybe three weeks to finish the job though. Mabel excused herself to go tend to her children, Betty watched her walk away. "Say, y'all wouldn't know anything about how much them horses are worth, would ya'?"

Both Hector and Mr. Bailey stopped what they were doing and looked over at Betty. "Yep, that's what I thought. Looks like y'all have yourselves a problem." Hector didn't like what Betty had said and immediately went into a rant concerning the welfare of man's rights. "Whoa, hold on a second, Hector. Listen to what Betty has to say. I want to hear it." "Sell the Sullivan's a horse or two and there won't be any problems. Refuse their offer and they're just going to take 'em any way. Just take the money, give 'em what they want. You'll still have the rest and you'll have more money to invest. Huhhh, whatcha say?"

Mr. Bailey scratched the back of his neck and leaned up against the water pump. Hector on the other hand was not so calmly collected. "You got to be kidding me. Just who the hell are you, little Miss britches. I have you know that I'm a board-certified Veterinarian and I will not tolerate being extorted by you or any other person on this ranch."

Betty smiled and tipped her hat. "Good day, Mr. Bailey." Betty walked back to the farm house and told Mabel and the kids good bye. "Please look after the garden back at the house for me,

Betty." The both hugged and Betty ruffled Arthur's hair. "Sure, thing Miss Mabel." Betty got back into her truck and drove off while Mabel went back into the house to help her mother prepare dinner. Betty watched Hector and Mr. Bailey argue as she drove away.

Mabel and her step-father, Mr. Bailey, were unusually quiet that night over dinner. Mrs. Bailey could feel the tension and began to tell everyone a joke that she heard on the talk-box. "Y'all know why the Easter Bunny never talks about his wife?" Mabel and Mr. Bailey shook their heads no. "It's all because he's too ashamed to admit that she's a chicken." All of them laughed, that is except for Arthur. "Is that why he has colored eggs, Granny?" Mrs. Bailey ruffled his hair and said, "sure is honey. It sure is." She winked at both Mabel and Mr. Bailey and they laughed out loud again.

Later that night on the front porch, Mabel sat down beside Mr. Bailey smoking his pipe. "What are you going to do, Pops?" Mr. Bailey took a couple of puffs off his pipe, blew some smoke, and shook his head. "We're going to have to sell them Sullivan's a horse I reckon. Hector is refusing to even bargain with them. He doesn't know them Sullivan's like we do." "I'll try to convince Hector in the morning, Pops. I don't want this either but you're right. Hector doesn't know what they're capable of. I'll try to talk some sense in to him." Mr. Bailey smiled and thanked her but it didn't ease his tension. He knew that Hector was as stubborn as an old mule.

The next day Mabel tried her best to convince Hector but to no avail. No matter what she said, he just wouldn't budge from his earlier position. "Dammit Hector, y'all are going to have to sell them a horse or they're just going to take them. You don't know them Sullivan's like we do, Hector." "Thank you, Mary, for the advice. These horses are not going anywhere, darling, and that's that." Mabel shook her head. There was nothing she could do or say that would persuade him otherwise.

Except for maybe something else. As Hector was leaving the stables, Mabel caught up to Hector and stopped him. Without saying a word, she reached for his face with her hands and gave him a very intimidate kiss. "Do it for me Hector. Please." He was suddenly confused but delighted all at the same time. "I don't know, Mary. I don't think..." She gave him another passionate kiss.

"Please." Hector's face was completely flushed. He didn't say another word but stood there silent and dumbfounded. Mabel heard her mother's voice calling her, so she kissed Hector again and went back to the house. Hector was still confused, yet excited. He kept to himself for most of the day, trying his best to figure out his possibilities. However, the more he considered having to sell a stallion or brood mare the more determined he was not to go through with the deal. By early that evening Hector called Mr. Bailey and told him that it would be a bad idea but Mr. Bailey should do what he thought was necessary. Mr. Bailey was pleased and relieved.

Little did Mr. Bailey know that Hector had no intentions of allowing the Sullivan's to purchase or obtain any of the horses. Instead, after he got off the phone with Mr. Bailey and asked to be connected to the Sullivan's, he rang up the operator. Even the operator knew who he was referring to which just added to his surprise. Byron Sullivan answered the receiver after a few rings. "Hello." "This is Hector Davis. I need to explain something to you folks." "I'm listening, Mr. Davis." "Y'all ain't getting any of our horses. You understand? There ain't no way in Hell you or any of your partners are going to ever step foot on the Diamond B Ranch or I will call the law on you for trespassing." "Is that so?" "Yes Sir, it is. You can take that to the bank and shove it where the sun doesn't shine, mister. I'm recording everything that's happening and I will personally make sure the law and the newspapers hear what's going on if you try anything stupid. You hear me, Sir?" "Yes, Mr. Davis. We hear you just fine. Have a good night, Mr. Davis."

Hector hung up the phone and felt proud of himself. He told them off and it felt good. He went to bed that night as proud as a peacock, content in his confidence that things would work out. He couldn't have been more wrong. Sometime in the late hours of the night, Hector heard someone knocking on his window. He got up and looked through it. Mabel was standing outside the window, trying to get his attention.

Hector opened his window and looked outside. Mabel walked away, saying something but he couldn't hear her well. So, he put on his pants and shoes and quietly walked out of the house to speak to Mabel. "Mary, where are you?" "I'm over here Hector." He began to walk over to where he thought Mabel was standing. Giger sneaked up behind him with a rag that was soaked in knock-out-gas. Hector never saw it coming. Betty was disguised as Mabel and doing her best to imitate her voice. It successfully worked.

Within a few minutes, Betty and Giger brought Hector to her truck and loaded him up in the back. It didn't take them very long to find a creek. It's amazing just how quick a person can drown while they are unconscious and being held under water by two people. Hector simply didn't have a chance. As soon as Hector's body stopped moving, Betty and Giger carried his body to the side of the creek. Together, Giger and Betty were as efficient killers as a fine tuned mechanized war machine.

The deal went through the next morning with Hector's absence. Mr. Bailey was relieved that Hector didn't show up and make a scene. One of Matilda's sisters was sold. It was a brood mare named, Bright Sunday. Mabel was anxious to see Hector, so she had saddled Blue-Sky Bruiser and left before the Sullivan's arrived. When she arrived at the Davis's farm that morning, Mabel discovered that they were looking for him around the farm.

"Have you seen Hector, Mary?" "No, Ma'am. I was just coming over to see him." "He wasn't home this morning when we woke up. He didn't get dressed and he obviously didn't take the automobile or tractor. We've searched all over the place and can't find him." Mabel's heart began to race and she furrowed her eye brows. "I'll look around." With that said, she kicked her feet and Blue-Sky took off like a bat out of Hell.

Mabel searched everywhere and couldn't find a trace of Hector. She thought, maybe perhaps he was at the wildflower field and directed Blue-Sky in that direction down towards the creek. What she found when they got to the place where she usually crossed the creek made her heart drop like a rock in the water. Hector's body was lying face down and he wasn't moving.

Mabel jumped down from her horse, raced over to his body, and flipped him over. Hector's eyes were wide open and his face was white as a ghost. Mabel began to scream bloody murder and wail to the top of her lungs. "Oh God, no! Oh Hector!" She continued to scream and cry over his body. She sat with his cold body all day and cried until the Davis's found her. They too were in shock when they discovered their son. By the time the law arrived at the Davis's farm, the Sullivan's had already boarded their new brood mare on a train headed to Jacksonville, Florida. Their mission would be completed but they would soon discover something new.

Betty brought Mabel and her children back to their home in town to get ready for Hector's funeral. When they all got home, Mabel took Betty out on the front porch and asked her who killed Hector. "Who do you think Miss Mabel?" "Did you have anything to do with it, Betty?" "Hell no, Miss Mabel. I wouldn't do something so despicable in all my life." "Why would they have to do it?" "I have no idea, Miss Mabel. That's not how the Sullivan's usually do business. Something must have been said or done. I don't know. But I do know one thing, you have a family that loves you and a husband that's going to be back any day now."

Mabel wasn't pleased with what Betty said. The open admission of the Sullivan's guilt just made her even more angry. However, Mabel kept her composure during the day but fell apart during the funeral. A dark cloud began to grow deep in the recesses of Mabel's subconscious. By the time they placed Hector's casket in the ground, Mabel had silently sworn an oath to pay the Sullivan's back for what they had done.

Betty kept a close watch on Mabel but had to continue doing her regular job for the phone company and was already back to work the next day. After Mabel finished hanging the clothes on the line. She decided to investigate the back of her husband's make shift barbershop. He kept a back room that he always had locked and hidden from view. Mabel also knew that he kept the key to the door hidden somewhere near, so she immediately began to look around for a place to hide a key.

She found a key in a match box right next to the wood stove furnace that Ed used to melt his lead fishing weights. The key fit. Mabel was completely confused at what she saw.   There was chemistry equipment, multiple weapons, and film making equipment as well. She just stared at everything completely amazed at what she was seeing. Her mind began to race at what she was seeing but she also knew to start looking for something that could give her an edge. She knew next to nothing when it came to mechanical weapons but she did find a few tool boxes that had bottles of liquid and powders with labels on them.

She eventually found a bottle labeled cyanide. That was the only chemical she recognized. So, she took it back to her kitchen, poured half its contents into another little glass bottle and returned the poison and key back to where she found them. Mabel was now armed with a weapon she felt certain would do some damage or if she was lucky, would kill the men that took her Hector away.

The next morning, she had Betty drive her and the children downtown so she could do some shopping at Woolworths. Mabel decided it was high time that she got a brand-new set of dinnerware, a new reclining chair for Ed and a whole lot of boy's clothing for Arthur. After she picked out everything that she wanted she told the store clerk to charge it all to the Sullivan's account. She then waited at the lunch counter with her children. The clerk made a call upstairs to his manager and waited for a few minutes while he watched Mabel place an order at the counter.

Thirty minutes later, Byron Sullivan came walking into Woolworths. The San Carlos wasn't too far from the department store, so Mabel figured that Mr. Sullivan must have run or walked rather fast. "Mrs. Goodwin. I see that you've been enjoying Woolworths today." Byron removed his hat and sat down at the counter while he motioned for the soda jerk to bring him a glass of water. He was breathing heavily so she thought he must have run.

"I've taken it upon myself to acquire some necessities for the silence you're going to need when Ed returns." "Excuse me." Arthur and little Charles were laughing at the soda jerk that had dropped a milk shake at the other end of the counter. "Hector was a friend of the family, Mr. Sullivan. You don't think his death will be so easily forgotten, do you?" Byron couldn't believe her brave attempt at extortion. He smiled at her and said, "of course not, darlin. Where are my manners?" He motioned for the store manager to come over and told him to put Mabel's purchases on their account.

Mabel's children began to make a mess so she got up and began to clean up around where they were sitting. While Byron Sullivan was leaning over talking to the store manager she poured half of the contents of the cyanide from a little glass vile into Bryon's water glass without anyone seeing anything. After cleaning up both of her children she thanked Byron for his understanding and kissed him on the cheek. Byron was surprised but relieved. If this was all it was going to cost him and his brother to keep the peace than it was a cheap price to pay he thought as he picked up his glass of water and drank down the rest of its contents.

Mabel was out of the door of Woolworths and was walking down the sidewalk toward the San Carlos Hotel when Byron Sullivan's chest began to constrict and his breathing became impossible. Within a few minutes of leaving Woolworth's he had fallen down on the sidewalk clutching his chest in downtown Pensacola. By the time she and her kids made it to the San Carlos, Tom Sullivan was walking out of the hotel and greeted her. "Good morning, Mrs. Goodwin." Tom removed his hat as Mabel began to cry in front of her children. "There, there, please Mrs. Goodwin." Tom Sullivan offered her his handkerchief and Mabel took it. As she was wiping her false tears she turned around and poured the rest of the contents onto the handkerchief, then turned around and handed it back to Tom Sullivan. Arthur had noticed everything and scratched the back of his head.

"It's alright, I'll be fine. I need a taxi, please?" Tom put the handkerchief back into his coat pocket and went back inside to get Bob from Bob's Taxi to take her and the children home. Within a minute or two, Mabel and her kids were in Bob's 1931 Buick, driving back to Brownsville. By the time they arrived back at their house, Tom Sullivan was given the news about his brother's death. By the time Betty arrived for dinner that night, she was given the news that Tom Sullivan had died too after he went to go identify his brother's body in the morgue. Betty was wide eyed and paranoid when she told Mabel before dinner.

"What do you mean, it must have been God?" Betty was shocked but suddenly scarred of Mabel. She knew that Mabel obviously had something to do with their deaths but didn't know how she had pulled it off. Betty didn't even think Mabel had the nerve to do it, much less the bravery of doing it in broad daylight. What stuck Betty even more profoundly was that Mabel was as calm as a cucumber. Dinner that night was a rather strained experience for Betty but then again, she had, after all, been the one that created it.

Chapter 24

Ed and his men were watching the horses race around the track at Idle Hour Stock Farm when Ed first met George Reamus. Mr. Reamus was already a well known person to anyone that had ever read the newspapers back then. His face was on the cover of every newspaper during that time. It was a famous court trial where Mr. Reamus pleaded temporary insanity for killing his wife after he had discovered that she stole millions of his money. Amazingly, he was acquitted and set free. A feat that was still fresh in every American's mind.

"Excuse me, fellows, I'm looking for a Mr. Paul Godwin." Ed pushed his hat back on his head and grinned from ear to ear. "What can I do for you, Mr. Reamus." George smiled back. "Oh, not much. I've just been paid a whole lot of money to find out what you folks are doing and why you're here." "I reckon we've caused enough of a racket, huhh?" "You can say that. What I hear is that every time people are sent to take you and yours out of the game, they simply disappear, never to be heard from again. Without so much as a trace or a word."

Ed continued to smile. Mr. Reamus shook his head. "I surely hope I'm not in any trouble. Am I?" Ed motioned for the fellows to head back to the trucks. "Nah, Mr. Reamus. You ain't in any trouble. Unless you are planning to do me and mine any harm?" "No Sir, Mr. Godwin, no Sir." "Good." "So, what I really want to know as well as other folks too is, who do you work for? What operation do you represent?

Ed smiled, took out a cigarette and lit it. "I'm glad you're here, Mr. Reamus. You've asked the right question and I'm mighty pleased to know that someone is finally paying attention." Mr. Reamus took off his hat and wiped his forehead. Ed immediately knew that he was being trapped. It was obvious that Mr. Reamus was nervous but Ed knew that he would also be cautious and probably had a shooter hidden nearby. "Mr. Reamus, you should know that right now as I speak one of my men have discovered a good location to shoot your brains out as soon as I toss my hat here." Ed took off his hat. Mr. Reamus swallowed his pride and raised his hand over his head and waved it.

"How did you know this was an ambush?" Do you not remember what you said about people disappearing that are sent looking to hurt me? Now it's just my personal assumption but when

I see men or a man approach me and mine with guns then it's just not very likely that they plan on not doing me any harm, you see. We're always ready to interrupt such nonsense."

Ed tossed his dwindling cigarette and began to walk back to one of the trucks that was parked nearby. "Follow me, Mr. Reamus, if you want any answers and want to stay alive." Mr. Reamus quickly began to walk in his direction. Ed walked back to the back of his truck and lifted the back-canvas cover. "Sheamus and Leonard still tracking 'em?" Miguel picked up the head set and asked Leonard in the other truck if Sheamus was still tracking the men that were following them. There was a loud crackle noise than Leonard's voice could be heard saying something into Miguel' receiver. "Yes Sir, boss. He's got them in his scope."

"Tell him to knock the hat off the nearest man, then close shop and meet us back at the safe house in Lexington." "Yes Sir." Miguel relayed the orders and waited for a reply. Mr. Reamus watched in awe. "Come on, Mr. Reamus, let's jump in the back here." Ed got into the back of the truck and reached down to help George get in the truck. Mr. Reamus was not a small man. Ed had to use all of his strength just to get him up in the truck.

Miguel got out, jumped into the driver's seat and drove away. "What kind of instrument is that?" Mr. Reamus pointed to the giant two-way radio sitting in the back of the tuck. "Oh, that's just something we tinker with when we want to get the jump on someone." You mean you can talk on it like a telephone?" "Yep," was all Ed said as he lit another cigarette. "What are you, Paul, some type of special telephone man?"

"I hear and see everything that's important, Mr. Reamus. Remember that when and if you ever speak on the phone again. How much do you know about the Commission?" Mr. Reamus smiled and began to tell Ed everything that he knew about the Commission including New York's Lucky Luciano, Cleveland's Frank Milano and Frank the Enforcer in Chicago. Apparently, after Capone was imprisoned a few months earlier, Frank, the Enforcer, Netti became the next in line and was given a contract by Frank Milano. He had just been appointed as the head of the Commission to seek and destroy the people responsible for the disappearance of the men from the Arrowhead Inn and the Old Kaintuck Castle.

"Is that so?" Ed tossed his cigarette out the back of the truck and reached down to retrieve the footlocker from underneath the bench that Mr. Reamus was sitting on. He then, took out a piece of beef jerky from a little tin inside his coat pocket and began sticking some of it inside the sliding door on top of the footlocker box. Mr. Reamus looked at the box and was curious. "What's in the box Mr. Telephone Man?" Ed looked up and smiled.

"It's a Norwegian Wharf- rat. We call her Percilla. She helps us get to the truth. Don't ya', girl?" Ed kicked the box and laughed. Mr. Reamus's eyes began to bulge. "Don't worry George. You've been very cooperative. There's no need for using old' Percilla any more so I need to feed her." It was getting colder as the truck drove on down the road. They were feeling the chill as Ed began to tell Mr. Reamus what he wanted and needed him to hear.

"I'm a representative of what you would call the American Family's of Industry. They are sort of like a very old cartel." George crossed his arms and carefully listen to what was being said. "Mr. Reamus, they are the ones that rule and control this country. They are always watching, waiting, listening, and they are very good at collecting information.

You see, Mr. Reamus, it's information that they're always seeking. Information is what makes them more powerful and power is what they really crave. Hell, they have all the money they need plus more. These hoodlums and gangsters that have created this so called "Commission," or those other quasi syndicates are simply small potatoes to the Families. The power of life and death of over hundreds and thousands of people is what they wield in their hands Mr. Reamus. If I'm not mistaken, I do believe that Mr. Lansky knows a thing or two about this subject."

Mr. Reamus's eye-brow rose at the mention of Lansky's name. "You mean, Myers Lansky?" Ed nodded his head and said yes. "He's familiar with whom I am talking about." The truck slowed down and turned down a dirt road. "Tell the people that contracted you that we are everywhere and we are always watching and listening. This so-called Commission is operating within the Families territory with their good graces. When and if the time comes, and the Families need something. The Commission will respectfully comply. You don't want to know what will happen if they don't."

The truck stopped in the middle of an airfield. Sheamus and Leonard had already arrived and were unloading their truck. Ed got out of the back of his truck and helped Mr. Reamus. "As a way of insuring the Family's trust, they're going to need a to take a person from this group as a hostage. Preferably, someone that's at the top. If you know what I mean?" Miguel and Leonard began unloading his truck as George and Ed began to walk over to a small building with a gas pump in front of it. Mr. Reamus did his best to keep up with Ed.

"What do you mean hostage?" Ed could tell that Mr. Reamus was nervous again. "Relax George. They're going to take someone from this new Commission as a way and means of making sure they keep their promise. That ain't you." "They haven't made any promises yet." Mr. Reamus turned around at the sound of a Ford Tri-Motor airplane coming in to land on the airfield runway. "They don't have any choice in the matter George. Either, someone from this Commission either honorably complies or they will choose someone for them. Either way, they're going to have to make a decision." The airplane landed as Ed shook Mr. Reamus's hand. "Here's the keys to one of the trucks. It's yours. Just remember what I said and make sure to tell the men that sent you everything I've said. Understood?"

George Reamus wasn't exactly the kind of man that liked to be ordered around but this time was something very different and the sly fox could sense it. "Yes Sir, Mr. Telephone Man. Yes Sir." Ed doffed his hat and walked over to where the plane had stopped after landing. Mr. Reamus watched as they loaded their equipment on the plane. Within a few minutes the plane was taxing down the runway and taking off again. With total bewilderment and complete astonishment, Mr. Reamus got into one of the trucks and drove away.

Ed and the fellows were once again in the air, flying back home or so he thought. The pilot headed toward the eastern seaboard. Six hours later and they were landing on an air strip in Newport, Rhode Island. They had no idea why they were taken here but would soon find out. A group of men and trucks were waiting for them and their equipment. As soon as everything was loaded up they were taken to a warehouse at a local seaport. There was Rolls-Royce limousine with a driver sitting in the front seat waiting to take Ed somewhere for a debriefing. The men were provided with food and told to stay behind. Ed did as he was told and got into the back of the limousine and was driven away.

The limousine drove along the side of the Atlantic Ocean. The car began to pass by mansions that were as big as the one he visited in Jacksonville, Florida. Ed suddenly remembered Epping Forest and his meeting with the real bosses. Ed was excited and anxious as the car drove into what looked like a castle to him. There was an attendant waiting to show him to his room where he was able to clean himself and dress in a new set of clothes that were laid out on the bed.

After a quick wash and change, Ed felt like a new man. His clothes fit perfect. How they knew his measurements was just more proof to him that they were always watching and listening. He chuckled to himself as he thought about that when he heard a knock on the door. Ed opened the bedroom door and was greeted by a butler who was waiting to take him to the drawing room and library. The mansion's decor overtly advertised the wealth and power of the people he worked for, which gave him the confidence he needed during his debriefing.

There were a few old men, a young boy, and a couple of middle-aged men sitting and drinking while the young boy pointed on a map with his stick. The butler announced Ed's presence as the hired help. A distinguished looking older man corrected the butler. "From now on you may address this person as the Telephone Man, Jameson." The butler nodded his head and withdrew from the rooms.

"News travels mighty fast these days. I hope that name doesn't stick." The older gentlemen in the room began to introduce Ed to everyone. "I regret to inform you that is the name you've been given. Sorry chap. It's just easier this way." Ed shrugged his shoulders. "You may call me Neily, this young man is David. That's his father John, J.P. Jr., Andrew, and Willie here," Neily pointed to a gentleman with a thick mustache that shook his hand with vigor. "It's nice to meet you Sir." Ed was handed a drink and told to sit down.

Ed knew the drill. He'd been doing this for quite some time for the Sullivan's. He took out his leather-bound note book, drank a large gulp of whiskey and then began to debrief everyone in the room, leaving absolutely nothing out. "My goodness." replied the man named Andrew. "What a nest of nasty little rats. So, they know that we expect a hostage for such a fetid affair?" "Yes Sir. They know now. However, I doubt any of them are going to volunteer themselves." Neily explained to everyone that they were still waiting to discover whom their most important member was. "It won't matter no how. As soon as we're sure then, he'll be taken."

It seemed to Ed that they really didn't worry much about the crime syndicates that were springing up all over America. They were more concerned about hearing who had the best race horses and the breeding farms. The man named Willie was especially keen on hearing everything that Ed had to report on the farms that he'd investigated. Now he suddenly understood why he was given that order. Apparently, horse racing had long been a family obsession. Sending him to Kentucky to investigate the organized criminal factions was just an incidental thing for these fellows. It was thoroughbred horse racing that was really on their minds. Yet, they didn't forget their other important business.

The young boy named David pointed to the map. "So now that we know who's operating in these places, how about California?" Ed didn't say a word. Neily looked at Ed. "Looks like the Telephone Man has another job to do." Ed tried his best to act indifferent. However, he didn't like being gone from his family and home town too long. "I need to check on my home front and family. If y'all don't mind?" The man named John stood up and lit a cigar. "Pensacola is a fine little city. The Navy boys are having a time of it with that new air station of theirs."

"You've done well, Mister Telephone Man. However, you've got six weeks to get your affairs in order. Time is of the essence now days, I'm afraid. We need more information." An unassuming attendant that was standing in the room the entire time refilled Ed's glass. "Perhaps he should look into the Pleasanton Fairgrounds outside of San Francisco." "Of course, Willie, but don't forget the film."

The Hollywood film stock market and its newly found industry was a very sensitive topic for the Families. For them it was essential to maintain control of what they considered to be America's newest propaganda tool. Such power was never left freely alone. In fact, the Families even considered it paramount to support Dupont industries in making the best film stock that modern technology could produce. Keeping the Hollywood movie makers and moguls as close as possible was of extreme importance to them. William Randolph Hearst had always been in cahoots with the Families but newspapers alone just weren't enough anymore. By the 1930s, newsprint, and radio had learned to share the spotlight with the Hollywood movie mills.

The Families wanted to control all of America's communication tools. To them, the American media was simply an important type of power that they understood and could appreciate. "We want you to make sure the Hollywood boys appreciate and understand for whom they are working. Nothing vulgar mind you, just a little demonstration of our will. Do you understand?" Ed nodded his head up and down toward the man named John. "Yes Sir."

"Good, we will send you the proper reports and the materials needed for this job. You supply the labor and together we will acquire what is needed." Ed got up and thanked them for their hospitality and asked to be excused. "You don't want to stay a little while, Mister Telephone Man?" Ed looked over at the teenager named David. "I'd rather be back with my men. We all have a long flight tomorrow morning."

The industrialists were very proud of him. He could tell that they appreciated his professionalism. It was after all their own subordinates, the Chief and Gunny that had apprenticed and shaped who he was and the man that he had now become. Perhaps, it was that name they gave him that made them feel like they had created him and now possessed him like so many of their other belongings. Their pride however made him feel proud as well. It didn't matter to Ed if he was their possession. At least he belonged to the right side of success and not to the beggar's side of life, he thought. "Take care, Mister Telephone Man and God's Speed. Keep up the good work. Your efforts will be rewarded." Ed thanked them again and was soon ushered away by Jameson.

Chapter 25

Ed and the fellows flew back to Pensacola at the break of dawn the next morning. It took them five stops to get there and everyone was tired of being cramped up in the airplane. They landed in Corry Field at Pensacola late in the day and were greatly relieved to be on the ground again. Winter never last very long on the Gulf Coast. Ed was happy to be back home as he was dropped off at his house in Brownsville. Arthur and Bo Peep were the only ones that greeted him. Mabel was removing the clothes off the clothes line when Ed sneaked up behind her, then hugged her, turned her around and kissed her.

It was a lackluster response. He immediately could tell something was wrong. Mabel's feeble attempt to smile was an obvious clue. "Where's Fred?" "She cutting hair in the garage." Ed asked if everything was alright. Her response was simple. "Go talk to Betty." His eye-brows rose with curiosity. "Okay." Betty was just finishing with her last customer as Ed walked in and sat down in the church pew. "I'm all ears, Fred." Betty nodded her head and began to tell her boss about everything that had happened. While telling her story, she removed a hidden bottle half full of whiskey and poured them a glass. By the time she was done debriefing him about the Sullivan's sudden deaths, Ed drank all the whiskey in his glass and motioned for Betty to pour him another.

"Holy Hell, Fred. Have you spoken to Goldring yet?" "No Sir. I was waiting on you to return before I do or say anything to anyone." "Hot-to-mighty Damn! This is one hell of mess. I didn't know this Hector Davis very well but I think Mabel's mother once said that they used to be childhood sweethearts or something." Betty looked at her boss. "Do you really think your wife is capable of doing such a thing?" "Of course, I do, Fred. Just look at what you've accomplished already." "Yep, that's what I was thinking too. Just needed someone to say it out loud."

Dinner that night was a strange affair. Mabel was unusually quiet and had a hard time looking at anyone at the table except for her children. Tending to her kids became a protective cover for her. Mabel twitched and became cold and aloof every time Ed touched her that night. She even made an excuse to sleep with Charlie and Arthur in their bedroom because she thought little Charlie was coming down with something and she wanted to stay close to him and watch. It was an obvious lie but Ed didn't argue. They all went to bed, wondering and worrying about what was going to happen. There were no pleasant thoughts.

The next day, Betty and Ed went back to work for the telephone company as usual. Mr. Johnson gave them a few work orders on Bay Street when the phone rang in his office. "This is Johnson." Ed and Betty watched their boss listen and answer, "I'll tell them right away sir. Apparently, y'all are needed in Ferdinand Plaza as soon as you can." They looked at each other. "Did they say who to meet?" "Nope, just said to get there now. Don't forget to do them jobs sometime today." They took the work orders and left.

After parking their work truck on Jefferson Street, Betty and Ed began to walk toward the middle of the park when they noticed Mr. Ball and Mr. Goldring sitting on a bench talking together. "Good morning Mr. Ball. Saul." The two men turned around and greeted them. "I wish I could say the same, Paul. However, there's a situation that needs to be addressed. The Sullivan's are dead. It looks very much like it was an inside job, if you know what I mean." Ed took out a cigarette and lit it while Mr. Ball got up and told them all to walk with him. They head towards City Hall, just across the street.

Two men were waiting at the front entrance as they ascended the front steps of the building. Mr. Ball was escorted to one of the back offices and sat down in a big, comfortable, leather chair. "Have a seat." Mr. Ball motioned them to a couple of chairs in front of a large desk. "So, tell me what happened up north?" Mr. Ball sat back in the chair and listened as Ed briefed him on everything that happened, including the next job in California and why it was important.

"Yeah, I know about the film stock market. It's actually quite important. Well, six weeks is enough time. I'm placing Mr. Goldring in charge until there is a suitable replacement. You're to report everything to him directly. Collections will be sent to Lodge 15 treasury until further notice." Ed and Betty looked at each other. "Sir, I am the Master of the Lodge." Mr. Ball looked directly at Ed. "Exactly, there is already a new accountant on the family pay roll that will handle the books. Mr. Goldring is only temporary." Mr. Goldring wiped his fore head with his handkerchief. "I'm going into the soda pop business, folks. That Volstead Act ain't going to be around much longer. Too much money being wasted and not made."

Betty clicked her tongue and shook her head. "They ain't going get rid of that any time soon. Mr. Goldring simply shrugged his shoulders. "Think what you want, my dear. I'm inclined to think that it's going to happen soon, one way or another." Betty rolled her eyes. Mr. Ball interrupted them. "I'll get a plane to take you and Betty to California in a few weeks. In the meantime, I want it to be business as usual."

"If the job is a simple scouting and investigative nature then I would rather take my wife if it's alright with the you, sir?" Mr. Ball scratched the back of his head. "Why?" "I believe, she's been unnecessarily involved in our business and it has affected her in a bad way. I think this trip might be good for her right now." Mr. Ball furrowed his eye brows and put his hands delicately on the desk. "Did she have anything to do with the sudden deaths of our dear Sullivan brothers?" "Maybe, I'm not sure. That fellow the Sullivan's got rid of was her first boyfriend."

"Good God! Are there any more knock-off-men or women that I need to know about?" Mr. Ball looked around the room. Everyone was quiet. "Jesus Christ on a Bicycle. Take your wife with you but remember this, she's either in or out with what we do. There's no in between. Got it?" Ed nodded his head. "Yes Sir."

Betty was staring a hole into the floor. The mood in the room shifted to an uncomfortable atmosphere.

Mr. Ball got up and excused himself. He was heading back to Tallahassee to meet with some corrupt Florida legislatures that were hoping to get pay-offs for a new vote in the House. Mr. Goldring told Ed and Betty to report to him in the back of his brother's shoe store on Palafox street that afternoon. Everyone left at the same time. People at City Hall never even gave them any notice as they bustled about with what they were doing.

They finished their work orders on Bay street by two o'clock and had enough time to make the collections. When they walked into Goldring's shoe store, they were greeted by Sal's brother.

After a quick introduction, they were ushered to the back where Sal was finishing putting together his research for the new assignment. "Sorry, I don't have anything to drink for you." Ed shrugged his shoulders. "That's alright. Looks like this place is relatively successful." Mr. Goldring grinned at him and shrugged his shoulders as well. "Looks can be quite deceiving, Mr. Telephone Man." Ed chuckled, Betty looked at Ed with her eye brows raised.

"Never mind all that, Betty here is going to drop off the collections and I'm heading back to the barbershop." Mr. Goldring smiled and told them that from then until Mr. Ball chose a replacement that he would be at the shoe store. He was still working on the assignment report and would have it ready for Ed by the end of the week. Little did Ed know that his new assignment was going to a humdinger of job and one that would forever change him.

Ed was worried about Mabel, she was still acting cold and aloof toward him and Betty. For the next couple of days Ed stayed close to his home, keeping a careful eye on his wife. It became abundantly clear to him that she was upset with him. No matter what he did or said, she was not going to change her mood. A few weeks had passed when Mr. Goldring finally had the needed research and assignment placed neatly together in a leather folder. When he read the report in his barbershop later that evening Ed was completely dumbfounded.

The Families wanted Hollywood insiders that would funnel information back east. The Families had previously accepted Edison's defeat in the movie industry and they knew perfectly well that the American Jewish movie moguls were better film makers, more successful, and wanted desperately to be accepted as loyal Americans. The Families investigators found only patriotic intentions and the studios' boss's fervent obsession to promote popular American culture. The movie moguls wanted in and they seriously wanted to prove themselves as real true American citizens to the Families. It was a perfect opportunity and the Families were not going to miss it.

His bosses had already identified and located all of the potential candidates and had made arrangements for a rendezvous. It was at an estate called Pickfair located near Los Angles in an area known as Beverly Hills. There were going to be Hollywood elites and movie stars present. Ed immediately thought about his wife as he read the list of the people he needed to meet. Maybe he thought, this would be just the ticket to bring her back around. Ed chuckled at this new prospect. California was definitely going to be interesting, he thought as he closed up shop.

Later that week Ed watched as Betty proved herself at the shooting range on base. Sergeant Hickum was watching her targets with his binoculars as Betty hit a bull's eye on each one of them. Ed was watching too, he was impressed. "Good golly. That's a perfect set." Betty reloaded her rifle and waited for further commands. "That's enough, Sugar-pants. Now empty your weapon, break it down, clean it, and put it away." Ed gave Betty a wink as he lit a cigarette. "She's passed her training and surprised us all." Ed took out an envelope of cash and handed it to the sergeant. "Thank you, Sergeant Hickum. The Gunny would be proud of your work." The sergeant took the envelope and put it in his pocket. "What do you mean by that?" Ed tilted his head to the side. "You've done a good job with Betty's training is all." "Oh yeah, she's done good with her training, she'll do well."

Betty did as she was told and remained silent as her boss finished talking with the sergeant. "I'll see you in a few days, I'm heading out to San Diego. General Pendleton is pulling a lot of strings on the training out there, so I'll be flying with you." Ed smiled and thanked him again. "See ya' later Sergeant." Sergeant Hickum put his index finger to his right temple, then pointed it up and tilted his head. Betty was proud of herself and quite happy with her success.

On the way back to the barbershop Betty felt confident enough to ask her boss if it was alright to miss dinner. "If you don't mind boss, I'd like to take Mary Jane to the movies tonight." Ed lit another cigarette. "Naw, I don't mind. What movie are you going to see?" "It's that movie everyone was ranting and raving about, "The Champ." They say it's a real humdinger of a movie." Ed scratched the back of his head. "You know, I never been one for the movies. Hell, I don't think I've even seen a talky yet." Betty looked her boss. "Gosh, it's been several years since they've been making talkies, boss." "Yeah, I know." Betty smiled to herself. Tonight, was going to be special.

That evening Betty picked up the Merritt's youngest daughter and took her to the Saenger Theater in downtown Pensacola. Giger and Sheamus hung outside the theater and smoked cigarettes while waiting for the girls to come out. Ed wanted to make sure nothing happened to Betty if she decided to flaunt taking a girl out on a date. Pensacola was just like any other city in the South, you never knew whose jealous attentions were going to be roused by one's emotional frustrations.

A couple of hours later and the girls came back outside all giggly and holding hands. It was obvious that they were into each other. The fellows froze in their model A and watched the girls walk back to the plaza. A couple of blocks south of the theater proved to be exactly what Betty's boss feared would happen. Sure enough, a couple of wharf rats otherwise known as the unemployed yolk of the young and restless decided that the two unaccompanied women were the perfect type of victims, soft targets.

Suddenly two young transients jumped behind and in front of the girls. Betty was not amused. As soon as the two boys surrounded her and Mary Jane, Betty pulled out a small steel pipe from the inside of her jacket and smiled.

"So, you boy's want to dance, do ya'?" Before the first guy said anything, Betty swung her pipe over, then under and stepped into the blows coming up behind the fellow in front of her. Before the man could turn around he was knocked out by a blow to the back of his head with Betty's pipe. The guy behind them reached over and grabbed Mary Jane from the behind and held a knife to her throat. Betty walked slowly with purpose directly toward the two. Right before she got to them Betty stopped and smiled. "Run away, kid. Run as fast as you can." As soon as the guy began to speak, Betty whipped her pipe underhandedly, crushing the man's right temple causing him to immediately fall to the ground.

"Holy shit, Betty, are you, all right?" Betty turned around and saw Sheamus and Giger running over to her and Mary Jane. "I hope like Hell that you fellows weren't keeping an eye on me, were you?" "Ah come on Betty, you know the boss, it's our nature." Betty ignored them and concentrated her attention on Mary Jane. "Are you alright, darlin?" Mary Jane grinned and smiled. Then reached up and whispered something into Betty's ear which made her blush. "Alright fellows, get out of here. I'll be just fine.

Sheamus shook his head from side to side. "Yeah, apparently so. You girls have a good night. Don't stay out to late." Betty and Mary Jane just walked off back down Palafox street giggling to each other as if they were oblivious to what had just happened. "Come on, Giger, your partner Betty is more than enough for anyone in this old town." Giger smirked and let out a laugh. "You have no idea, Sheamus. That girl is more capable than most men." The fellows kept their distance knowing full well that Betty and Mary Jane were in no harm but remained at their post and vigilantly made sure nothing bad happened. Before it was too late, Mary Jane was taken back home and the date was over. After some heavy petting and a very long drawn out kiss the two departed, Betty headed back to Brownsville with a shit eating grin and Mary Jane went to bed that night with a mind full of fantastic fantasies.

The next week came by faster than expected. Mabel was beyond apprehensive. She really didn't want to come along. It took Ed quite a deal of convincing before he was able to talk her into going with him out to California. However, the air plane ride was a whole other issue that he hadn't expected. Mabel had never been in an airplane much less ridden across country in one. The very idea of it terrified her down to her core. "This ain't right. If God wanted us to fly, he'd have given us wings." Ed smiled at his horrified wife. "God did give us wings, sweetheart. He gave us the United States Navy and they now have wings, my dear." That didn't help ease his wife's anxiety nor did it quell her apprehensiveness as they boarded the airplane that would take them to Texas. There was going to be multiple stops on the way to California but Ed didn't mention it.

He made sure that his wife was as comfortable as possible during the entire trip, which didn't go unnoticed by Mabel. She was still upset at him and tried her best to remain aloof during her ordeal with the first few flights. By the time they reached the Pacific Coast, Mabel was grateful beyond belief as the plane touched down for a final landing. Sergeant Hickum thought that Ed's wife had done rather well considering how nervous she had been back in Florida. "Looks like our rides are here and someone really wants to impress you." Sergeant Hickum pointed to the military truck that was waiting for him and the Rolls-Royce limousine that was waiting for Ed and Mabel.

Ed smiled and shook the sergeant's hand. "Good luck, sergeant. Looks like I'm going to be enjoying this visit." The sergeant snickered at him. "Don't get to lazy, friend, that's how things go south." Ed immediately turned his head in the sergeant's direction. "That's exactly what the Gunny used to say." Sergeant Hickum began to walk to his truck. "That's just the way it is, partner. Keep vigilant and always be prepared. That's just the Marine Corps way of life. See ya'."

As soon as Ed and Mabel's luggage were removed from the plane, the driver of their limousine came over and helped them carry it to the car. Ed introduced him and his wife as Paul and Mary Godwin. The driver introduced himself as Clifford and told them that he was expected to drive them to Los Angeles so they wouldn't have to take the train. Ed was pleased. It would be better to just get to where they were going quickly so they could enjoy themselves for a little while before they had to head back to Florida.

The trip to Beverly Hills was longer than anticipated but the long ride gave Mabel and Ed an interesting view of Southern California. It was just like Florida except there was no humidity thought Ed as they turned onto Summit drive. Beverly Hills was like no other place Mabel had ever seen before. The Ponce De Leon Hotel in Florida was the fanciest place she had ever seen but in

Beverly Hills everyone seemed to live in their own private hotel or so that's what it looked like to her.

The Rolls-Royce drove right up into the drive way of Mary Pickford and Douglas Fairbanks Jr.'s mansion. They were taken inside the front entrance and greeted by "America's Sweetheart". "Good afternoon, Mr. and Mrs. Godwin. I'm Mary and this is my home. I'm glad to see that you have arrived before tonight's dinner party. Oh, we are going to have such a wonderful time. So many old friends are going to be here. Happy times are here again!" Mabel was tongue tied, Ed smiled and shook her hand.

"It's very nice to meet you, ma'am, my wife and I are fond of your movies." Mary Pickford scrunched her nose at the sound of the word ma'am. "I'm no matron Mr. Godwin, I've still got a few movies in me yet." She chuckled at his perceived embarrassment. "Mr. Smith from Dupont say's you're a real deal true Southerner. From the sound of it, you are every bit the part. You both just relax and enjoy yourselves. We Hollywood folks are no different than everyone else." She rang a little bell on the end table and a servant appeared. "Show Mr. and Mrs. Godwin to their room so they can freshen up.

They were both escorted upstairs to a beautiful guest room. Their bedroom window looked out onto the swimming pool. Mabel had never seen a concrete recreation pool, which was what the attendant called it, when she asked. The very idea of it was such a novel thing for Ed that even he had to make a comment. "I ain't never in my life seen a concrete recreation pool. I wonder if it's ever been stocked with ducks to shoot?" Mabel was tired, felt out of place, and still angry with her husband. He never really told her that she would be meeting a famous movie star much less be staying at her house and she was none too happy about it.

Something snapped inside of Mabel and she simply exploded. "God damn you, Ed! You knew where we would be tonight and you think this is amusing. I left my babies home because you said this was really important. You lying, cheating, son-of-a-bitch!" Ed immediately told her to calm down. It didn't work. "So, who else do you plan on fooling around with? Are there any movie stars you'd like to screw as well?" Ed looked baffled. "What in the world are you talking about?"

Mabel tore into her husband with her words and the back of her right hand. Ed caught the slap before it landed and held Mabel's wrist while grabbing the other one. "I haven't fooled around on you sweetheart, I promise." "You are a dag-gum liar! I saw you downtown before your last trip. That floozy whore was all over you, kissing you, and you were kissing her back. Don't lie to me anymore. You ain't nothing but a cheating liar!" Ed let her go but pushed her onto the bed and just stood over her looking menacing but saying nothing. Mabel was still furious, she rolled off the bed and stormed out of the bedroom.

Mrs. Pickford ran into Mabel as she was heading out of the house while crying. "Excuse me, Mrs. Godwin." Mabel blushed and kept her eyes averted. "My name is Mary too but Ed calls me by my middle name, Mabel." Mrs. Pickford reached her hand out and lifted Mabel's chin. "Walk with me, Mabel. Looks like you need a friend right now." Mabel was in no mood to argue. They headed out to Mary's gardens and she showed Mabel her favorite flowers. "How about if I just call you May? I like that name." Mabel smiled and shrugged her shoulders. "Sure, I don't mind." "And you my dear just call me Mary. From the look on your face I say you're quite distraught.

Mabel smiled and tilted her head. "What makes you say that?" Mary raised her eyebrows and made a funny sound. Mabel laughed. "These damn men are nothing but a bunch of crude and rude animals. If it weren't for us gals, civilization would've never been created." Mabel's mood began to lighten as she listened to her new friend. Mary stopped at her rose garden and looked directly at Mabel. "I've known for more than a year now that my husband hasn't been faithful. He hasn't shared my bed since the discovery. He's a coward and I know it. I can't believe I'm telling you this. I just met you but I know what you're going through. I overheard the part where you yelled, "you ain't nothing but a cheating liar," I think that's it." Mabel blushed again and laughed while Mary Pickford tried her best to perform with a southern accent.

"That was a horrible performance." It was Mary's turn to laugh. "Yeah, I know. I've never been able to quite get the Southern lilt. Southern accents are really beautiful but they are not easy." Mabel chuckled at that remark. "If you say so." Mary looked directly at her and whispered, "what's good for the goose is also good for the gander." Mabel's eyebrow raised. "I'm stuck, May. I can't just end my marriage that easily. We women have our reputations to worry about but men just get slapped on the back and congratulated."

"There will be plenty of young handsome men tonight that would be more than happy to have your attention. Let your man see that you're nothing to slouch out. If he doesn't care then you'll know it and at least you'll know where you stand." Mabel was not too sure about that but was amused at the thought of making her husband jealous. Mary eventually showed her the concrete recreation pool. "If you didn't bring any bathing suits that's alright. We've got plenty in the pool house. Let's go get something to eat, I'm hungry." Mabel was a little hungry too and quietly followed Mary back inside.

Mary had a tray of food sent upstairs for Ed while they ate in the privacy of Mary Pickford's glassed in patio. "You must let my assistant fix your hair for tonight's dinner party. She used to be stylist, and makeup artist on our set but I've wrangled her away with more pay and better living conditions. She's a miracle worker I tell you, there are days I couldn't live without her." Mabel ate quietly while she listened to Mary talk and talk.

"You're a very good listener, May." Mabel smiled. "Thank you, you're a very nice hostess." Mary smiled back at her but paused to take bite out of her sandwich. "I know this is personal but I have to ask. How much do you know about what your husband does for a living?" Mabel nearly choked on her food, she looked directly at Mary and raised her eyebrow. "Enough to know, not to ask any questions, my dear. You apparently know too much from the look on your face, Miss Mary." Mary Pickford was somewhat surprised by that last remark. "You're not in the least bit frightened by it?"

Mabel began to relax and let out a soft chuckle. "If you mean am I'm afraid of what my husband does for a living in order to support his family, then the answer is no. I'm not the least bit frightened. Nor am I worried about it. What I am worried about is how long will his womanizing continue." Mary sipped her drink and looked over her glass. "You don't have to call me Miss Mary, just Mary will do." Mabel smiled and grinned at Mary. "Sorry, it's a Southern term of endearment." Mary laughed. "I do love your accent, though."

As they were finishing lunch, Ed appeared at the entrance to the patio. "We need to talk." Mabel excused herself, got up, and walked out with Ed following her. Mary sat there and finished her glass of wine. Mabel headed directly upstairs to lie down. When they got to their room, Ed immediately began to explain that he was simply picking up a collection when that so-called floozy tried to get fresh with him. "She's a whore, Ed! I know what that place is, don't lie to me."

Ed sat down and lit a cigarette. "I know you killed the Sullivan's. I don't know how you figured out how to do what you did but the bosses already know." Mabel suddenly cooled down and sat on the bed. "So what?" "They will want your loyalty now. Either you're in or out. There's no in between." For the first time in Mabel's life, she was suddenly afraid of her husband. Her mind began to race with thoughts of him killing her in California and making it look like an accident. Thoughts of her children and parents immediately crossed her mind.

"I promise you, this will never happen again. I'll make Betty pick up the collections at those places from now on. I need to know that you have got my back or do I have to worry about you too?" Mabel looked sternly at her husband. "Promise me, that you'll be faithful and I'll be good little girl."

Ed was shocked at her sarcasm. "We ain't been in Hollywood for more than a day and you're already catching an attitude. I promise you, Mabel, I will never cheat on you." Mabel didn't believe him for a second. His wide jaws flexed as he held his mouth shut. His body language spoke volumes to her, she knew with every fiber of her body what that look meant. He'd get sneakier and like Mary Pickford, she was simply stuck in a relationship that she couldn't just up and leave. Things were way too complicated.

"I've got your back, Ed. What's our job here?" Ed wanted to smile but knew better. "The big bosses want an insider. Mary Pickford is our target, she's already been cooperative but they want her loyalty too. There's going to be every important movie mogul and producer here tonight, I aim to set them all straight. The Families want patriotic films, that show American values. They don't want anything that might be considered un-American." Mabel was confused. "So, what would be considered un-American?" Ed scratched his head. "It all has to do with business and government. What they don't want to see is anything that would make our country look or appear bad and they don't want any red commie propaganda neither. I'm simply here to let those that don't already know, that they are being watched."

Mabel raised here eyebrow at that last statement. "You mean, if they don't do what the Families say, then there will be hell to pay later." "Exactly." Ed smiled at her and got down on his knees in front of her. "I'm sorry Mabel, I won't ever do that again. I mean it." Mabel wished he were telling the truth but once again, he had that same lop-sided grin that reeked of greater mischief. What could she do, her alternatives were not exactly bright, thought Mabel, as she looked at her husband, grinned, and then ruffled the hair on his head. "I guess that's what we'll do then."

Chapter 26

The Families already had people throughout the movie industry that were on the pay roll but they wanted something more. They wanted someone that could be there point man that would bring Hollywood on board. In effect, they wanted a pro American, no nonsense business man and someone that the movie moguls all knew and feared. The Families had already embedded just the perfect person and their man was none other than Joseph Patrick Kennedy. He was an Irish American Catholic but that didn't bother them. Some of the Family elites were still quite opposed to anyone that wasn't a White Anglo-Saxon Protestant but to the movers and shakers within the Families, it only came down to business and Joe Kennedy was as ruthless as they were. Which just made him even more endearing to them. Joe was their man and he knew how to get what was needed done.

Mary's assistant and stylist was every bit as talented as Mary had said. Mabel had never worn so much make up in her entire life. Her hair was given a pin curl wave that was tied up around her hair with tiny bobby pens that could not be seen. Mabel didn't recognize herself in the mirror. Mary Pickford giggled behind her. "This is my favorite part. The look on your face is priceless." She giggled again. "Come on, sweetheart, let's get you into that gown. You're going to love the way you'll look. I know."

Ed had already dressed in his tux and was enjoying himself with a drink in an authentic western saloon bar that Mary's butler brought him to. Ed couldn't believe what he'd seen so far. Pickfair mansion had not only a real western saloon bar but it also had a bowling alley, billiard room, large screening room for watching movies, and plenty of bedrooms to spare. People started to arrive and he was greeted by a man with round glasses and large teeth. "Excuse me Sir, might I have something to drink? A sarsaparilla will do." Ed looked over at the gentleman and introduced himself. After shaking the man's hands, he introduced himself as Joe Kennedy. Ed didn't have to explain anything. Mr. Kennedy already knew who he was and was already briefed about the job.

Mr. Kennedy looked around the room and took a sip of his drink. "So, I finally get to meet the Telephone Man. Your reputation proceeds you, Mr. Godwin." Ed kept a poker face and took another sip of his drink. "So, you're a teetotaler?" Mr. Kennedy looked at his glass and shook his head. "No Sir, I just don't like to drink when I've business to do. Besides being an Irish vice, I'd rather not prove that to be too true for the sake of my own ilk." Ed understood his meaning and put his drink down. "Let me know what you want, Sir." Mr. Kennedy smiled. "Let's go for a walk. I'll fill you in on all the details."

"After the dinner tonight, there will be a screening of a movie made for this meeting. After it's over, I will pitch them the ultimatum. They're not going to like it. You may have to demonstrate your skills Mr. Telephone Man, when that time comes. I really don't think it will be too difficult. Most of these types just want to fit in and be accepted. They're no different than the actors they use. They too are starved for attention and want nothing but admiration and money. Besides, we've got Uncle Sam on our side with this one." Ed listened quietly as they reentered the house amongst a sea of Hollywood celebrities and movie moguls.

"Joe, is that you." "Well of course it is, my darlin. How's American's Sweetheart?" Mary Pickford swayed in and around her guest leaving behind her new daughter In-Law whom she never liked. It was no secret to everyone in Beverly Hills; Mary thought Joan Crawford was nothing more than a low-down rattlesnake that would slither her way to the top and Mary's step-son was just another notch for the she-snake.

Ed looked around the room and couldn't see Mabel. Perhaps she was in another room. Before he had an opportunity to leave, Greta Garbo put her arm through his and gave him a wink. "What's a man with square chin doing in a place like this?" Ed looked over to her and raised an eyebrow. "Are you with Joe?" "I'm not with anyone, pal. I just don't like crowds or large parties. Come on, mister man, keep me company so the wolves stay away." Miss. Garbo led him back to the western saloon where most of the younger people were drinking.

He kept his eyes peeled the entire time but still could not locate Mabel. That is until he heard a bunch of men laughing while a woman with Mabel's voice sang Camp Town Lady in a seductive southern accent. It was obviously her voice but he simply didn't recognize the woman sitting at a table surrounded by a group of young good-looking actors. Mabel had been powdered, painted, pampered, and produced. Greta introduced herself while the bar tender handed them their drinks. Ed kept his eye on his wife as he introduced himself to Miss Garbo.

"I'm Godwin, Paul Godwin." Mabel was sitting between Charles Buddy Rogers and none other than John Wayne. She was dressed in a bright red evening gown that accentuated her red hair, bright red lips, and her emerald green eyes. She was having a ball in her newly established Hollywood look. However, Mabel was clueless of whom she was drinking with because Mr. Wayne had introduced himself as Marion. All Mabel knew was that Ed had been looking for her and couldn't find her until she sang that last tune and now couldn't keep his eyes off of her.

Greta Garbo was watching Ed stare at Mabel and all the attention she was receiving. "So, who's the little red robin? It's painfully obvious that you know her." Ed finished his drink in one entire gulp. "That's my wife." Miss Garbo shook her head and sipped her drink. "They'll be the death of us, pal. Do yourself a favor and just let her show out. They always regret it later. Trust me." Ed wasn't really listening any more as he excused himself and walked over to the table where Mabel was sitting.

Ed walked over behind Mabel and whispered, "I need to have a talk with you." Mabel ignored him. Mr. Wayne drank another shot of tequila. "Alright, just one more tune and I'll know for sure what state you're from." Mabel began to sing the ballad of Dixie when Ed leaned down and whispered, "now." Mabel stopped singing, nodded her head then started to get up. "Now hold your horses' little lady. We had a wager." Ed looked down at the two men. "Mind your own business."

Mr. Wayne stood up from the table and towered over Ed as he looked down on him. Excuse me, pal, but I don't think the little lady is done here." Ed smiled and extended his arm for a hand shake. "I'm Mr. Godwin, it's nice to meet you." Mr. Wayne raised his eyebrow, extended his arm and grasped Ed's right hand then said, "& I'm John Wayne." As soon as Mr. Wayne introduced himself, Ed reached over with his other hand and squeezed the actor's wrist with such force that he was able to bend the wrist forcing Mr. Wayne onto the floor.

Ed looked directly at the actor and smiled. "That little lady is my wife, pal. Now if you will excuse me." Ed extended his arm to his wife, she placed her hand delicately on his arm and together they walked out of the room while everyone else in the saloon watched. Mr. Wayne was tending to his sore wrist and cussing up a storm under his breath as they left. For the first time in Ed's life he was suddenly very possessive of his wife. The abruptness of this new-found emotion was not wasted on Mabel. She quickly gained his attention with, "are there any targets here, or are we just scouting for information?" He couldn't believe his eyes or ears, Mabel knew too much and Ed simply didn't recognize his wife looking this sexy and glamorous.

Before Mabel could say another word, Ed grabbed her by the curve of her back, held her tightly to himself, and kissed her. She didn't resist. When he finally let go and released her from the kiss, Ed put his hand under her chin then said, "scouting my dear. But remember this, you're bait. So, watch your back and ease off the booze. I want you in the back of the screening room watching everyone when the point man makes his pitch." Ed led her to the screening room as Mary Pickford's butler and attendants began to usher certain guest that were privately invited for this specific occasion.

The screening room filled up quickly. Mabel and Ed were completely clueless as to who they were sharing space with but it didn't matter. They had a job to do and these people were no different from anyone else to them. As far as Ed was concerned, they were all a bunch of wolves in sheep's clothing. The bosses had already warned him and he was ready to set things straight. Within half an hour the room was filled with nearly every important movie producer in America. Joe Kennedy walked out in front of the screen and stood there, quietly, until the room began to quiet and he had everyone's attention.

"Good evening ladies and gentlemen. You may have already guessed that you all have been either invited or coerced into attending this meeting." A few people began to talk at the same time before Mr. Kennedy interrupted them. "You may have also guessed that you all are movie producers of the highest ranks and would not have been asked to attend if you weren't. You may also know that I have thrown my hat in the ring for Franklin Roosevelt." Suddenly, the room lit up with cheers and clapping. Although, there were some that remained seated and did not share his politics. Mabel and Ed observed their demeanors as Joe Kennedy resumed his speech.

"There is a movement making itself known over in Europe. The National Socialist German Worker's Party has been gaining a tremendous amount of popularity. This has been a result of the depression and propaganda, the likes of which you've never seen." Mr. Kennedy motioned for the projectionist to begin and the lights became dim as a movie began to play on the big screen. Joe Kennedy sat down as the movie began to show the brown-shirts of the Nazi party in Germany bully other Germans in their country. A narrator's voice began to speak, explaining what was being seen. The German people that were being picked on were all Jews. The narrator began to translate what the Nazi brown-shirts were shouting and chanting. Ed looked around the room at all the shocked faces. This was something that apparently hit home with this audience.

When the film ended the lights came back on and there were hushed voices throughout the screening room. Mr. Kennedy got back up in front of the screen and waited for everyone to quiet down again. "This industry is an advertising business. You people deliver to people all over the world what you see as the American Dream. This has not gone unnoticed by the boys back east. You know of whom I'm speaking, the industrialists, the bankers, old American partnerships that have been so entrenched into the fabric of this country that no one even notices any more. So far, all of these associations have been pleased with this industry, even though nearly most everyone here in this room is a Jew. That's right I said it. It wouldn't surprise me a bit if I were the only Catholic present. Being a papist has never gotten in the way of doing business for me. Just like being a Jew has never interfered with you doing business with Gentiles. That is except for now.

As you may already know, most of the Bolsheviks were Russian Jews. Mind you they're an atheistic lot and see no problem killing other Jews. However, there is a rise of antisemitism, the likes of which hasn't been seen in many years in Europe." There was absolute silence in the screening room. No one said a word as Ed looked around the room at all their surprised faces. Mr. Kennedy continued. "The fact that nearly all of Hollywood is owned and controlled by Jews has a lot of these old American business associations a little on edge, even though they know you're just as American as the Model A. You all have remade yourselves in an Americanize version of what you think this country should be and these business families know this.

What I've been sent here for is to let you all know to keep doing what you're doing. Everyone love's your movies. You've created a fantastic industry but don't ever make this country look bad and don't ever side with the Marxist Communists. What is it you call it? The rags to riches theme. Now that's American. Work hard, be smart, and anyone can succeed in America. That supports our capitalistic constitution and that's the kind of stuff they like."

Charlie Chaplin had been squirming around in his seat during the entire spill. It was painfully obvious that he wanted to say something. So, Mr. Kennedy pointed to him and told him to go ahead. Mr. Chaplin got up and raised his hands above his head. "There's no difference than this and what Mussolini is doing in Italy. This is a totalitarian demand from a fascist group of people." Mr. Kennedy put his hand up to object. "I've already told you that I've thrown my hat in the race for Mr. Roosevelt. You need to think again if you think the boy's back east want anything to do with a military takeover of our government. That would simply usurp their power." Mr. Chaplin was still hot under the collar over being called a Jew. He suddenly stood up and pointed his fingers around the room. "You're all a bunch of hypocrites if you believe this shit. I tell you right here and now. This is exactly what the fascist would say. He, my friends, is an American Fascist!"

Ed had heard enough. He stood up and walked directly over to Charlie Chaplin and began to speak loud enough for everyone to hear. "Call the Family a bunch of fascists and watch them cut your throat open while the band continues to play, Mr. Chaplin. Go ahead and try your bullying and see what happens but know this; Far greater & stronger people than you have tried & failed. They're now all dead. Do yourself a favor and stop acting like your opinion is relevant. I will forget that you ever said anything." By the time Ed reached Mr. Chaplin, the actor was cowering in his shoes. Ed simply put his hand on Mr. Chaplin's left shoulder and gently pushed him back down onto his chair, then gave him a wink.

Ed walked back to where he was sitting and continued speaking as he sat down. "All you folks have to do is show your patriotism in your films and prove to them that you're red-blooded Americans. I promise you, you're not going to like what nasty things they have in store for you if you try to undermine their Authority. They will torture and kill those that do not learn to respect our American way of life." Ed lit a cigarette and looked over at his point man and nodded his head.

Mr. Kennedy continued with his pitch. "Give me freedom or Give me death," wasn't just something that was dreamt up in a Hollywood movie. It's real history, folks. Trust me, you don't want to mess with the Families." Walt Disney was the first person to stand up and speak out. "I'm a red-blooded American and I vow to support the Constitution of the United States." Howard Hughes immediately stood up as well and he, too, declared himself a red-blooded American that vowed to support the constitution. Cecil B. DeMille stood up at the same time as Louise B. Mayer and they made the vow followed by other movie mogul's intent on declaring their allegiance to America.

Mary Pickford looked on as one of her closest friends got up and stormed out of her screening room with only a hand full of producers. Charlie Chaplin and the other movie producers were not missed. The majority stayed and swore the oath. Eddie Mannix approached Ed and shook his hand. They made their introductions and Mr. Mannix handed Ed his business card. "Call me some time, Mr. Godwin, I would like to hear your opinion on a few things." Ed nodded his acceptance and waited for Mr. Kennedy to get done speaking with everyone.

Mabel eventually skirted the room back to where Ed was at with Mary Pickford in tow, giggling something into her ear. "I may have been born in Canada but I'm just as red blooded as anybody here." Ed smiled at Mary Pickford's attempt to speak with a southern accent. He simply shook his head and smiled at her. By the time most of the movie moguls had finished declaring themselves loyal to the republic, Mary and Mabel had excused themselves to go powder their faces and no doubt gossip over what was happening.

Eventually, the last of the movie moguls passed him on the way out of the screening room and shook his hand appreciatively. Ed smiled back at the movie mogul and simply said, "show 'em your patriotism, partner, that's all you have to do." Mr. Mayer laughed at that. "I was born on the fourth of July, friend. I couldn't be more American than the stars and stripes." Mr. Kennedy laughed at that as he and Ed walked back outside the screening room with Mr. Mayer.

While they were walking outdoors, John Wayne walked over to where Ed and Mr. Kennedy were talking in the garden and punched Ed in his chin with a right upper cut. Ed spat out blood as he was knocked backward. It didn't knock him down though as Mr. Kennedy stepped to the side and watched him begin to laugh. "That's the best you got, mister?" Ed couldn't stop laughing as he felt his sore chin. Before John Wayne had a chance to move out of the way, Ed swung his left leg up and down on top of Mr. Wayne's left thigh making a loud snapping noise. Ed had earlier contemplated wearing a pair of iron knuckles but that would have been too obvious and easily seen so he decided on wearing his metal shin grieves under his pants instead. It was a move that the Gunny had learned from the French in the war.

Mr. Wayne let out a scream so loud that everyone's attention was directed to him. "You've broken my leg, you maniac. You've broken my leg!" Ed squatted down beside to the fallen actor. "Naw, I've just given you a little fracture to remember me by, good night, Mr. John Wayne." There were other fellow actor friends that helped carry Mr. Wayne back inside. Mr. Kennedy clapped his hands and congratulated him. That was the first time Mabel ever saw her husband get punched in the face, most men couldn't do what he just did, much less keep standing, then walk over and fracture the man's leg. She was repulsed yet attracted to him all at the same time. Mabel couldn't help herself, she simply smiled at her husband as he made his way to her. He may not be perfect or completely loyal she thought, but he was hers and no one elses.

The night eventually wound down and all the guests left with much to gossip about. In the wee hours of the night, Ed and Mabel made love with a passion that they hadn't felt since they were first newlyweds. Down the hall, Mary Pickford and Charles Buddy Rodgers had secretly shared their own frantic love making with noises that filled the night with sounds of passionate bliss. Once again, the servants at Pickfair practiced the art of ignoring the sounds of carnal pleasure while vigilantly keeping the house secrets to themselves. Beverly Hills had seduced them and done the trick. At least that's what Ed thought as he laid in bed smoking a cigarette.

The next morning before breakfast Ed and Mary Pickford were able to come to an agreement in her glassed-in patio. The deal would favor Mrs. Pickford for the rest of her life, so long as she continued to keep being the Family's informant in Hollywood. Mary wanted her investments protected and she wanted help to push through her payroll pledge program that would bankroll her pet project, the Motion Picture's Relief Fund. That had always been her main objective and the reason why she was willing to work with the Families from the very beginning. It was the single most important thing she wanted and the Families would give it to her and then some. What she had already surmised but kept to herself was that the boys back east all had crushes on her and were still fascinated by her because of her films. No one ever said she was clumsy at business. In fact, it was just the opposite. By 1933, Mary Pickford had become one of Hollywood's most powerful women.

By the middle of the breakfast, it became abundantly clear that Mary Pickford was having an affair with Mr. Rogers and was falling in love. Mabel and Ed couldn't stop smiling at the two love birds as they kept making silly gestures at each other during the meal. Mary's husband, Douglas Fairbanks, was already in an affair in Europe and Mary had no intentions of being alone, much less, unloved. Until Shirley Temple came along she had been "America's Sweetheart" and that was not something that she would allow her husband to forget. Both Mary and Buddy invited them to stay and take a trip with them in Benedict Canyon on horseback. According to Mary, "the weather was gorgeous and love was in the air." However, Ed had business to attend in San Francisco and wanted to finish it as soon as possible.

"I appreciate the offer and invitation but I have pressing business elsewhere. Can I have your driver take us to the train station so we may catch the Santa Fe. Mary looked at them and smiled. "Sure thing. Sure, you don't want to stay for a little while longer?" Mary looked at Mabel and shook her head up and down, trying to get a response. Mabel smiled. "Well alright but if you change your minds and want to stay for a few days, I won't mind." Ed was determined to get to his next assignment so he politely declined.

Chapter 27

Mrs. Pickford's chauffeur drove them to La Grande Station in Los Angeles to catch the first train to San Francisco. By noon that day, they were both heading north on the Santa Fe railway. Ed made a phone call from the train station to his contact person in California before they left. He was given more instructions and was also given a new assignment. The Dupont family wanted him to procure for them, the world's fastest thoroughbred race horse and they didn't care how much it cost. Ed was not exactly sure how he was going to accomplish this new assignment but he had his orders and he never disobeyed the bosses.

By the Spring of 1932 the world of horse racing was completely taken by surprise with Australia's most prized thoroughbred race horse, Phar Lap. The horse was a gelding that had been originally purchased in New Zealand and trained in Australia. Phar Lap was essentially, the modern world's first true Dark Horse. In a time when the world needed a winning champ that made the common man money on a cheap bet, Phar Lap's consecutive wins became a sign of hope to everyone that believed in the underdog.

The hero, however, had entered a world full of desperate men and desperate times. To everyone's surprise, Par Lap, overnight had blown every other horse away in the horse racing arenas in Australia. The young gelding won nearly every race it ran in Australia and was eventually brought to Mexico to race in the Agua Caliente Handicap. The purse was set at one hundred thousand dollars. Now, the entire world was experiencing severe economic depressions, but Tijuana, Mexico, which happened to be conveniently located right outside of California's border and had the largest payouts at that time. Every horse-bookie, trainer, strapper, and breeder took notice when Phar Lap left his competition in the dust.

Suddenly, the dark horse had everyone's attention and the breeders in the Families wanted him, had to have him, and if they couldn't, then no one would. Which sadly was exactly what would happen. Phar Lap was the heroic horse that became a legend but his life would not be long. There were simply too many power-brokers that stood in the way.

Ed and Mabel sat in the dining car and watched the tranquil scenery pass. The waiter poured them a cup of coffee. "Where are we going next?" Mabel sipped her coffee as Ed began to tell her about the next job. "I've got to see a man about a horse," was all Ed said as he lit a cigarette and drank his coffee. Mabel didn't want to hear anything about horses because it brought her too many bad memories of Hector so she refrained from further inquiries.

The train ride to San Francisco was a pleasant experience that gave them time to reflect. Mabel handed her husband back the newspaper that they shared. "Those poor people. I dearly hope the Lindbergh's get their little boy back. What a horrible ordeal and to think what that child must be going through right now." Mabel put her hands over her mouth and tried her best to compose herself but she could only think of her own little boy back home with the exact same name and was about the same age as well. She began to cry and she was unable to hold her tears back.

After reading the latest news on the kidnapping of the Lindbergh boy, it had hit too close to home for Mabel and she simply couldn't get it out of her mind. Ed could sense her unease, so he held her hand and pulled her closer to him as he quietly reassured her that he would never let that happen to his family. She eventually fell asleep in his arms only to be awaken by the sound of the train whistle as it pulled into the next station.

They were able to catch a taxi cab that took them first to downtown Pleasanton, California, where Ed made sure they were able to get a room for them as he continued on to the Alameda County Fairgrounds. He arrived at the home of Mr. Rodney McKenzie. The Pleasanton race track had been a sponsor of harness horse racing for quite some time but lately, there were rumors that the California legislature was due to legalize the pari-mutuel wagering in the horse racing world. Suddenly, all the big horse-bookie establishments, underground, began to scramble for their share of the new market and all horse owners and trainers wanted a piece of the pie.

Mr. Rodney McKenzie was the son of a wealthy Canadian railroad mogul and he had the same Midas touch as his father. It was Mr. McKenzie that created the Alameda County Fairgrounds, twenty something years earlier, and had purchased an already established successful race track just inside the fairgrounds. Ed had been invited to attend a meeting that night at Mr. McKenzie's residence where he was hoping to run into David Davis, the owner of Phar Lap, the wonder race horse.

Ed left Mabel at the Riverside Hotel in Pleasanton, before going to the meeting. Mabel was pleased to be left to her own devices and far away from any race horses. She checked into the hotel and immediately called her mother to check on her children.

Ed continued on to the meeting and was taken directly to the Mr. McKenzie's house. Upon arrival, Ed could sense that the air was thick with tension and he felt that he was not wanted even though he was invited.

As soon as he knocked on the door, Ed could hear yelling and screaming from inside the house. An attendant opened the door as two businessmen stormed out of the house, giving Ed a glare, as they got into the taxi that had brought him. Mr. McKenzie and some business associates stepped outside as the taxi drove off. Ed introduced himself and asked why the business men were so angry.

Mr. McKenzie shook his head and sighed. "That was the owner of Phar Lap, he actually thinks that his horse is going to continue racing." Ed's eyebrow rose as he lit a cigarette. "Hell fire, and damnation." Mr. McKenzie's associates both began to laugh simultaneously. One of them took off his hat and introduced himself to Ed. "Let me guess. You, too, have an offer to buy the wonder horse and now you know that's never going to happen. Am I right?" Ed sat down in one of the chairs on the front porch and simply said, "yep." All the men shook their heads in defeat.

"It's a damn shame that some people can't be bought, persuaded, or reasoned with." Ed put out his cigarette and looked up at Mr. McKenzie. "I presume that Mr. Davis thinks he's going to get his way but no one's going to get the horse." Mr. McKenzie looked directly at Ed. "You presume correctly, Mr. Godwin. I'm sorry that you had to travel this far to be thwarted so quickly but others have already beaten you to the punch. I'm afraid that Mr. Davis is going to be a very disappointed man sometime very soon." "Yep, that's what I thought." With that said, Ed got up and asked if he could call a taxi to take him back to his hotel.

"I'll take you back to your hotel." One of Mr. McKenzie's business associates introduced himself as Mr. Conroy and motioned for Mr. McKenzie's attendant to bring his car around to the front of the house. Mr. McKenzie shook Ed's hand and apologized again for the embarrassing situation. Ed nodded his head and agreed with him. "You're right, it's a shame that some men can't be purchased, persuaded, or reasoned with.

The next day during breakfast, Ed and Mabel read in the newspaper about the sudden death of the wonder horse Phar Lap. The sensational news declared that he had died under mysterious circumstances. Everyone in the horse-racing world knew that the horse had obviously been poisoned. The whole world thought that Australia's national hero had been snuffed out by American gangster's intent on protecting their investments. Little did they know that it wasn't just American gangsters, but also American Industrialists, that would rather see a dead-horse than a successful champion. Ed simply sighed as he handed the newspaper to his wife.

By the time Mabel read the paper she was taken back by the sudden news. "You didn't have anything to do with this, did you?" Ed took a drag from his cigarette and looked directly at her. "Are you kidding me? Hell, I didn't have a chance to talk with Mr. Davis, much less get to warn or threaten him. Sometimes, folks are just too damn bull-headed to know what's good for them." Mabel figured as much, clicked her tongue and shook her head. "You can say that again, darling. Some folks are just too stubborn for their own good." Mabel put her hand on his as Ed chuckled and put out his smoke. "Come on, sweetheart, let's go catch a train."

No one would ever really know how the race horse died but everyone would believe that he was murdered by those that couldn't have him or control him. It was simply a sad ending for a real hero during a time when the common man really needed one. By the time they made it to the train station, the weather began to become dark and dreary as the Santa Fe Chief left the station. Once again, they sat in the dining car as the train made its way along the tranquil scenery of California's beautiful back county.

The Santa Fe Chief rolled on as the rain began to pour down in torrents obscuring the view from their window. After sometime she excused herself and left the dining car to use the restroom. Ed waited and waited but Mabel never returned.

An hour later and Ed was panicking as he searched the entire train for his wife to no avail. She couldn't have just disappeared, thought Ed, as he made his way to the front of the train. As soon as Ed opened the door and stepped inside the train conductor's office, a steel pipe landed on the back of his head and he immediately fell. He eventually opened his eyes to see a couple of goons lean over him with smiles on their faces. "Looks like he's coming around, boss."

Ed opened his eyes wider and could see three men with their shirts rolled up and his wife hanging from a rope behind them. "Mabel!" The men looked at Ed and began to smile. "Oh, she's not going to answer you, pal. You see, she didn't last very long, like you will, I'm sure." Ed's heart sank into the pit of his stomach as he stared at his wife hanging before him. "Yep, that bitch is as dead as a door nail." The man pushed Mabel's hanging body making it swing back and forth from the rope. "Now I know that you think you're going to get out of here alive but I can tell you right now that you're not."

Ed's blood began to boil as he listened and watched his dead wife swing back and forth in front of him. "Who do you work for?" Ed couldn't stop starring at his wife. One of the goons punched him in the jaw. "Who do you work for?" He spit blood out and began to laugh. "You might as well kill me cause I ain't going to talk." They kept punching him. "Who do you work for?" He gasped for air as he came to and heard their repeated question. So, he laughed again as he caught his breath. "I might as well join my wife in the hereafter, so y'all can just kiss my hairy-ass, you sorry son's-of-bitches." They began to stuff the rag back in his mouth when one of the men stopped them and took it out again. "Who do you work for?" Ed grinned wide with his bloody mouth and laughed again. "Know this; None of you fuckers are going to live for very long after this is over."

Ed tried his best to flex his muscles and tear out of his restraints but it was no use. "My fucking wife is dead! Dead! I have no purpose or point to live any more you fucking idiots! Just go ahead and kill me and get it over!" They began to rough him up more until he was knocked unconscious. Then they began to spray water on him to wake him up. It worked and they continued to repeat their question. Ed never relented, he continued to threaten them while he was being tortured never giving them a single shred of information until his body simply gave up and he slipped into unconsciousness.

He awoke to the sound of the radio playing a soft sounding tune from far away. Someone was wiping his wounds with a warm wet cloth and whispering something to him as the pain from his recent ordeal crept back into his mind. Ed could hear the familiar sound of a woman's voice say his name. "Wake up, sweetheart. Try to open your eyes." Ed tried his best to open his swollen eyes but he could barely see who was washing his wounds. He did recognize the voice though and quickly reached out with his hands to touch the woman. "Mabel? Is that you?"

Ed's wife reached out and grabbed her husband's hands to reassure him that she was indeed alive. For the first time in Mabel's life she witnessed her husband begin to cry. Ed sobbed like a little baby, he simply couldn't stop until he heard his wife sooth him with her words again. "Hush now, sweetheart, everything is going to be alright." Ed tried again to open his swollen eye lids but they were too sore to move. "It's not alright if that's what you mean." Mabel stood up and began to remove the blood-stained clothes in front of him. Thankfully, Ed couldn't see the blood dripping from his wife's dress as she began to wipe the blood from her face but he could sense and smell that there was something amiss and not quite right.

"I smell blood. What's happened, Mabel?" As she wiped off all of the blood from her body Mabel began to tell her husband what had happened. "We were ambushed. I remember someone gagging me after I left the bathroom and I just blacked out. Then I came to sometime later and was stuffed into a mail bag and was being carried off the train. I started to scream and something hit me over the head and everything went dark again. I woke up and was hanging from a rope tied to the ceiling of some strange room and there were these men beating you to a pulp in front of me." "Then suddenly there were gun shots being fired outside and all the men left the room. Next thing I know there was an old man cutting me down from the ceiling and then the stranger handed me a knife and told me to lay low and play dead. That's when another feller ran into the room and was shot in the back by the man that saved me. When the old guy shot the last goon, blood splattered all over me and that's why I'm covered in blood."

There was something not quite right about his wife's recollection and he could tell that she was not completely telling him the truth. He didn't care though, as long as she was alive and unharmed. What really happened was that the old man that had saved her had indeed handed her the knife and told her to cut Ed loose while he looked for the others. However, as the old guy left to further investigate the situation another goon came into the room and pointed a gun at her. She backed away while hiding her knife as the man came closer and motioned for her to stay quiet.

Mabel kept the knife concealed behind her as the man walked by her to the next room where the old man had gone. As soon as the fellow passed Mabel, she jumped at her chance and ran up behind him and pounced. Mabel latched onto his back, sliced open his throat and began stabbing the man in the chest as fast as she could, until he fell to the floor while his blood gushed out of him. Seeing her husband being tortured, awoke a deep desire for vengeance that had simply overtaken her. When the man stopped moving on the floor, Mabel jumped off and immediately ran back to her husband.

"The old timer told me to clean up and then left. I don't know what's happening Ed. We got to get out of this place and quickly." Ed's body was sore and completely bruised but the story she told made his adrenalin begin to flow and he was able to rise and open and partly open his eyes. "Let's go." Mabel was wearing only her slip as they walked out of the ware house building and was greeted by the old fellow waiting by the opened door of a Model A car. "Get in, we don't have much time."

They got in the back seat as the old man got into the driver seat and drove off. Ed immediately could sense something familiar about the man's voice but he was too distracted to recognize it. However, as they began to drive down the road the old fellow told them that they were needed back home and were being taken to a nearby air-field. He knew that voice, it was a voice that he had recognized back when he first began his training years ago on Pensacola beach. Ed immediately reached over and grabbed the old man's shoulder. "What have I always told, son?" Ed couldn't believe his ears. It was the Gunny's voice!

They simultaneously said, "Always observe your surroundings." The old fellow pulled off his fake mustache, fake beard, then looked back at his young protege and smiled. Ed couldn't believe his eyes and ears. "I thought you were dead. I saw Goldring shoot you in the back. There were brains and blood all over the place." Gunny laughed and shook his head. "Pig brains and blood were packed into that blank bullet. It was the only way to survive that awful situation. The General wouldn't have stopped until he knew I was dead. It's just the way it is, Paul. Sometimes you got to fool the ones closest to you if you want to fool those that are hunting you. It was simply a necessary diversion. General Butler is no longer in power. So, I don't have to worry about that shit anymore."

Ed was still stunned by this new realization but it did help him forget his pain as he smiled and held his wife's hand. They drove into an open-air field where there was another Ford Tri-Motor airplane waiting for them. They drove right up to the air plane and began to board it when Mabel saw the car with men standing on the side floor rails holding machine guns. Mabel began to say something when she turned around and saw the Gunny climb up on top of Model A car and lay down while holding a long-range rifle. It didn't take him long to aim and pull the trigger. He hit his first target and immediately reloaded, aimed, and shot his next target. The third shot stopped the car in its tracks and the Gunny reloaded, aimed and shot again two more times. "You both go ahead and get in the plane." Captain Riley bent his head outside the cock pit window and yelled toward the Gunny.

"What do I do?" The Gunny got down from the car and told him to start the plane and pick him up before he took off. Captain Riley didn't have to be told twice. Gunny Fletcher reloaded his gun and drove the car over to his victims. Ed could see the Gunny inspect the damage as the Gunny began to write something down in a note pad. Then Ed saw something that he'd never seen the Gunny do before. The old Marine ripped a piece of his note book and placed it into the mouth of the driver.

Captain Riley pulled the plane close enough to the scene and the Gunny boarded. "Let's get the Hell out of here." Captain Riley nodded his head and pushed down on the throttle and they flew away. Mabel looked down and was glad to be flying in the air again.

They had to stop several times to refuel but this time no one seemed to care about the distance or the amount of time that it took them to get back to Florida. By late that afternoon Captain Riley was landing in Corry Field at Pensacola. Betty was waiting for them in her truck as the plane landed. Mabel got Betty to help Ed get out of the plane. His body ached all over as he was helped into Betty's truck. Mabel sat next to Ed as they drove back home. Betty noticed that Mabel had dried blood stains on her face and hands and she wore only her dress slip and a man's suit coat. It was apparent that they had been in the thick of it and was in serious need of a stiff drink and hot shower.

"Gee, boss, you sure look worse for wear." Ed tried to smile but it simply hurt too much. He chuckled and said, "You have no idea, kiddo, you have no idea." Betty lit a cigarette as she drove home and handed it to Mabel to hand to Ed. Ed's face had swollen but he still managed to smoke while they drove back to Brownsville. When they finally pulled up in front of their house on U street, Mabel and Ed had never thought they would be so glad to return to their modest and tranquil home in Pensacola. Ed was cleaned, dressed, and put to bed within a few hours. Mabel climbed into bed to cuddle with her passed out husband. She had sent Betty over to her mother's house to retrieve her children while she waited in bed next to her sleeping man. It was good to finally be home.

Chapter 28

"We will kill every one of your God-damned race horses, one by one, and then we will devour them in front of you. It's your choice, make a smart decision and don't disgrace yourself." Ed jerked in his sleep then awoke from his nightmare in his sweat drenched bed. He got up, lit a cigarette, dressed, and made his way to the kitchen in his house. Mabel was cooking breakfast as Betty fed little Charlie at the dinner table. "Hey, boss, looks like Mr. Roosevelt has won the election." Ed sat down at the table and put out his cigarette. "Let me see the newspaper." Mabel walked over to the table and handed him the paper. Ed grabbed his wife and made her sit in his lap. "Did I tell you how much I love you today?"

Mabel rolled her eyes and kissed him on his forehead. "No, you haven't but I'm sure you will." She got up and he smacked her on the behind as she walked back to the stove. Betty smiled at her boss as she finished feeding little Charlie. "So, have you thought about any baby names yet?" Mabel turned toward Betty and placed a hand on her pregnant belly. "Nope, not yet. Ed thinks it's going to be another boy but I surely hope it's a little girl."

"If it is a girl, I think I'll name her Joyce. She might bring some joy to this world." Ed looked over his newspaper, "What if he's a boy?" Mabel looked at Betty, then her husband. "How about Gus?" Ed laughed as soon as she said it. Betty began to laugh as well. Ed got up from the table, walked over to his wife, grabbed her face gently and kissed her. "It doesn't matter what we call the child, darling. As long we're together, the kids going to be alright."

Ed pulled his wife closer and kissed her again. Mabel melted, and let him hold her tight while they passionately kissed. Arthur began to clap his hands while Betty let out a whistle. Little Charlie began to clap his hands mimicking his older brother. Ed picked his wife up by the hips and swung her around then put her back down with another kiss. "Gus will work but I prefer Paul. It reminds me of the Apostle and I've always liked the name." Mabel this time laughed back at what he said. "Paul's a good name darling. If it's a boy, I'll name him Paul, sweat-heart. Just for you." Mabel shook her blushing face as she began to prepare the plates of food.

"Now y'all hurry up and eat before your eggs get cold. Betty and Ed said, "yes ma'am" simultaneously as they dove into their food. Mabel chuckled at their voracious appetites. "Slow down, y'all, or you'll give yourselves indigestion." Mabel picked up little

Charlie. "Looks like my little boy needs changing." Mabel put her nose close to his diaper and responded, "Oh yeah, sure does." Betty and Ed smiled at each other as Mabel took her child down the hall to change his diaper. "It's good to see you both happy again, boss." Ed smiled back at Betty. "Oh, you have no idea. That woman is the best thing that ever happened to me. I'd do anything to make her happy and content. Anything." Betty smiled back at him as she finished her coffee.

"Now that Gunny is back in charge, things will get back to normal I hope." Betty looked directly at Ed. "Gunny scares me, boss." Ed smiled at what she said. "Good. You should be scared, Fred. That man has much to teach us. I've never stopped learning from the old feller. He's dangerous and highly intelligent. So, do everything he tells you and you'll become a better professional, sweat-heart." Betty cocked her left eyebrow and Ed returned it.

A few months had passed since their ordeal in California and everything had gotten back to normal for Betty, Ed, and Mabel. Gunny Fletcher was made the new underboss of Pensacola even though Mr. Goldring had known that would happen the whole time during his short stint. Ed soon found himself back on the beach giving his boss the weekly debriefing.

On his way over to the bridge, Ed stopped at a gas station to fill his truck when one of the older men that usually sat out front, waved hello to him. "Howdy, Paul." said one of the men sitting outside. "Looks like it's going to be another sunny day." Ed smiled back and agreed with the old-timer. "It sure does, Sir. It sure does." Ed knew every one of the fellows that hung outside the old gas-station and he always greeted them. It was definitely nice to be back home, thought Ed.

Mr. Novak had to make room for Gunny and was given an office at the Casino, right next to Gunny's. Mr. Novak apparently knew Gunny Fletcher from another time and place and they liked each other so it wasn't too hard for Mr. Novak to stand aside for the new boss.

Gunny had just finished reading three different newspapers when Ed walked in and sat down. "Looks like old' Capone was the one that sent those men after you in California. He's in prison but still able to issue orders. Frank, the Enforcer, is now head of the Chicago boys and he's not interested in losing any more men, so the hunt is over." Ed lit a cigarette. "Why would Capone be interested in us?" Gunny Fletcher put the newspaper down and took off his reading glasses. "The Family wanted you to shake things up in

Newport and Cincinnati. Right?" Ed shook his head to confirm what Gunny was saying. "Well, it was some of Capone's men that you guys wasted. That fat fucker took it personally and wanted you dead and wanted to know who you worked for, but don't worry. That asshole is done for now and his new man in charged isn't likely to continue down that road anymore."

"What's bothering me though is there is a schism within the Families, Paul. Most of them are not too worried about this new President and his liberal thinking. Hell, he defeated that Norman Thomas, the Socialist representative, as well as Hoover, too. It's just them God damned Bolsheviks over in Russia has all of the elders scared to death. The Family has become obsessed and concerned about the spread of communism. They think it's contagious or something. I don't know how soon things are going to go south but I do know that they have been creating something over in Europe and want to do something here in America."

"We need to find out what's going on in Germany. The Family elders want to create something that will hurt them Russian Commies. They haven't forgotten about the loss of their properties and investments in Russia and they're still quite sore about it. They want vengeance. Reports are coming in that these Commie Reds are starving millions of people into submission."

"The Family may sometimes act cruelly but this is just down right crazy. Can you imagine if our government starved a few million people to death while denying them fuel for the winter? Apparently, millions of Russians are dying by the minute and them atheistic commies are quite content about it. Things are getting out of hand on the world front and I'm feeling them cold winds of discord are beginning to blow again. It's time we prepared ourselves for another inevitable world war."

"What! Another great war, you can't mean it. Can you?" "Did you hear anything I just said, Mr. Telephone Man, or were you day-deaming again?" Ed blushed in front of his boss. "No Sir. I heard it clearly. I'm just in shock over what you just said."

Gunny grabbed his hat, wiped his forehead with his handkerchief, then looked directly at Ed. "You ain't just a woofin', pal. Come on, Paul. We got ourselves some work to do." With that said, Gunny Fletcher walked outside to where his favorite horse was tied up. Gunny climbed up on his horse while Ed got into his truck and followed Gunny Fletcher down the beach to where another ship of booze was being unloaded. It would be the last load of illegal booze that was directly delivered to Pensacola Beach before the end of Prohibition. Mr. Goldring and his brother had already started their bottling company and were all set to make a mint when the Volstead Act was repealed.

By the end of the day, Ed and Betty had finished working for the telephone company and Betty had begun to make her collections while Ed headed back to his barbershop. No sooner had he turned on the radio box, tuned to his favorite station and turned on the barbershop light when in walked one of his loyal customers. "Whatcha' say, Mr. Goodwin?" Ed wiped clean his barber chair and smiled at Mr. Levine. "Oh, nothing much, partner, just another day at work and another hot day in the sun. Have a seat, Mr. Levine. A shave and a haircut?" "Just a haircut friend, just a haircut."

The radio played "Why Waste Your Tears," by Lew Stone's Dance Band as the older gentlemen sat into the barber chair and Ed wrapped a sheet around him. "Sure thing, Mr. Levine. So, how's life been treating ya'?" "Ahhh, not so bad, not so bad. We finally got ourselves another Roosevelt in the White House and it looks like happy days are here again." They began to laugh together at Mr. Levine's attempt at political humor. "You got that right, pal, you got that right." Ed began to cut hair as another customer walked into the shop. "Yes Sir, for now, happy days are indeed here again but

let's keep our fingers crossed just in case," said the Telephone Man.

THE END

Shannon Blake is a Southern Historian. He lives in his home town of Pensacola Florida where he was once employed as a butler for his great-uncle he barely knew. His uncle had Alzheimer's and thought Mr. Blake was his brother the (Telephone Man) and divulged much of what would later be collaborated as "The Good O' Boy System," in the South. As a caregiver / historian, Mr. Blake learned about the secret underground network called the Family. However, due to legal matters, he has had to write this novel as a work of historic fiction in order to prevent future litigation.

Made in the USA
Middletown, DE
29 April 2018